Catherine Simpson has been shortlisted in the Mslexia Women's Novel Award and the Asham Award. Her short stories have been featured in anthologies and she has performed them at various festivals (including Edinburgh International Book Festival) and on BBC radio. She was named as one of Edinburgh UNESCO City of Literature's emerging writers in both 2012 and 2013. Her journalism has appeared in *The Scotsman, The Herald, The Daily Mail, The Sun* and many magazines. In 2013, she won a Scottish Book Trust New Writers Award for the opening chapters of *Truestory*. She was raised on a Lancashire dairy farm and now lives near Edinburgh with her husband and two daughters. *Truestory* is her first novel.

TRUESTORY

Catherine Simpson

SANDSTONEPRESS
HIGHLAND | SCOTLAND

B000 000 016 2354

First published in Great Britain
and the United States of America
Sandstone Press Ltd
Dochcarty Road
Dingwall
Ross-shire
IV15 9UG
Scotland.

www.sandstonepress.com

Editor: Moira Forsyth

The moral right of Catherine Simpson to be recognised as the author
of this work has been asserted in accordance with the Copyright,
Design and Patent Act, 1988.

The publisher acknowledges support from
Creative Scotland towards publication of this volume.
Creative Scotland logo.

ISBN: 978-1-910124-59-8
ISBNe: 978-1-910124-60-4

Cover design by Jon Gray, London
Typeset by Iolaire Typesetting, Newtonmore.
Printed and bound by Totem, Poland

For Tricia, Missed Always

ACKNOWLEDGEMENTS

Thank you to Hilary Hine who has asked me on a regular basis, since I was twelve years old, 'Have you written that book yet?'

Thank you to Sonja Cameron and Jules Horne, from the Open University Creative Writing courses, for setting me on the right path.

Huge thanks to the wonderful Sam Kelly and David Bishop of Edinburgh Napier MA Creative Writing programme whose difficult questions, spot-on observations and unwavering support helped *Truestory* spring into life. Thanks to Stuart Kelly, James Robertson and Rob Shearman, also part of the Edinburgh Napier Creative Writing MA dream team, who gave generous support and advice.

Loving memories of Uncle Gerald whose legacy paid for the creative writing courses.

A million thanks to Scottish Book Trust (whose existence, is proof – if proof were needed – that we live in a civilised country). With special thanks to Caitrin Armstrong, Claire Marchant-Collier, Will Mackie and

Helen Croney. Receiving a New Writers Award was like winning the lottery, especially being given the opportunity to work with my mentor, Kathryn Ross, who spent hours discussing *Truestory* with me over cups of tea in the Scottish Storytelling Centre – and who always managed to put her finger on the nub of the matter.

Thanks so much to my lovely agent Joanna Swainson of Hardman & Swainson, another in a line of straight-talkers without whom *Truestory* would not exist in its current form.

Thanks to Prof Sue Black, of the University of Dundee, who gave her advice generously.

Biggest thanks of all to Sandstone Press and their wonderful team who turned my words into this beautiful book. Special thanks to Moira Forsyth for her sensitive editing and her grace when dealing with my text.

Thank you to my dad, Stuart, who is an inspiration (and a handy farming consultant).

Much love and gratitude to my husband Marcello Mega without whom I would never have found the time to write this book.

And lastly to the two most straight-talking women there are: Nina Mega and Lara Mega, thank you.

Chapter 1

I watched my jailor, Sam, all four foot five of him. He was straining with effort and concentration, his tongue sticking out the corner of his mouth as he drew a map of our world.

I gripped my coffee cup. I wanted to smack it off the table, hear it crack and smash and see the coffee splatter all over the kitchen, but I couldn't because loud noises and sudden movements were NOT ALLOWED.

Lots of stuff was NOT ALLOWED in our tiny world, including wrapped presents, wasps, flies, cloth hankies, the colour yellow, nettles, plug holes, uncovered ears, boiled eggs, balloons and a never-ending, ever-growing list of other random craziness.

On his *Map of the World* Sam drew Backwoods Farm, the farmyard, the barn, the workshop and The World of the Jungle at the Bottom of the Orchard. From the farmyard he drew a lane wending away between Big Hill and The Wildwood and past Wayside Cottage with its row of little gravestones. When the lane reached the edge of the paper he drew a skull and crossbones and wrote in red letters: DANGER: HELL FIRE PASS.

I forced a smile.

He'd eaten the omelette I'd given him for lunch after he'd smeared it with tomato sauce to make it red – icing it slowly, meticulously, like a precious cake, squinting at its yellowness through his sunglasses to stop his eyes from burning. Then he'd smoothed out a big piece of paper on the table and run his hand over it looking for lumps, bumps and creases. God forbid there should be any lumps, bumps or creases. Especially creases.

I closed my eyes. I didn't need to watch him draw the confines of our tiny world – I'd seen him do it a thousand times and I knew it, every inch.

I left the house at two o' clock and not a minute before. That was the deal; I was allowed out for a couple of hours at two o'clock on a Tuesday. I pulled the door to and Bess shot out of the barn, zigzagging on her chain and barking so hard her front feet left the ground.

'Go to bed, Bessie!'

The racket she made jarred even though Sam wouldn't hear it because by now he'd be lying under his quilt, tucked in on all sides, his earphones on and his bobble hat stuffed with cotton wool and pulled right down over his face.

There used to be hell to pay when I went out on a Tuesday. For years he'd beg me not to go, he'd start crying, pleading – the lot. It wasn't that I was leaving him on his own – his dad did jobs round the farmyard on a Tuesday afternoon to be near and to keep an eye on him.

That might have been half the trouble.

Sometimes I wouldn't go. I'd say nothing and put the car keys back on the hook and feel the walls close in another few feet. Or I'd tell him 'I can't be here *all* the time'. I'd try to keep calm, not to let the anger and the resentment and the frustration leak out of every pore. 'I've got to get away some time.'

'*Why* can't you be here all the time?' He'd say. '*I* am.'

But the last time he asked me not to go my patience snapped. I flung down my carrier bags and kicked them across the kitchen, where they sent a pile of Farmers Weeklies slithering under the armchair, and I yelled 'For God's sake, you're going to kill me, you are. You're going to drive me into the Royal Bloody Albert,' and then I started crying – big snotty tears, like a kid.

When I calmed down I went to apologise. I tried to put my arm around him.

'I didn't mean to shout, Sam. I'm sorry.'

But he shrank away, as if he didn't trust me – as if he didn't even like me – and I started crying again.

Later his laptop was open on the kitchen table and I saw he'd Googled 'The Royal Bloody Albert'. He'd found it was actually the Royal Albert Psychiatric Unit '*with individual rooms and en suite bathrooms in a Grade 2 listed building, set within landscaped gardens.*'

Put like that it didn't sound so bad – a single room with space to think, space to breathe, space to be nothing but yourself – if you could still remember what you were supposed to be.

After that he didn't ask me not to go into town on a Tuesday anymore. Instead when it headed towards two o'clock he concentrated on drawing a *Map of the World* – there was a pile a mile high next to the kitchen range – or he hid under his quilt tucked in tight all round and with the full bobble hat and cotton wool routine. Or sometimes he went on his computer.

But whatever he did I could tell by the look on his face when I got back that he'd been truly terrified of me driving away down HELL FIRE PASS where unspeakable terrors lurked, too terrible to fully form in his mind, and that he'd believed the whole time I was away that he might never see me again.

I lobbed two carriers into the back of the car and climbed in. I squinted into the rear-view mirror; smoothed the frizz around my temples, examined my eyes, my teeth, my forehead, the baggy neck of my baggy jumper. If I kept my eyes half shut I couldn't see how old and knackered I looked. Or how disappointed.

The car stank. The roof had let the rain in and the carpet had gone rotten. I'd chucked it on the bonfire but the smell lingered and I wondered if it clung to me. I sniffed my jumper: fried onions, fried bread and a whiff of bleach from my hands. I opened the window.

As I backed the car down the yard, the two carrier bags rolled around spewing stuff out. Today I was taking the bright yellow curtains I'd bought for Sam's bedroom before he was born, before I realised yellow burnt his eyes, before I realised how easy it was to make mistakes with a kid even when you were doing your utmost to get it right. I'd also brought Duncan's old suit – the one he wore at our wedding – there was no point in having that thing cluttering the place up. I couldn't remember the last time I'd seen him in a suit.

The car jolted over the potholes. I didn't look up at Sam's window. I felt bad enough; if he'd got out of bed to watch me leave I didn't want to see him.

I glanced at the garden. It was a tip. The only things thriving were gooseberries because nothing can kill bloody gooseberries. On the yard weeds sprouted between the cobbles, poking through the cow muck. From the shed by the gate a cow shouted. It poked its head out and looked at me. Its newborn calf must have been taken away. It shouted again, a long, sad bellow, like cows do.

I turned up the radio.

Driving down the lane I acted like it felt good to be out; I tapped to the music and mouthed a few words. But it didn't feel good. A sick feeling crept up my throat, down each arm, down each leg. I was a bad person, a bad mother, a monster, driving away, abandoning Sam like that and leaving him to suffer.

Every week I felt the same and I was right to worry because often I'd get back and find the place in chaos. Duncan would have said something to kick Sam off; tried to make him do something he couldn't or joked about something he shouldn't. There was endless stuff that could go wrong when it came to Sam and Duncan. Then Duncan would expect me to step in and make everything right.

Sometimes I thought it wasn't worth going out in the first place.

Except it was. It was always worth going out if I wanted to stay sane and to stay alive.

I pulled up at the tip. A man was dragging old floor boards from his boot. I grabbed my carriers and climbed up the steps to the skip. I didn't chuck the bags in, or empty them over the side because that would have been a waste – no, I made the most of it by rolling up each item, throwing it for all I was worth and watching it slap down among the rubbish.

The man lobbed wood on top of the curtains and I thought that's right, bury the bloody things. They were specially made those curtains – not cheap either – in what the woman in the shop called a 'nice neutral colour, good for a girl or a boy'.

Only thing was I didn't know I was going to get a boy like Sam.

I bundled up Duncan's suit jacket and flung it as hard as I could. The bloke with the wood was chucking old paint tins now and one crashed onto it and the lid flew off and brown paint splattered onto the jacket's shiny lining and dribbled down.

I remembered Duncan in that suit on our wedding day, twenty-three years ago. He'd been propping up the bar with his mates, talking about shooting and fishing and cars and motorbikes. They were all farmers and they looked like they'd put their suits on with shovels; too tight round the shoulders, too short in the sleeves, shirts poking out. He'd been knocking back the pints while I danced with the bridesmaids in their emerald frocks. The bright green bridesmaids were folk I worked with in the bank – the type who invited you to Tupperware parties and Pippa Dee parties and every other kind of party: jewellery, make-up, plastic shoes, there was nothing those girls couldn't sell from their settees.

I'd lost touch with them ages ago.

I lobbed the suit trousers.

It felt good to get rid of stuff. The farm was full of ancient possessions that had never been cleared out because farmers don't retire and move to the seaside, they die in the job and the next generation steps in. Duncan's family had been at Backwoods Farm for five generations. Six if you counted Sam.

I used to drop it at charity shops: tea sets, sherry glasses, gardening books, wool – endless bags of un-knitted wool – and every time I dumped a bag I felt a bit less tied to Backwoods Farm, a bit freer. But I hated those smelly shops with their battered books and bobbly tops and saggy trousers and anyway, after a while it hadn't been enough.

Since then I'd been coming here.

Duncan had never noticed. Except for that jumper his

mother knitted him and some plastic shooting trophies, oh and the old jigsaws from when he was a lad. He'd wanted to know where they'd got to. When he asked, I shrugged. How should I know? If they were that important he should have looked after them, shouldn't he?

Chapter 2

Welcome to U Chat

Home   **Chat**   **Message Boards**   **Rules**   **Contact Us**   **Log in**   **Sign up**

How safe am I?

Truestory
Date: 3 June 2014
Time: 14.11

My father, Duncan Gordon McCabe, is firing a gun through the bathroom window. It is 168 decibels, which is 40 decibels above the human pain threshold. In between each shot he is shouting 'for fuck's sake' and throwing things and kicking the bedroom wall. I have been alive 11 years and 10 months and it is the loudest noise I have heard. I don't know how safe I am in this house. I do not have any ear defenders. I think I may be 30% safe. But that is only an estimate. Estimates are not very satisfying. Because they are only guesses.

Re: How safe am I?

Boodyqueen
Date: 3 June 2014
Tme: 14.19

Hey, Honey. Where's your mom?

Re: How safe am I?

Diamondsky
Date: 3 June 2014
Time: 14.19

Man, where you at?

Re: How safe am I?

Truestory
Date: 3 June 2014
Time: 14.20

I am at home. I am in my bedroom. My mother has gone away and left me.

Re: How safe am I?

Chocolatemoustache
Date: 3 June 2014
Time: 14.23

Get out of there, Truestory. Call Childline.

Re: How safe am I?

Boodyqueen
Date: 3 June 2014
Time: 14.26

Call 911 honey. A kid should not have to deal with this kinda shit.

Re: How safe am I?

Truestory
Date: 3 June 2014
Time: 14.28

911 does not work in Lancashire. My father has just shouted: 'My best fucking gun,' and run downstairs. The last time he fired the gun there was a crash. I think he dropped it out of the window.

Re: How safe am I?

Truestory
Date: 3 June 2014
Time: 14.32

He is now in the yard opening and closing his gun and pointing it at the sky. His mouth is moving fast and his face is ugly. It is the sort of face that makes me want to hide under the quilt and hold my breath with my bobble hat on and cotton wool in my ears. I will take this opportunity to go and search for my mother. Thank you for your help.

Chapter 3

I didn't want a stupid biscuit, but I chose one anyway, putting it on a china plate with a little pair of tongs.

I inched towards the till, waiting for a fat woman to pay for a load of cake. I was going to have to choose what tea I wanted. Peppermint? Camomile? Blackcurrant-flavoured Rooibos?

Who cared? I didn't even want a cup of tea. But I had to have a cup of tea because a cup of tea and a biscuit in a café was my weekly treat for being trapped at Backwoods day in day out, year after year.

'Earl Grey, please.' I smiled at the girl but she didn't smile back and I felt stupid. I bit my lip; the back of my throat tightened and burned. I'd better not start crying. I snatched the change, resenting her sticky fingers all over it, and without saying thanks went and sat by the window.

I broke the biscuit into crumbs and stirred my tea until it went cold. I watched the shoppers trail past with their miserable faces. What was keeping them trapped in their dreary lives? Maybe they weren't trapped. Maybe they wanted to traipse about the grey precinct on a Tuesday afternoon carting their carrier bags of cheap crap from the pound shop with only a trip round Farmfoods to look forward to.

11

Maybe it was only me who might start screaming and never stop.

I was thinking about Duncan's suit in the skip dripping with paint and slipping between the floorboards and I wondered if there was such a thing as a council incinerator. Perhaps I could throw my old junk into a fire and watch it burn, see it singe and smoulder and burst into flames until there was nothing left but a pile of ashes.

My phone beeped and I jumped. A text from Sam. My heart raced as if I'd been punched. I stopped breathing. What now?

MUM BUY EAR DEFENDERS. URGENT.

What the hell? I stared at the phone then chucked it in my bag.

The pull back to the farm was immediate and irresistible; I had a panicky urge to wave a magic wand and be back there straight away.

Sometimes it took days to calm Sam down after a bad do, days that stretched and swirled around me, holding me fast, suffocating me. Days like the ones after Duncan lit the fire with Sam's map and we were forced to turn the house upside down searching for every map he'd ever drawn – and he could remember every single one. Days like the ones after Sam's first computer died and he wouldn't stop crying and refused to eat or sleep and barricaded himself in his room biting his hands and his arms until they bled and his sheets were all stuck to him and the scabs turned septic.

I don't believe in God but I started praying. Oh God let it be all right. Please, God, let it be all right.

I couldn't get back to the farm fast enough yet I had an overwhelming urge to head in the opposite direction

– trees and hedges whizzing past in a blur – my foot flat down, air ripping through the car window, and never stop, never have to face the day-to-day reality of life with Sam.

I mean, ear defenders? What the hell was going on? Was Duncan yelling and storming about in a temper? Had he started some half-cocked building project? Had he picked up that guitar he'd bought in the pub and never played? Or, God forbid was he trying to bully Sam into learning to box again?

Would I never learn that I couldn't leave them together, even for an hour?

I jumped a red light, squeezing through as the other lights turned green and I hammered it back to the farm. I shot through the gate, crunching over the potholes, stones flying. I pulled up and took a couple of deep breaths.

After the panic of getting back I didn't want to go inside. I gripped the wheel. I wanted to lean my forehead on it, close my eyes and let life wash over me, but I couldn't. I glanced up at Sam's bedroom window, but he wasn't looking for me; there was no shadowy figure hovering behind the curtains. I let a second of peace pass, then another, but I couldn't hide in the car all day; I had to go and pay the price for that cold cup of tea and crumbled up shortbread biscuit.

In the kitchen Duncan was squatting beside his stupid new cartridge press, muttering. He had a spanner in his hand, which was a bad sign.

'Fuckin' thing's fucked – '

I took in the scene and for a second was torn between ignoring him and yelling at him. I'd told him that cartridge press was another waste of time and money – which had been obvious all along unless you were Duncan.

Duncan lived in a world where you could Get Rich

Quick – he really believed it. No matter how many times his daft schemes didn't work, he kept coming up with another, and another – endless new ways of wasting what bit of ready cash we had.

This cartridge press was the latest. With this contraption Duncan was going to manufacture shotgun cartridges. In the kitchen. Like *that* was going to work. He'd come back one night with a mouldering pile of junk that was 'all he needed'. Casings, shot, caps, gunpowder, everything. Bought from someone in the pub. Obviously.

'This fucking thing's knackered me gun.'

I dumped my bag on the table.

'Where's Sam?'

Duncan bobbed his head about, squinting up into the machine.

'It's fucking warped – '

I went to the stove and picked up the omelette pan from lunchtime and looked at the other greasy pans, the sauce bottles, the buttery knives and the scattered crumbs.

'I said, where's Sam?'

He glanced at me for the first time since I'd come in.

'Sam?' He went back to his cartridge press. 'He'll be about.'

I gripped the pan handle so tight my knuckles went white. I wanted to crash the pan onto the stove, knock the crap on the floor, smash up the cartridge press and bash the pan off the corner of the table until either the table or the pan or my arm gave way. But I couldn't because – as I well knew – loud noises and sudden movements were NOT ALLOWED.

I forced myself to put down the pan. I took a deep breath. Held it. Let it out slowly.

Duncan dropped his spanner. 'Would you believe this fuckin' pile of shit.'

'What have you been doing?'

'Trying out some cartridges.'

'Where?'

He wrenched at the press and avoided my eye. 'Using that knackered weather vane on the barn end for target practice,' he said. 'Cartridge wasn't right. I dropped the effing gun out the bathroom window.'

So this was what Duncan got up to when he was supposed to be looking after Sam – the kid who was terrified of loud noises.

Flinging my coat over one of the armchairs by the range, I marched across the kitchen and ran upstairs. If Sam was chucking a fit somewhere, one of us had better go and sort it out. And as usual it had better be me.

He wasn't there. I flew from his bedroom to the bathroom and back – pulling off his quilt to see the rumples and grooves left by his body, his woolly hat stuffed with cotton wool, his headphones – but no Sam.

I glanced down the side of the bed where he hid his worn-out trainers in case I threw them away. They'd gone. They were old aerobics trainers of mine from twenty-odd years ago – they'd been blue then, they were grey now, like everything Sam agreed to wear, and they were worn soft and thin on the sole. Sam could run fast in them – like the wind when he wanted to. In fact he told me he could fly in those trainers and that only one step in every two or three actually touched the ground.

I'd explained Newton's third law of motion to him – not that I understood it myself – but we'd Googled it together. I told Sam he didn't have the fixed wings and high speeds to generate the lift and thrust to take off over Backwoods and soar away over The Wildwood. He wasn't convinced. As logical as Sam was about some things, he was stubborn and pig-headed about others, and there was no arguing with him when he got certain ideas in his head.

I clattered through the kitchen and out the back door. Duncan didn't look up – his bum was stuck in the air, jeans sliding down.

I jogged down the lane.

Sam had to be with Jeannie. He had to be. But that didn't stop my heart from racing and my imagination running riot. Was he crying? Was he hysterical? Was he hurting himself? Had he got there in exactly 823 steps?

I slowed to a walk, out of breath, my throat stinging.

He must have been terrified by Duncan's shotgun blasts and run off as far as he dared down Hell Fire Pass – to Jeannie's cottage. He always counted his steps as he hurtled along to make sure he got there in exactly 823.

He believed he *had* to make it in 823 because this would keep his world safe but if he took 822 or 824 he'd lose control of his world which would spin off into chaos. Like I said: there was no arguing with him when he got certain ideas in his head.

There was a new grave by Jeannie's front door. A home-made wooden cross had been hammered in, knocked up from an old floorboard with words on it done in a fancy stencil: *Here lies the dust of Banjo Patterson.*

I tapped at the front door and went in.

Sam was sitting at the kitchen table and Jeannie was in her wicker armchair by the range. They were drinking Jeannie's homemade lemonade – proper lemonade made with proper lemons – not like the fizzy junk I bought at Lo-Cost that had never seen a lemon. Sam was gulping it down.

'You all right, Sam?' I said, but he didn't answer and carried on gulping and gazing about him.

I could tell right away he'd got here in 823 steps.

'He's fine,' said Jeannie. 'Sit down.'

I dragged a chair out and slumped on it to let my thudding heart subside.

Jeannie's cottage always looked like a bomb had exploded in a jumble sale. It was the very opposite of Sam's own room which had everything in its place: the pens in separate tubs all sorted into colours; the paper lying flat and smooth on shelves; his laptop folded on his desk; and his trainers hidden six inches apart down the side of his bed.

Sam's room could not have been more different from this and I wouldn't have expected him to like it here, but there was nothing straightforward about Sam, and he did like it, he definitely did.

I quite liked it too. Jeannie's cottage had candles all over the place, usually in things not made for candles – saucers, jelly moulds, tea pots, shells – and at night she lit them and sat in the twinkly dark.

If Sam came down she told him stories.

She told him all sorts; she said she was a fabulist, a myth maker, a reader of auras. I wasn't even sure what those things were and sometimes I wished she wouldn't fill his head with all sorts of rubbish, but he seemed to like it – and at least spending time with Jeannie was *something*. She told him about time travelling and visiting other planets and revisiting former lives. She had one heck of an imagination; there was no doubt about that.

A few weeks ago she told us she'd had visions of spaceships landing in the Nevada Desert – a visit that had been verified by NASA. I'd sat there half-smiling and keeping schtum but Sam had drunk it all in and later at home he'd brought it up again.

'Jeannie saw space ships. In the Nevada Desert.'

I wasn't in the mood and carried on reading my 'True Life' magazine story about a woman with two wombs giving birth to clones.

'She saw spaceships,' he said again.

I didn't look up. 'I think Jeannie's got a bit of a screw loose.'

Sam was silent and I was immediately gripped with regret. I tore my eyes from my magazine and could see he was weighing up the phrase 'a bit of a screw loose'. I flicked my magazine shut.

'A bit of a screw loose only means being a bit different.'

Sam said nothing and slipped away to his room.

Since then he hadn't mentioned any of Jeannie's stories.

Jeannie shuffled to the dresser and took the jug of lemonade to refill Sam's glass.

'Lemonade?' she said.

I nodded.

She picked up a glass on the table, examined it for dregs and filled it for me.

Then she plopped the jug back on the dresser beside a rusty safe with its door open. The safe was full of chocolate biscuits. On top was a puppet with its strings in a knot. The dresser shelves were full of hard-backed books and an ancient radio that was wafting with cobwebs.

She took the biscuits and passed them to Sam. It was no wonder he ate next to nothing at home.

We sat munching and sipping.

I think it was this that Sam loved as much as the lemonade, the biscuits and the stories – the silence, the peace, and the chance just to be.

I gazed at the giant dresser. Jeannie always said she never swept cobwebs away because it left spiders homeless and hungry. She'd told us many a time about her pet spider,

Septimus, who lived in the top corner of the dresser and was 20 years old.

Next to the radio was a bowl of cookie dough. Today it was green, which I hoped meant it was peppermint. There were also carved wooden boxes that Jeannie claimed to have brought back from the Orient full of priceless treasure. Sam rooted through the priceless treasure from time to time and said it looked like buttons, buckles, pins and brooches. There were binocular cases with no binoculars, lanterns full of fir cones, copper jugs so dusty I could see Sam's initials written on them, and ticking clocks that she wound up every day or two.

Stuck in between were postcards from the Taj Mahal, Table Mountain and Ayers Rock. There were curling photos of dogs and cats, each marked with a name: Leaky, Tombstone, Janet – the same names as on the graves outside. One of the armchairs was piled with kindling that Jeannie had dragged back from The Wildwood. The walls were covered in paintings and framed photographs of a woman wearing long silk or velvet dresses covered in jewels and feathers, which Jeannie said was her.

Stuck between the paintings and the photographs were Sam's maps: all the same, all of Backwoods Farm, Big Hill, the Wild Wood, The Pile of Rubble Covered in Weeds, and the lane to Jeannie's cottage, 823 steps down HELL FIRE PASS.

'We buried Banjo Patterson,' said Sam, and he took another swig of his lemonade. 'He's going to turn to dust, like we all will.'

'Oh, that's a shame.' I said. Although neither of them looked very upset. It wasn't as if Jeannie was short of animals – I could spot at least five pairs of eyes from where I was sitting. They were tucked away among Jeannie's

19

stuff – dogs and cats she'd rescued from outhouses and waste ground and car parks; dogs and cats with bad habits and no manners that scratched and bit and only had one ear. They found corners and gaps to nestle in and to watch and to hide. One cat was hunkered down on top of the dresser, its shoulders sticking up like a gargoyle's, watching Sam drink his lemonade. On the bookcase a tabby cat was curled up neatly on a round fruit cake which made a perfect camouflage.

Yes, there were plenty left all right.

Jeannie made a toast with her lemonade.

'Here's to Banjo,' she said. She bent down and picked up a basket with a sleeping cat in it that looked all flat and stiff. For a second I thought another one had bit the dust. Then she flipped the basket and the cat over and wound a key on the bottom. It started purring – a loud ticking that for a second made Sam put his hands over his ears. She dropped it on the floor and rested her feet on it. The cat's belly was rising and falling.

'In't it sweet?' she said.

I wouldn't have expected Sam to like it in Jeannie's cottage but he did, he liked it a lot because it was peaceful and because Jeannie was there.

Sam had trusted Jeannie since before he could remember. He was a toddler when we were walking down the lane together and one of Jeannie's cats scratched him. It was sitting on a tree stump by her cottage and he'd tried to stroke it and the cat swiped at him. He tried a second time and it swiped again, this time catching him with a claw. Sam was part furious and part frustrated that he couldn't stroke it.

He started yelling – a real bawl – that brought Jeannie outside. I'd sort of known Jeannie for years as the crazy old cat-woman in the cottage down the road, but I'd barely had a conversation with her. I was going out to work every day before Sam came along – and Sam didn't come along until we'd been married thirteen years.

Anyway that day she was wearing a purple dressing gown with an orange flowery towel wrapped round her head. She cut quite a figure and I expected Sam's crying to get worse but she rubbed the cat's ears in a way that turned the animal into an ecstatic jelly. She nodded for Sam to stroke it. He stopped sobbing and buried his little fist in the cat's furry belly, a beam spreading across his face. The whole time he kept his eyes fixed on Jeannie; this vibrant vision who could entrance cats, do magic and make his dreams come true.

I felt pretty similar myself. Even at that age – two years old – Sam could not tolerate strangers and as a rule curled up into a ball, like a little hedgehog, until they left him alone, but not Jeannie.

I watched, amazed, as Sam stroked the cat and made his first and only friend. After that Jeannie's cats and Jeannie's cottage became fixtures on our walks. As Sam got older and his world shrank to almost nothing there were times I wondered if he'd leave his bedroom at all if it wasn't for Jeannie and her cats.

Chapter 4

Welcome to U Chat

Home　　**Chat**　　**Message Boards**　**Rules**　　**Contact Us**　**Log in**　　**Sign up**

How strong is my mind?

Truestory
Date: 3 June 2014
Time: 16.40

Is it possible to use the power of my mind to make people do what I want?

Re: How strong is my mind?

RootToot
Date: 3 June 2014
Time: 16.49

Sure. Why not? Psychos do it all the time.

Re: How strong is my mind?

SpiritLove
Date: 3 June 2014
Time: 16.55

Come over to Spirit&Soul Spiritual Community. We can show you the power of the mind. You'll be amazed what you can achieve with the right guidance. And if you like us and become a full member you'll get the gift of an in-depth numerology report for only $25. Just click here.

Re: How strong is my mind?

Truestory
Date: 3 June 2014
Time: 17.01

In particular I want to know how to control people's movements with the power of my mind. For instance stopping them from leaving me.

Re: How strong is my mind?

Fizzy Mascara
Date: 3 June2014
Time: 17.05

Nice try Truestory but if someone's gonna leave you they're gonna leave you – there's lots of mad shit on the internet and none of it's gonna sort that out!

Re: How strong is my mind?

JC
Date: 3 June 2014
Time: 17.08

Jesus Christ Almighty taught us to use the power of the mind – it calls upon God the Father to love us and care for us and guide us in our times of need. IT IS CALLED THE POWER OF PRAYER. Try it Truestory and you may find the FIRE OF CHRIST JESUS BURNING IN YOUR BELLY.

Re: How strong is my mind?

SpiritLove
Date: 3 June 2014
Time: 17.11

Just click the link here Truestory and come and join us. The Spirit&Soul Spiritual Community is right here waiting.

Re: How strong is my mind?

Truestory
Date: 3 June 2014
Time: 17.15

It would have to be accurate though because there are some people I want to leave and some I do not. For instance I do not want my mother to keep leaving me but I would prefer it if my father left me alone all the time.

Chapter 5

The cock-up with the cartridge press felt like the last straw. It may not have been the daftest thing Duncan had ever done, or the most expensive, but it was the wrong cock-up at the wrong time.

He'd wasted a hundred quid on that press and now his gun was knackered. He'd dropped it twenty feet out of the window because of the dodgy cartridges and it would cost a fortune to put right – except we didn't have a fortune to put anything right.

I'd brought Sam back from Jeannie's and I was in the kitchen with Duncan and the stupid cartridge press.

'You never give me a fuckin' break.' Duncan ran his hands through his hair. 'You *want* things to go wrong so *you* can be right.'

'Want things to go wrong!' I spun round to face him. 'Want things to go wrong! I pray for the day when things round here *don't* go bloody wrong.'

'You think you're so fucking clever,' said Duncan.

I crashed a dirty mug into the sink and the handle came off.

'So fucking clever,' he said again. 'What do you want me to do, eh? What?'

I opened my mouth, but the truth was I didn't have a clue what we should do about the failing farm and the mounting bills. Not a clue. I stood there holding the cup-less handle.

'What?' yelled Duncan. 'What the fuck should I do? If you fucking know everything. Fucking tell me.'

I flung the handle towards the bin. It hit the side and bounced off across the kitchen floor.

One thing I did know – Duncan should stop wasting time on half-baked schemes and concentrate on the farm proper. I drew breath, but before I could speak he was off again.

'Go on, tell me.' He was attacking the press with a spanner, clattering and clanging about.

'For Christ's sake,' I grabbed the broken mug and threw that at the bin too. It smashed straight in and the lid crashed to and fro. 'Shut up!' I yelled and readied myself for another yell only to see Sam staring at me with his hands clamped over his ears and his bobble had pulled down past his eyebrows. He walked over to the stove and gazed into the greasy frying pan.

'Where's my pasta?'

Duncan threw down his spanner and it clanged and skidded across the kitchen floor.

'I'll fucking shut up when you've told me what the hell we should do.'

Sam scrunched up the hat into his fists covering his ears.

'I want my pasta with just butter on.'

'*Then* I'll fucking shut up!' Duncan snatched the spanner back and lobbed it into the scabby box next to the press.

'Not tomato sauce, not grated cheese, not Philadelphia, just butter.' Sam had his eyes shut now as well as his fists over his ears and was speaking extra clearly as if I was deaf or stupid or something.

25

As Duncan kicked the scabby box, Sam started bending over as if he was toppling face forward in slow motion.

'Jesus Christ!' I looked from Duncan to Sam. Were they going to drive me into the Royal Bloody Albert after all? Sam peered at me through his crazy mop of hair poking out of the hat and covering half his face. I tried to drag my thoughts back from cartridges and broken guns and wasted money. I looked at Sam.

'What?' I said.

'For Chrissakes! What time is it?' Duncan straightened up and looked at the kitchen clock. It was past milking time and the cows would be shouting.

Duncan strode to the back door and shoved his feet in his boots. Muttering and swearing under his breath he grabbed his jacket and marched out, slamming the door. Sam flinched at the crash of the latch and for a moment he looked as though he might buckle at the knee.

'Just butter,' he whispered. 'Nothing else.'

I squeezed my fingernails into my palm and felt the sting. I must sound calm.

'It'll be ready in a minute.'

'Pasta takes twelve minutes,' said Sam. 'It is now 17:20hrs. And I want it with just butter.'

He staggered to his place and gazed at me from under his hat.

I turned back to the stove and took a deep breath. *In for three, hold for three, out for five.* That's what the magazines said. It was vital I stayed calm or Sam might have a meltdown himself. I had to pretend everything was all right even though my heart was thumping and my head was spinning.

I forced a smile. I needed to distract Sam for twelve minutes. I switched the kettle on and said:

'So what did you get up to this afternoon?' Then I

caught sight of the cartridge press and the broken gun. Shit, I didn't want to go *there* again. Change the subject. But it was too late; Sam had squeezed his eyes shut and was clinging to the edge of the table and holding his breath.

I needed a better distraction.

'Here, count out nineteen pieces – you don't want to end up with the wrong number, do you?' I held out the bag of pasta and a bowl. Sam's eyes opened, he looked at the pasta and the bowl, and then he took them. As he picked out the pasta pieces one at a time and placed them quietly in the bowl he started to breathe again.

And so did I.

I didn't say anything that night when Duncan went off to the pub even though he never went to the Dragon on a Tuesday. He sometimes went on a Wednesday and always on a Friday, but never on a Tuesday. I didn't care. I kept out of the way until I heard the back door crash and the Land Rover pull out of the yard.

I liked being at home on my own anyway. The fire was lit and I never felt alone when I'd got a fire. Spring was turning into summer outside but it never got very warm inside the stone walls of Backwoods. A fire was nearly always welcome and the way it crackled and shifted in the grate was company. It was mesmerising; I could stare at it for ages.

Strictly speaking I wasn't on my own of course: Sam was upstairs, probably on his computer, but I didn't count Sam as company. He didn't see the point of conversation. Talking was for passing brief information only and not to be engaged in lightly. Or sometimes it was for a one-sided imparting of lengthy, possibly technical, information whether the audience was interested or not. Unless it was David Attenborough on low volume – so you practically couldn't hear it – he hated the noise of the telly and the radio too.

I put my feet up on the range and felt the heat on the back of my legs. I closed my eyes. I was aware of the cartridge press sitting all innocent beside me with the stacks of casings and shot and all the other crap that had come with it. The boxes were bashed up and filthy as though they'd been dumped in someone's garden shed for twenty years waiting for some idiot to come along and buy them.

Well Duncan was your man – after all he'd bought the caravan that was currently rotting away in the orchard. Five hundred quid he'd given for that. A scabby old tourer, for God's sake, the thing was forty years old.

He'd turned up last summer as pleased as Punch with it hooked up behind his Land Rover. It could be rented out for holidays, he said. Lots of people wanted to go to the country on their holidays. Or it could be used for the overspill if the Green Dragon was full. I was speechless and gaped at him as he patted the stupid thing and smiled at it. The pub was four miles away. Did it even take guests? And what about a bathroom? Who the hell went on holiday where there wasn't a proper bathroom?

Duncan said *we* had a bathroom and people could use that or they could use the outside washhouse – people liked it authentic nowadays – and I had to roll up my sleeves and get stuck in if we weren't going to lose the farm.

I nearly threw something at him then. In fact I thought I'd heard him wrong. Roll up my sleeves and get stuck in? I was stuck in all right – I was stuck in the middle of home schooling our son, a boy who had refused to leave the farm for over six years and didn't look like he was planning to leave it any time soon.

But Duncan ignored that and said it was all about

diversifying. Farming was in the doldrums and it wasn't going to get any better, not now, not ever, and so farmers like him had to explore all the options for maximising income.

He'd read it in the Farmers Weekly.

I shook my head and asked when exactly the Farmers Weekly had suggested lumbering yourself with a heap of junk like that old caravan.

He'd hooked up some long trailing electricity wires to the caravan, and brushed it out and got me to put the curtains through the wash. He'd whistled as he worked like Cinderella or Snow bloody White or whoever it was. Then he'd run over the outside with the power washer. But it still looked shabby and depressing and, despite all the scrubbing, not much cleaner. In fact, all the cleaning had done was to show up the rust spots, the chips and the worn-out bits.

After a week or two he'd stopped going on about it.

The caravan was still there mouldering away like the bloody eyesore it was.

Sam wasn't allowed to play in it mind you, even if he'd wanted to. Because at the end of the day Duncan said it was an investment and you never knew, you just never knew what opportunities that caravan might throw up.

He landed back from the pub after midnight and I could hear voices as he opened the kitchen door. I couldn't imagine who he was talking to. His drinking pals stayed in the pub and he hadn't brought them back since Sam was tiny and woke at the slightest sound and shrieked at the glimpse of a strange face.

He stuck his head round the door to see if I was still up and kind of raised his eyebrows in acknowledgement. I wouldn't have been up if I hadn't fallen asleep in the armchair and now I had a crick in my neck and a sore back. I struggled up, trying to look awake, as Duncan came in followed by a scruffy bloke I'd never set eyes on before. He was carrying a big rucksack.

'This is Larry Dougal,' he said, and the homeless-looking bloke raised his hand.

'Could I borrow your lavvie?' he said. Duncan pointed him to the outside washhouse.

'He'll be a good help around the place,' Duncan whispered to me. He looked excited. 'He reckons he can turn his hand to anything: welding, fencing, anything.'

'Who is he?' I hissed. 'And where's he from?'

'He's a good bloke,' he said.

'But who is he?'

Duncan hummed and hawed but the upshot was the guy was some kind of travelling worker he'd just found in the pub.

'You've brought back a bloody tramp?' I said.

'No, he works here and there. Knows his stuff.'

'So he's a drifter who's washed up in the pub on his way to friggin' nowhere, and you've brought him here. Bloody great.'

Duncan looked pissed off, but hell, I was pissed off too. In fact, I wanted to strangle him.

'What about Sam?' I said. 'How's Sam going to take it?'

Duncan's face closed. 'It's about time he met a few folk. It'll do him good.'

'And where the hell's he going to sleep? Our spare room's empty except for three buckets catching the rain.' I fixed Duncan with a hard stare. 'And he's *not* dossing on the sofa.'

Most of the farmhouse downstairs was taken up with one big room with a massive table in the middle, cooker and kitchen stuff at one side and easy chairs, a sofa, range and a telly at the other. I wouldn't have put it past Duncan to shack this bloke up in a sleeping bag in the corner.

'He'll sleep in the caravan.' A look of triumph passed over Duncan's face. 'The caravan will be just right for him.'

This was worse than holiday makers.

'We can't afford to pay him,' I said. 'We can hardly afford to pay *ourselves*.' I muttered this last bit because Larry had come back from the loo. He wandered across to the range to warm his hands over the embers, pretending he couldn't hear.

'It's all taken care of, isn't it, Larry?' Larry smiled a bit. 'We'll explain in the morning,' said Duncan. 'We'd better go and get the caravan sorted.'

When they went outside with torches and a stack of old blankets, Duncan was whistling.

Larry smiled at me as he pulled the door to and I couldn't tell if he was smirking or trying to apologise but it didn't matter; he was leaving first thing in the morning and that was that.

Chapter 6

I got up next morning to find Duncan had already finished milking because Larry had been a Good Samaritan since first light.

They'd got the frying pan out and the minute I came downstairs I was presented with a doorstep bacon butty.

It was hard to turn down – it had melted butter running out the side and the bacon looked lovely and crispy – but I managed it. They couldn't buy *me* with a butty.

They didn't seem to register my protest; they cut it in two and polished it off between them. They were deep in conversation about crop yields and optimum temperatures and other farming stuff they seemed to be animated about.

I leant against the cooker nursing a cup of coffee all knotted up inside worrying about what Sam would do when he came down and saw this bloke with his feet under the table.

I willed them to talk quietly, not to laugh too loudly, not to ask him any questions, not to pass comment on his food or his appearance or anything else, not to touch him, for God's sake, not to even look at him.

I watched the clock tick round to 8.25, straining to hear Sam padding down the stairs. I got his favourite bowl and spoon ready and put them on the table beside the

Weetabix and the sugar and milk. I clattered the bowl down and clanged the spoon to show how pissed off I was. Duncan hadn't even got Larry to sit at the other end of the table, he was sitting right next to Sam's place.

When I heard Sam trotting downstairs I froze. What was it going to be? A tantrum? Hiding? Hurting himself? Not eating for 24 hours?

Sam came through the stair door and stood there for a long, long moment looking at this weird guy with a blue bandana and a gold earring eating a bacon butty with brown sauce dripping out the side, and who had a map partly spread out on the table in front of him.

Sam glanced at me.

'You're all right,' I said. I tried to make it sound like this happened every morning. 'Come and get your breakfast.'

He stood stock still, gazing at Larry and his butty and his map.

'Get your Weetabix,' I said, pushing his bowl as far from Larry as I could. 'Come on.'

He sidled up to the table but he did not sit down. He stood as far away as possible and in slow motion put the sugar and milk on his Weetabix then picked up his spoon and mushed it up like he did every day. Except today his eyes were fixed the whole time on Larry and his map.

I'd have put money on a scruffy stranger at the break-fast table making Sam do a runner, but no. He took in the bandana round Larry's head, the stubbly face, the pierced ear, the sunburned arms, the dirt under his fingernails, the partly-folded map, staring and staring like I hadn't told him a thousand times it was rude.

Larry didn't seem to care – or even to notice at first – then he looked up and wiped his mouth with the back of his hand and grinned at Sam.

'How's you, son?'

33

I froze. Shut up, I thought. Shut up. Shut up. Shut up.

But Sam kept staring as he scooped up his Weetabix at arm's length from the table and posted it into his mouth.

'What are yous up to today, then?' said Larry.

Duncan bashed his mug down and said:

'Answer him, Sam!'

Sam took a step back.

'Stop shouting,' I said. 'That's not going to help.'

'Sit down, Sam,' said Duncan a bit more calmly. 'And answer him.'

Sam sank straight to the floor in one rather graceful movement and sat cross-legged, his spoon poised in mid-air. In a faint voice, he said: 'Those sentences did not make grammatical sense. And I am not his son.' Duncan scowled but Larry burst out laughing. Pointing at Sam, he said:

'I bet you're right, son.'

Sam blinked at him.

Sam saw next to nobody: the vet and the milk-tanker driver and the odd travelling salesman flogging cow food or whatever. But when they were about he'd only watch from the window keeping his distance so they couldn't see him. Then there was Jeannie, Dr Watts – when we'd called him out a couple of times – and the bloke from the education department who came to make sure I was teaching him something. That was about it. When other visitors came – and let's face it there weren't many after years of not being asked – Sam stayed out of sight.

Larry tried again. 'So what you up to today then?'

Sam was still sitting on the floor too far from the table to reach his Weetabix, his spoon still hovering.

'I am doing geography,' he whispered.

Larry nodded: 'A million years ago when I was at school geography was my favourite subject. Nowadays rather than study the world in a book, I travel it.' And he tapped his map.

Sam wrapped his arms round his knees. 'One million years ago you would not have been at school. You would have been living in the Palaeolithic period with bands of other Homo sapiens, collecting plants and making tools out of stone.'

Larry laughed and Duncan snapped: 'Come back to the table and get your breakfast eaten properly!'

Sam ignored Duncan. He strained to see onto the table and his attention was fixed on Larry's map. As though speaking to himself, Sam said:

'I have seen that map on the internet.'

'Aye,' said Larry.

Duncan cut in obviously thinking enough time had been spent on Sam: 'So what do you reckon the crop yield will be in the first six months if we can get it sown this week or next?'

Larry turned away from Sam and scratched his chin to think about it.

'Well . . .'

I threw what was left of my cold coffee into the sink.

'Sam, I've got you some studying sorted. I've sent a link. Geography.'

By now Sam had curled himself into a small ball and hutched himself halfway to the bottom of the stairs.

Duncan and Larry scraped their chairs back and put their boots on to go outside.

'Thanks for breakfast,' Larry said, even though I'd had nothing to do with it. He gave a little salute to Sam who covered his head with his arms. When they'd gone I took Sam's spoon off him.

35

'Have you had enough? Do you want to come and sit at the table properly?'

He gave a tiny shake of his head and, scrambling to his feet, he scuttled upstairs.

I sat among the dirty pots and greasy pans. I knew I should be grateful Sam had not freaked out at the sight of Larry. I should be relieved that the worst had been a bit of bluntness and curling into a ball – but I wasn't grateful or relieved; I was reeling and jittery. There would be a price to pay for this. Of that I was certain. There was always a price to pay with Sam.

I was tempted by one of Larry's roll-ups, even though I hadn't smoked in years. I slipped the lid off the battered tin of Golden Virginia he'd left on the table, chose one he'd rolled earlier and lit it with one of his matches.

I took a drag, put my head back and let the nicotine do its stuff. The smoke drifted across the kitchen. What had Sam really made of Larry? With Sam there was no way of getting inside his head; no way of knowing. That was hard. It was sad to have a child who was a closed book to you, a child who was a baffling enigma.

I heard Sam trotting downstairs and I knocked the ash off my fag and put it in Larry's saucer. He came in and examined the table, ignoring the smoking fag. Then he gazed about the rest of the kitchen searching for something.

'How's the geography?'

He didn't reply.

'That man might still be here at lunchtime,' I said. 'But I'll make sure he's gone by teatime.'

Sam stopped scanning the work surfaces and looked at me.

'No,' he said. 'Larry is an acquaintance of mine. I do not want him to go.'

I was so surprised I gaped at him, waiting for the punchline.

But Sam said nothing else. He looked around Larry's chair and up and down the kitchen then, giving up his search, he went back upstairs.

Chapter 7

Welcome to U Chat

Home   Chat   Message   Rules   Contact Us   Log in   Sign up
Boards

I want it but I do not know where it is.

Truestory   What shall I do? I want it but I do not know where it
Date: 4 June 2014   is.
Time: 9.25

Re: I want it but I do not know where it is.

Fizzy Mascara   Huh?
Date: 4 June 2014
Time: 9.32

Re: I want it but I do not know where it is.

Sweet Cheeks   We all want it babes, don't u worry!! ☺
Date: 4 June 2014
Time: 9.35

Re: I want it but I do not know where it is.

SpiritLove
Date: 4 June 2014
Time: 9.41

Hi Truestory, Don't think of the item as lost, think of it as ready to be found. So the first step is to relax and stop looking. Then take some deep breaths and imagine – what does it feel like, what does it smell like? You will begin to resonate with the object and it will be found. I've got a great little booklet on this and other visualisation techniques described on our Spirit&Soul website, which can be <u>purchased here</u> Only $2.50. Plus p&p.

Re: I want it but I do not know where it is.

AuntieMaud
Date: 4 June 2014
Time: 9.45

My mother used to use divining rods to find lost things – actually they were wire coat hangers but they did just as well. She held one rod/hanger and repeated the name of the lost thing until the rod/hanger moved to point in a direction. She would then hold both rods/hangers and walk in that direction. When the rods/hangers crossed she would find it!

Re: I want it but I do not know where it is.

AuntieMaud
Date: 4 June 2014
Time: 9.51

By the way, my mother once found a diamond ring even though she was only looking for her sandal. She has been dead for 26 years now though so I'm afraid I can't ask her for any more details.

Re: I want it but I do not know where it is.

NoShitSherlock
Date: 4 June 2014
Time: 9.55

My mum always said – it's where you left it, is where it's at!!

Re: I want it but I do not know where it is.

AuntieMaud
Date: 4 June 2014
Time: 9.59

My mother was a very wise woman too. I used to wonder how I would manage without her. I still wonder that. She was my best friend.

Re: I want it but I do not know where it is.

Truestory
Date: 4 June 2014
Time: 10.03

An acquaintance of mine has a map. I want it but I do not know where it is. It is correct to refer to him as an acquaintance because an acquaintance is defined in my on-line dictionary as a "slight friendship". I only have a slight friendship with Larry because my father only found him in the pub last night.

Re: I want it but I do not know where it is.

Truestory
Date: 4 June 2014
Time: 10.07

The map is one of the Ordnance Survey Explorer range with a scale of 1:25,000, which means it is 4 centimetres to every kilometre. It is of the area of Backwoods Farm, which is Number 296 in the Ordnance Survey index. I have never seen this map in real life. I have only seen it on the internet. I want it, but I do not know where it is.

Chapter 8

'Cannabis!' I stared at Duncan. He'd finally lost it. 'We're going to grow cannabis?'

'Yeah, Larry's an expert.'

My wooden spoon dripped over the soup pan. This was a joke, right?

Duncan was full of it: going on about crop yield per square foot and polytunnels and ventilation requirements. I hadn't seen him like this for ages. Not since the caravan episode. He was striding round the kitchen bombarding me with details, ridiculous, stupid details about thermostatic fans and carbon filters, a big daft grin on his face. This was going to sort out all our money worries. This was going to be the answer to everything. This was it.

'What the hell do you know about growing cannabis?' I threw the spoon into the pan, and soup splattered up the wall and across the stove.

'Larry's worked in a market garden.'

'Larry's a bloody hobo you found in the pub last night, for Christ's sake. And what's all this about polytunnels? We haven't got a polytunnel.'

'We're taking the trailer this afternoon.'

I grabbed the spoon and stirred again, so fast the soup splashed and spat on the stove.

'It's *illegal*, for a start.'

'That's the thing about being stuck out here – who's going to know?'

'And this is all Larry, is it?'

'No, *he's* a stroke of luck.'

Some stroke of luck. I took a deep breath. This wasn't the time for ranting; Sam would be down in a minute. I could see Larry through the window, mooching up the yard, throwing his fag end down and screwing it into the ground with the toe of his boot. I wanted to strangle him. I wanted to strangle both of them. When I thought the worst that could happen was Duncan wasting money on crappy caravans and cartridge presses, it seemed we were setting up in business as cannabis dealers.

'Yeah, it was lucky finding Larry,' Duncan said. 'I've never set eyes on him before and as a rule I don't go to the pub on a Tuesday, but if I hadn't met Larry this couldn't have got off the ground. It's one of them chances in a million. You've got to grab them while you can.'

I had to stop myself grabbing *him*. I felt like wielding the wooden spoon like a club, brandishing it and telling him he was an idiot who never learned and to wake up and see some sense while he still had the chance. But it was nearly half past twelve and Sam would be down any second.

I grabbed some bowls and shoved them round the table – pushing Duncan's towards him so fast it nearly shot off the end. He was telling a long-winded tale about how it had all come about: how Bill Webb's mate, Dob, had heard about the stuff from his son's pal, Smash, up past Lancaster, who said he knew a guy near Penwortham who had the stuff going cheap, seeds and everything. The fella's neighbours were getting nosey but for folks out in the middle of nowhere it was a chance too good to miss, a real opportunity.

42

'Larry's sticking around for a few days – going to help me get everything set up in return for bed and board. Won't cost us a penny.' Duncan looked like he'd won the lottery. 'He's welded the yard gate this morning too. Good as new.'

I drew breath to point out that for a scheme supposed to be secret, a lot of dodgy folk seemed to know about it. But Sam was running downstairs and Larry was tapping on the door. It'd wait. As I came back to the table with the soup pan, Duncan grabbed my wrist.

'The cannabis will pay for the cows, Alice. It's a chance to keep this place going.' I sloshed some soup into his bowl. Sam was standing at the bottom of the stairs watching Larry wash his hands at the kitchen sink.

I nudged Duncan's hand off. Would Sam come in or would he leg it back upstairs?

'Sam, it's your favourite – mushroom. Come and sit down.'

'My favourite is French onion. My second favourite is mushroom.' Sam's eyes were fixed on Larry who dried his hands and smiled at him.

'Yous done your Geography, son? Keep at it and you'll soon find your way around the world, like me.'

Duncan didn't seem to register that Larry and Sam had arrived. He touched my arm again.

'This could fix everything, Alice.'

I shook him off. 'Sam, come and eat your dinner,' I said.

Sam glided across the kitchen and slid into his place. He picked up his spoon and poked it round his bowl.

'Larry Dougal sounds like two first names put together,' he said.

Larry dragged his chair back and sat down, smiling.

43

'Aye, you're right, son.' He grinned at me and nodded thanks for the soup.

'I Googled to discover if there are any famous Dougals,' said Sam. But a song came on by Dougal and Gammer which was 160 decibels and made my heart beat at 110 beats a minute.'

Larry nodded at him and slurped his soup. 'Aye?' he said.

'The song was called "Fuck Me I'm Famous".

'Sam!' Duncan rounded on Sam: 'Don't talk like that!'

Sam dipped a piece of bread in his soup and put it in his mouth. He didn't look at Duncan and I wasn't sure he'd even heard him.

'Soup okay?' I said to divert attention. Duncan was great at ignoring Sam most of the time but came down on him like a ton of bricks when he stepped out of line.

'Aye, it's a nice drop a' soup,' said Larry.

'Aye, it's a nice drop a' soup,' parroted Sam.

'Sam!' I shook my head.

He went on. '"Fuck Me I'm Famous" was even louder than my mother shouting at my father "YOU DRIVE ME BLOODY MAD BRINGING A BLOODY HOBO INTO THE HOUSE".'

'SAM!' Both of us yelled that time.

'Yahoo Answers says that the symptoms of being mad are "Yelling, clenched face and slanted eyebrows".' He went on, 'In which case I think both my mother and father may have been driven mad.'

Larry kept a straight face, but I saw the corner of his mouth twitch. Duncan appeared to be doing the impossible – eating his lunch through gritted teeth.

Sam was looking around the kitchen like he'd lost something. Suddenly his spoon clattered to the table and he slithered down in his seat and disappeared from view.

'GET BACK ON YOUR SEAT!' Duncan jumped up. He strode round the table, knocked Sam's chair backwards and bent down to grab him by the scruff of the neck. He hauled him up by his sweatshirt yelling 'GET. BACK. ON. YOUR. SEAT.'

I felt both anger and tears well up. The situation between Duncan and Sam could boil over in a matter of moments – but who was the adult? Surely Duncan should be able to keep his temper for more than five seconds.

Sam was spluttering and choking, his eyes swimming as Duncan dropped him back on his seat.

I screamed 'You're going to kill him!' Sam clamped his hands over his ears to block out the noise. I wiped my eyes on the bottom of my jumper. 'You'll bloody kill him.'

Larry patted Sam's back.

'Get it up, son, get it up,' he said as Sam retched and coughed a piece of bread onto the table. 'That's it.'

'Why are you always like that with him?'

Ignoring me, Duncan sat down and started shovelling his soup in with a face like thunder. I dropped my head into my hands. I couldn't be bothered keeping up appearances – I didn't know Larry from Adam anyway. What the hell had Duncan expected, inviting strangers into the house?

'It's okay, Sam,' I said. 'You don't need to eat any more.' Sam was still gazing about the room absorbed in his search for something and as though the nasty choking scene had never happened. 'It's okay, you can go to your room,' I said, and Sam left the table in slow motion and disappeared upstairs.

Larry finished his soup and said he was off for a smoke before they went for the stuff and he went outside. This was my chance to kill the stupid cannabis idea once and for all.

45

'This cannabis thing's not going to work. Can you not see that?'

'It's the answer, Alice. Just wait and see.'

'Is it bloody hell!' I picked up Sam and Larry's bowls and clattered them on top of mine.

'*Something's* got to stop the money draining away,' said Duncan. 'We could start making some money again. Imagine that.'

'You're driving me mad. Honest to God, this is the last bloody straw.'

'Larry says it's piss easy growing cannabis. He says it grows like weeds. He says you can't go wrong. Honestly, you can't go wrong.'

I looked at him. Can't go wrong? Really? If there was one thing I knew after being married to Duncan for twenty-four years, it was that he could always go wrong.

'It's illegal, for a start,' I said. 'And I'll say right now that it's going to be another bloody waste of time and money. *Another* one.'

'It's what we've been waiting for.' Duncan folded his arms. 'You wait and see.'

Duncan shoved his boots and jacket on and crashed the door closed behind him. After a few minutes I saw him and Larry mooching across to the Land Rover. They were chatting away like there'd been no swearing and choking and screaming and crying in the kitchen. Like it had never happened. That was the thing: Duncan always over-reacted but then he recovered and moved on leaving me with my stomach in knots.

The Land Rover pulled out of the yard. I sat at the kitchen table drinking coffee and smoking a roll-up I'd found on the kitchen units. It had been left next to my coffee cup with a box of matches.

I could hear the Land Rover juddering down the lane and I cursed them both. I was so furious and lost in thought about how I could get back at Duncan and get rid of Larry that when Sam walked through on his way outside I couldn't get to grips with what he was up to.

'Are you all right, Sam?' I said, but he didn't answer. 'Where are you going?' I squashed the cigarette out in a soup bowl.

'Outside,' he said, pulling the door to behind him.

He came back ten minutes later when I was wiping the crumbs off the table. He was carrying a pair of yellow pliers by his finger and thumb and wearing a pair of sunglasses.

Where've you been?

'The workshop,' he said. 'Dad says: "Don't let me catch you in my workshop". But he's not here. So he couldn't catch me.' And he headed upstairs.

I had a shaky feeling that things were about to get worse. Sam had stared at Larry a lot during lunchtime; in fact he seemed mesmerised by him. The whole Larry thing was unnerving me – I didn't think he was having a good effect on any of us and I wanted him gone.

It took Duncan and Larry over two hours to get back with a great trailer-load of metal lengths and hoops and plastic sheeting. When they pulled into the yard I didn't look outside. I stayed at the table with my back resolutely to the window.

I could hear them shouting to each other as they unloaded the trailer. They sounded like a couple of kids, laughing and joking and dragging stuff round to the back of the house.

If they'd been doing anything else – anything useful or sensible or not plain stupid – I'd have taken them a cup of tea in the can with some cake or something. But they

47

weren't doing anything useful or sensible, they were doing something ridiculous, so they could forget it. I sat tight.

From the washroom I watched them pace out the plot and whack posts in with the sledgehammer. I spotted Sam skulking round the orchard. He looked like he was concentrating hard on the ground. As I watched he headed off towards Larry's caravan. No, it *wasn't* Larry's caravan. It was *not*. I mustn't think of it as Larry's caravan – I wanted him out of there and back on the road as soon as possible.

An hour later they'd gone quiet. I strained to hear but the banging and the shouting seemed to have stopped. I went back to the washroom to unload the machine and through the window I could see them, hands on hips, puzzling over something. Good, I hoped they'd bought a load of old junk that didn't fit together. That would really make my day. I dragged the washing out of the machine and dumped it in the plastic basket.

Going out the back door, I saw Sam beside Larry's caravan. What *was* he up to? I threw the basket down beside the line and started to shake the washing out, making big slapping sounds. Larry and Duncan looked up.

'Can't get the hoops straight.' Duncan shouted.

I ignored him, keeping a poker face. Absolutely great. I hoped they'd never get them straight.

I saw Sam again coming out from behind the caravan still gazing at the ground. He was carrying lengths of what looked like thick wire, as though he was dousing for water.

Duncan and Larry saw him too.

'Come here and hold this post,' shouted Duncan. Sam kept walking, head down.

'I said come here!' Duncan raised his voice and there was an edge to it. 'We need some help.'

Sam jolted to a stop and looked up. He hesitated, looking towards his dad, then towards the wire things.

'Come here!'

Carefully Sam laid the wire things on the ground and walked towards his dad. 'Hold that post,' Duncan said. 'We need to get the thing square.'

Sam held the post and looked at the plot.

'You need Pythagoras's Theorem,' he said.

Duncan and Larry strode away from the post in different directions.

'You need Pythagoras's Theorem,' said Sam again.

Duncan hesitated. 'Eh?'

Sam pointed at the plot. 'To get it straight you need four right-angled triangles. X squared,' he pointed to the length of the plot, 'plus Y squared,' he pointed to the width of the plot 'equals Z squared.'

He looked at Duncan as though that explained everything about erecting a polytunnel. 'Z,' said Sam, 'is the hypotenuse.' And he pointed again towards the plot.

I shook a pillow case, making a satisfying slap, and then I did it again – to remind Duncan that I was watching him being humiliated by his eleven-year-old son. I squinted at the three of them gathered round the post. Duncan was rubbing the back of his neck. Any second now he'd lose his temper. Larry was gazing steadily at Sam.

'You need to make sure the diagonals are exactly the same length,' said Sam. 'Take the dimensions of the construction and calculate the hypotenuse using Pythagoras's Theorem.' Sam was now gazing back at where he'd left the wire things. 'Although in fact it was not Pythagoras who devised the theorem,' he said, 'it was one of his followers.'

'For fuck's . . .' Duncan was cut off by Larry.

'That sounds like a great plan, son. Why do you no' work it out for us?'

Sam looked at Larry.

'What are the dimensions?' he asked.

'Supposed to be 24 foot by 14 foot.'

'You need to convert it to metric measurements. Applying Pythagoras's Theorem to imperial measurements is an unnecessarily complex procedure.'

Duncan and Larry looked at each other.

'Well. I dunno – '

'If it is 24 feet by 14 feet then it is 7.31 metres by 4.26 metres,' said Sam.

Larry lifted his eyebrows.

'Which means your diagonal must be the square root of 7.31 squared plus 4.26 squared.' Sam let go of the post. 'It will be necessary for you to use the Pythagorean Theorem Calculator,' he said.

He walked off. He went back for his wire things and I watched him circling the orchard for the umpteenth time. He veered towards me at one point and I could hear him murmuring 'Larry's map, Larry's map,' as he disappeared back up the orchard and behind the caravan.

I could see Larry trying to calculate the length of his hypotenuse on his smart phone. Reception was crap – even if he knew what he was doing, which I seriously doubted. Duncan meanwhile was pacing to and fro rubbing the back of his neck again which was getting redder and redder. Honestly it would have taken a heart of stone not to laugh.

I decided to follow Sam. He was acting weird and he was making me nervous. I went behind the caravan and found the door swinging open. I peered round it and could see Sam holding the wire things above the table. On the table were saucers full of ciggie butts and plastic lighters and

a four pack of Carlsberg Special Brew. I glanced around
the rest of the caravan – there was the pile of blankets and
a sleeping bag on the bed with a bottle of Glenlivet and a
hard-backed book on top.

'What you doing?' I said.

Sam had his eyes closed and he said: 'Don't think of the
thing as lost. Think of it as ready to be found.'

'You what?' I felt awkward. Larry was an unwelcome
guest but the caravan was still his private room and this
felt like prying. 'Come on, you shouldn't be in here.'

'Take some deep breaths and imagine what does it feel
like, what does it smell like? You will begin to resonate
with the object and it will be found.'

'What? Sam, for God's sake, come out.' I was hissing
at him now.

Sam opened his eyes and stared at the wires for a few
seconds.

'I think it's time to draw a map,' I said a bit desperately.
'Come on.'

Sam came out of the caravan with the wires straight out
in front of him, he wandered off towards the back door
and I let him go.

'Alice!' It was Larry. I took a few steps closer. 'That
map of mine. It's in the Land Rover. Give it tae Sam,
would you?'

I left the map at Sam's place next to his tuna butty. He
was still carrying those wires when he came downstairs
and he put them on the table before he spotted the map.
He stood stock still and then said to himself 'They work'.
He stretched his hand out and stroked the shiny surface of
the map as if he half-expected it to disappear.

'That's kind of Larry, isn't it?' I said. 'You'll have to say
thank you.'

51

He unfolded the map, holding it like it was an ancient parchment – delicate and precious and worth its weight in gold – before laying the map open on the square showing Backwoods. He examined it minutely, poring over every detail – although he seemed to be doing it with his eyes half-shut.

Then he took a pen and wrote 'The Big Hill' on the small unnamed hill near the farm.

'Stop writing on Larry's map,' I said. But Sam was in a map-induced world of his own. 'The Wildwood', he wrote on the trees in Four-acre.

'I said, stop it!'

I grabbed more laundry from the basket. As I looked up I saw him write HELL FIRE PASS in great big red letters across the lane beside a skull and crossbones he'd drawn. I sighed; I might as well talk to myself.

He was map-daft. He could spend hours Googling maps. He knew where all the lines of longitude and latitude passed through each continent and the name of every city within a hundred miles of the equator. It wasn't down to my teaching skills either; it was Sam's own obsession with the subject. He spent hours examining maps on the internet, as though the rules and the keys and the symbols were a comfort to him. I think he believed if he studied the world long enough it would all fall into place and begin to make sense. Same thing with Maths: he was always searching for patterns that made his world a place of order.

Last September, when the man from the council came to make sure I was teaching him something and that the 'home schooling' really existed, the chap ticked a few boxes on his clipboard but by the time Sam had shown him the proof to Pythagoras's Theorem and explained why the square root of two was irrational and recited Pi to twenty-five decimal places he'd put his clipboard away.

Good job he didn't ask about Sam's life skills. He might well be able to map the world but he couldn't find his way to the shops to buy a carton of milk, or visit the doctor's, or get a haircut at the barbers – all these things were impossible for him. I was the only person who had ever cut his hair. The last time was over two years ago but the horrific screaming drama of it was seared on my memory as if it was yesterday.

He was still drawing on Larry's map – the row of little gravestones now, outside Wayside Cottage. I pretended not to notice. It was easier that way.

Sam admired his handiwork, and then started to unfold the entire map. He looked scared and for a few minutes clung to the edge of the table and seemed to be counting under his breath. Then he began again, unfolding slowly and carefully and with his eyes open a tiny fraction.

'It's a good map, eh?' I said. Hoping to take that slightly mad look off his face, but he didn't reply.

I tried again: 'Nice of Larry to lend it, wasn't it, Sam?' But there was no answer – he was in a world of his own and for the time being there was no reaching him.

By now he'd got the map fully open and he put his finger on our lane and followed it round Big Hill, past The Wildwood, and over the words HELL FIRE PASS and the skull and crossbones. His finger travelled slowly after that and kept stopping, following the wiggles in the B-roads and then the main road until it came to Lancaster, by which time his arm was stretched as far as it would go.

Then he traced the route all the way back.

He was following the journey I took every Tuesday on my trip to town. I could see the tears on his face and watched him rest his forehead against his sweatshirt until the sleeve was sodden with tears.

Chapter 9

That night I did a double take when Sam arrived back at the kitchen table after supper. He never came back when Duncan was eating; he stayed in his room messing with his computer or drawing maps, or sometimes he went to Jeannie's. But tonight he peered round the door at Larry and Duncan before sidling across the kitchen and sitting down.

He had that map under his arm. I felt nervous.

Sam had always had a hair trigger. When he was a baby, and I'd still been trying to take him out into the world, I'd felt as conspicuous and on edge as if I'd had a DANGER UXB sign strapped to the front of the buggy. I'd dodged and dived along the pavement praying for folk to get out the way and, God forbid, not to try to talk to him because it was people he didn't like. Me and Duncan and Jeannie were more or less all right, or at least he could tolerate us, but anyone else – or even the off-chance of anyone else – and he'd go mad, screaming and crying and looking as if he was working himself up to a seizure.

Almost all the time we were out he'd have his eyes shut, usually with his bobble hat pulled down to his chin. He'd worn that original bobble hat come rain or shine until it fell to bits. By that time he hadn't let anyone touch his hair for years and it had grown so long he hardly needed the hat anyway.

54

I'd enrolled him in a playgroup once but it was a disaster. He hated being with other children, refused to take his hat and coat off and spent all his time curled in a ball or with his face flattened against the wall. He refused to talk or eat or drink until I took him away again.

The staff were glad to see him go – they had plenty of regular kids who were happy to do normal stuff like slurping juice and gumming cookies and singing the necessary nursery rhymes. The last thing they wanted was some weird kid complicating things.

'Is he always like this?' one nursery nurse asked. 'Perhaps you should take him to the doctor.'

Other parents didn't help either: gathering their kids up as though Sam was contagious; looking relieved he wasn't theirs; raising their eyebrows in disapproval when he acted different. They tended to give both me and Sam a wide berth and managed to say an awful lot without saying a word. I was constantly on the verge of tears and longed for a smile or a kind word from anyone. No such luck.

One day I was grabbing stuff in the supermarket as Sam writhed and shrieked in his buggy – he always writhed and shrieked in his buggy – when an old woman told me I wasn't fit to be a mother. It was like being punched in the stomach. I stood there, not saying a word, as the woman took some biscuits off the shelf, tut-tutted and said: 'Poor little thing. I'm glad you're not my mother,' and walked off.

I took off after the old woman. For a split second I wanted to squeeze her scrawny neck, smack her skull off the shelves and see the blood vessels burst in her stupid watery eyes. I really think I wanted to kill her. Thank God Sam's screams stopped me. He'd heard me walking away and was trying to tear himself out of his safety harness, arms and legs flying. I went back to the buggy and clung to the handle. 'It's all right,' I said, 'It's all right.' I wasn't sure if I was talking to Sam or myself. I set off with the buggy, knuckles white, legs shaking, pretending I was like anybody else out shopping for biscuits.

I'd taken Sam into town less and less after that. Life was easier at Backwoods where we were not judged by anyone else and where Sam knew what to expect from life. Where he could ceaselessly line up his soft toys in exactly the right order, over and over again, all day if he wanted to, and no one would stop him or interfere.

When I did venture out, Sam's crying sometimes started as soon as we got in the car, but if not it would definitely start by the time we reached Big Hill. It was a long drive after that, with Sam screaming himself daft in the back. He could not have made it plainer that he wanted to stay at Backwoods, and only Backwoods.

The health visitor said it was a phase. She said I mustn't let Sam bully me; *I* was the adult and I had to act like one. I must be firm. I must put him in the car and take him wherever I needed to go, whenever I needed to do so. It was as simple as that.

For a long time I struggled into town for health visitor appointments and dental checks and God knows what – until that last time when I finally gave it all up as a bad job.

We'd been on our way to his five-year check, which was bound to be another pointless box-ticking exercise if ever there was one anyway, when he stopped crying.

I craned my neck to watch him in the rear-view mirror. It was such a novelty having a quiet child in the back I laughed out loud.

Then I realised his face was going purple and his eyes were rolling back in his head. I stamped on the brakes and dived out of the car, ripped the back door open and

56

scrabbled at his harness. 'Breathe!' Breathe!' I grabbed him, shook him, banged his back and begged him. 'Breathe!'

After several more seconds he gulped for air and looked at me steadily. He didn't cry or try to talk. He just gazed at me.

I put him back in his seat and stood by the car for a few minutes staring down the lane – a lane that might as well have had a portcullis clanging shut right across it. I got back in the car, turned it round and drove home.

I hadn't tried to talk to Sam about it; there was no point. Sam talked *when* he wanted, about *what* he wanted. He'd talk about maps and times tables and dinosaurs and comets and stars but talking about going into town or riding in the car or stopping breathing – forget it.

I told Duncan I wasn't taking Sam into town anymore. Instead I'd go on my own for a couple of hours on a Tuesday afternoon. Duncan hadn't said much. He probably thought it would blow over, that if he kept his head down and got on with his farming everything else would sort itself out. I noticed he didn't offer to take Sam out on his own, though. He wasn't that daft.

I'd taken Sam's name off the school register and told the education people I was going to teach him at home. Then I'd thrown myself into home schooling the way I'd wanted to throw myself into being a normal mum to a normal kid.

But he'd tripped me up there too. Whenever I got him a new book he either knew everything in it from the internet, or he'd finish it in ten minutes flat and want another. One day I lost patience and shouted: 'You can't have read it yet! How does it end?' Sam had gazed at me, deadpan, and recited the last two pages word for word.

Pretty quickly my world had shrunk to the same size as

Sam's. I lost touch with friends. It was easier to let go of my old life and to live the kind of life Sam demanded. And really what choice did I have?

After six years of dealing with all this I was highly tuned to stuff that would throw our world out of kilter.

Now here was Sam choosing to come downstairs to sit opposite some scruffy bloke that Duncan had dragged home from the pub last night. It was mystifying and disorientating and absolutely bound to end in tears.

Sam put the map on the table and stared at Larry. I'd told him about staring a million times. Larry did not look bothered and carried on eating his bacon and eggs as if he'd not been fed all day.

'Well, we got the hoops up,' said Larry to Sam, 'thanks to Pythagoras's Theorem.'

Sam gazed at him. He obviously didn't want to talk about hoops or Pythagoras's Theorem. Slowly he put his hand on the map.

'Dunno about any theorem,' said Duncan. 'A bit of trial and error, more like.' He took another slice of bread and smeared it round his plate. 'Should get the sheeting on tomorrow if the wind stays down.'

Sam gradually slipped his fingers into the folds of the map and opened it like a concertina, never taking his eyes off Larry.

'You like the map, son?'

Sam did a single nod of the head.

'Aye, well, when the table's cleared we'll have a proper look at it, shall we?' Larry smiled at Sam. 'We'll see what we can see.'

I cleared the dishes and wiped the table while Sam sat there clutching the map. Duncan lit the fire and made a big show of selecting some bottles of ale from his stock in the washroom. Larry went outside for a smoke. I could see him on the granary steps stroking Bess's ears. She liked him and butted his hand with her nose and licked his fingers.

When he came back Duncan said, 'Fancy a brown, Larry?'

'Aye.'

Duncan grinned but then stopped grinning when Larry took the brown ale to the table and sat down beside Sam.

I put the ironing board up and dragged out the teetering ironing basket.

Larry opened the map and pointed to all the places he'd stayed and talked about the jobs he'd done.

He could spin a good yarn that was for sure.

He said he'd worked at potato picking, haymaking, mushroom picking, knocking down a cottage, pheasant beating for some shooters, whitewashing outhouses, putting up hen cabins and goodness knows what else.

When he got to the bit about mushroom picking Duncan shouted from his chair in front of the fire:

'There's nothing like being kept in the dark and fed shit, eh?'

Larry laughed.

'Whereabouts are you from?' I asked.

'Wee place in Midlothian,' he said. 'That's Scotland,' he said to Sam. 'If I had a map I'd show you. But I havenae.' He took a long pull on his ale. 'I left so long ago I can hardly remember it.' He looked at me. 'I got out of there as soon as I bloody could, pardon my French, and I won't be going back.'

Sam gazed at him wide-eyed, waiting for more.

'Where's home now?' I said, hoping he took the hint that home was definitely not here.

'In the summer I pick flowers and fruit in the south of

59

England. It's a good life, keeps me fit and out of trouble.'

'So is that where you're heading?'

Larry gave a vague kind of smile and didn't answer.

He showed Sam different places on the map and embarked on stories about the slavers that sailed into Lancaster, the drunken boys press-ganged into the navy and the Pendle Witches hanged at Lancaster Castle. He ran his finger down the coast and told Sam about the stone graves cut from rock at Heysham where St Patrick landed from Ireland.

I watched Sam taking it in, a slight frown on his face. He wouldn't have sat so still if *I'd* tried to tell him stories. Although come to think of it, I couldn't remember the last time I had tried to tell him a story. We'd got out of that habit years ago – Sam had been able to read himself stories since he was about three. Nowadays our evenings consisted of me reading a magazine or some novel or other, Duncan watching the telly, and Sam clearing off to his room to go on his computer or draw a map.

I bashed the iron on the ironing board.

'You've got plenty of stories,' I said.

Larry smiled and said to Sam: 'I've got plenty of stories because I've been to plenty of places and seen plenty of things.'

I put the last bit of ironing on the pile.

It was that map that was doing it; Sam was mesmerised by that map.

Duncan had been rattling bottles of ale like a kid waving a bag of sweets most of the time the stories had been going on. He got louder and more persistent until Larry said:

'Well, that's maybe enough for tonight, son.' And Duncan, spotting his chance, said:

'I've got a Hobgoblin, or a Cockahoop, or an Old Rascal?' and he chinked a handful of brown bottles.

60

Larry helped Sam fold the map.

'So we'll need to dig that trough round the polytunnel tomorrow before we get the sheeting on,' shouted Duncan, who obviously didn't want Larry getting sidetracked by Sam again. 'Let's hope the wind stays down.'

Larry held the folded map out to Sam and said:

'Now you need to explore for yourself, eh?' Sam's hand faltered and a look of mingled terror and hope flickered across his face.

A knot tightened in my throat. The map showed a small corner of the world – a small corner of a flat and wet and windy Lancashire – within touching distance of this farm, but it was out of reach for Sam. It was a terrifying world through the Wildwood, past Big Hill and down Hell Fire Pass and he might as well have been planning a trip to the moon. My heart twisted at the fear and the hope on his face.

Larry put his hand on Sam's shoulder and Sam flinched. Duncan shouted:

'You heard the weather forecast, Larry?' and Larry turned away and took his ale over to the fire.

'No yet. You joining us for a drink?' he said, looking at me.

I shook my head.

Duncan flicked over to the news channel. Sam stroked the cover of his map and held it to his face as if he was smelling it. Cuddling it to his chest and with his chin down, he disappeared upstairs.

Duncan talked over the telly, droning on about the polytunnel.

'. . . it'll be a mob-handed job . . . It'll take us a bit . . . best get it done early . . .'

blah blah blah

Like *he* had a clue about it.

61

I picked up the wobbling stack of ironing and, peering round it, carried it upstairs. I hoped there'd be a sodding hurricane tomorrow. I hoped the stupid tunnel took off like a parachute and flew off over the hills and far away, and was never seen again.

I perched on the edge of the bed. It was like being locked in a prison cell. I jumped up, opened my wardrobe and pulled at stuff: going-out clothes, dresses – when did I ever get to wear dresses? – strappy sandals, clutch bags, a glittery belt. All useless. I threw them in a pile; they'd be next for the tip.

The heap on the floor made me feel a bit better, but it wasn't enough. I opened Duncan's wardrobe and pulled out a sports jacket. And there was his old T-shirt, pale blue and soft – one he wore when we were first married. I thought *that* had gone ages ago. I dragged it out. He'd worn this T-shirt when we went driving on summer nights in his TR7, the windows down and my hair whipping about. We sang along to *Downtown* and *Don't Sleep in the Subway* and other cheesy old songs he had on his eight-track.

That was when Duncan's dad was alive and we were both young – still only teenagers in the early days. The farm was busy then; there was money in it and nobody thought it would ever change. The place was a bustle of activity with contractors, delivery men, salesmen; folk coming and going all day long. It felt like a thriving, living, breathing business back then.

I worked at the bank. Dead boring, and the money was rubbish, but it was clean and warm. I planned to do it until I had a baby and then I'd throw myself into being a mum. I'd make a better job of it than my own mother, that was for sure. No way would any bloke come between me and my kid; no way would any bloke drive my kid from home so they ended up feeling like they'd got no family and had to get married at eighteen, to get one. Like me.

There was a shout of laughter from downstairs – Duncan and Larry must be on their second or third bottles by now. I buried my face in the T-shirt and wiped my eyes then, catching sight of the pile of rubbish, I flung it on top.

In the aching silence I heard Sam pacing round his room. Round and round he went. Sometimes he paced for ages – hours – sometimes it went on all night, with silences when I presumed he went on his computer or drew something or gazed into space.

I strained to listen and heard him open his window. He liked to stare out at the black night – there were no street-lights at Backwoods – and watch the light of the moon silhouetting the tops of the trees in the Wildwood and the infinity of stars stretching out overhead. I'd watched him do it. I'd sat in the pitch black garden and watched him silhouetted in the window, thin and young and vulnerable-looking, as he stared up at the sky and out at a world that fascinated and tempted him but that was so terrifying it was way out of his reach.

Chapter 10

Welcome to U Chat

Home   **Chat**   **Message Boards**   **Rules**   **Contact Us**   **Log in**   **Sign up**

How do I know what I want?

Truestory
Date: 4 June 2014
Time: 21.09

Is it possible to want something and not to want it at the same time? Is it possible to want something so much it hurts but to be so terrified of it that that hurts too. How do I know what I want?

Re: How do I know what I want?

JC
Date: 4 June 2014
Time: 21.13

Go have a conversation with God. Believe in him and you will find your way.

Re: How do I know what I want?

Fizzy Mascara
Date: 4 June 2014
Time: 21.15

Why the hell do you lot always bring god into it. God can't save you – only you can do that. Now get real and stop believing in magic.

Re: How do I know what I want?

Root Toot
Date: 4 June 2014
Time: 21.16

LOL. Chill Fizzy Mascara.

Re: How do I know what I want?

SpiritLove
Date: 4 June 2014
Time: 21.21

Hi Truestory There are so many things out there getting in our way. Desires for fast cars, fancy houses, beautiful clothes. None of these things matter unless we are happy within ourselves. Money cannot buy the things that are truly valuable. Come and find out more click here – this is what the Spirit&Soul Spiritual community is all about.

Re: How do I know what I want?

ChocolateMoustache
Date: 4 June 2014
Time: 21.30

Steve Jobs said you should do what you love – and he didn't do so bad did he?

Re: How do I know what I want?

DiamondSky
Date: 4 June 2014
Time: 21.44

Doing wot u luv is the DUMEST ADVISE. LOVE DON'T PAY THE BILLS.

Re: How do I know what I want?

PlainSpeaker
Date: 4 June 2014
Time: 21.50

WRITING IN CAPS IS SHOUTING. STOP SHOUTING DiamondSky IT IS NOT NECESSARY OR HELPFUL.

Re: How do I know what I want?

Truestory　　　　　　What if what you want might kill you?
Date: 4 June 2014
Time: 21.58

Re: How do I know what I want?

Root Toot　　　　　　Then you'd die happy, Truestory!! Go for it man.
Date: 4 June 2014
Time: 22.00

Chapter 11

Next morning I found Larry frying bacon, his fag propped against the open window.

'Morning.'

I didn't answer. I was dying for a drag but there was no way I was asking for one. I flicked the kettle on.

'Sit down. I can do it,' said Larry. I ignored him and grabbed Sam's bowl and Weetabix and plonked them at his place. I switched the radio on and turned it up.

Duncan came in from milking, stamping his feet to knock off the bits of clinging straw.

'Heard the forecast?' He lobbed his jacket at one of the armchairs and looked at Larry.

Larry shook his head. 'Naw.'

'We'll be lucky, I dare say,' said Duncan.

Larry had daubed butter on slices of bread and was dribbling bacon grease across the counter as he dumped the rashers on top.

'Great,' Duncan slapped another slice on and sat down. 'We'll have that tunnel up good as new today. No trouble at all.' And he took a big bite.

Sam came down at half eight and slipped into his place. He went through the Weetabix routine without saying a word. Duncan wolfed his bacon butty then said: 'Alice, I'm going to need you and Sam to give us a hand this morning getting this sheeting on the hoops.'

I stared at him, coffee cup halfway to my mouth. After all I'd said about his idiot scheme, he was asking me to help?

Sam said: 'Today I am studying two-dimensional shapes on the internet.'

'You can leave your work for this morning,' said Duncan. 'I don't see what difference it makes anyway.'

'He's got stuff to do,' I said. 'It's my job to make sure he does it and doesn't waste time putting stupid polytunnels up. That's what difference it makes.' I slammed my cup on the table.

Sam stared wide-eyed at Duncan; he put his spoon down and his hands hovered over his ears in case there was any more yelling. Sam's study of two-dimensional shapes was news to me but, so what, it was still more important than a polytunnel.

'What's so important about this shape stuff anyway?' said Duncan.

'It's Maths. Then he's going to do some History.'

'Well he doesn't need to bother. He's coming outside and helping us.' He turned to Sam: 'Get your wellies on.'

Sam didn't answer. I wasn't sure he'd heard – after all he did have his ears covered.

'I SAID NOW!' yelled Duncan, and Sam squeezed his ears tight. Then he slid off his chair and headed for the shoe cupboard by the door.

'You're a bully,' I said. 'He should be doing his schoolwork.'

'It'll do him good working outside with us. It's better than being stuck inside staring at a bloody screen all day, eh Larry?'

Larry pushed his chair back. 'I'll get the lad to help me

68

unroll the sheeting.' He went over to Sam. 'You give us a hand, eh?' But Sam didn't hear because he'd got some cotton wool from up his sleeve and stuffed it in both ears and was now pulling one of my old bobble hats over his face.

I sat at my laptop after they'd gone out. I was meant to be lesson-planning but my stomach was churning. This was vintage Duncan – throwing Sam in at the deep end and to hell with the consequences.

It was hopeless trying to concentrate. I needed to keep my eye on Sam, so I grabbed my gardening coat and my basket of tools and headed outside.

The vegetable garden had gone berserk and needed some serious digging if I was ever going to get some spuds in. I grabbed the fork and set to, pretending to be absorbed, but with all my senses tuned to Sam.

Duncan and Larry were manoeuvring a roll of plastic round the house on the wheelbarrow. Duncan was loving it – yelling instructions: 'Left a bit, left a bit, right a bit, right a bit,' while Larry got on with it and Sam hovered by the hoops.

Duncan got Sam to pull on the sheeting as he and Larry unrolled it and slowly the sheeting was spread out on the ground. They all stood and looked at it.

'I predicted the sheet would be a rectangle,' said Sam. 'That prediction was incorrect. This sheet is a 4-sided polygon or a tetragon or a quadrangle.' There was a silence. Duncan rubbed the back of his neck and Larry stroked his stubbly chin as though he was hiding a grin.

Sam went on: 'There is no line of symmetry, so it is not a rhomboid and none of the sides are parallel so it is not a parallelogram.' Another silence and by now I was biting my lip too. I thrust the fork hard into the soil and put all my weight on it. Sometimes I wondered if Sam was an actual comedy genius – a comedy genius with no discernible sense of humour.

'There's fucking algae on it,' said Duncan pointing at several green slimy patches.

'We can deal with algae, nae bother,' said Larry. He turned to Sam. 'We'll get an old sheet and when the tunnel's up we'll fix two ropes to the sheet and pull it backwards and forwards over the tunnel and wash it down.'

'Bugger that,' said Duncan. 'We'll use the power washer once it's up.'

'I'm no sure the power washer's a great idea on a poly-tunnel,' said Larry to Duncan, but Duncan ignored him and set off for it. Larry sat on the grass and took his tin of roll-ups out of his pocket.

'Alice?'

He indicated the tin to me but I shook my head.

After a minute he squinted up at Sam through the smoke.

'You still liking that map of yours?'

Sam nodded. 'I have looked at it twenty-six times since last night,' he said. Larry raised his eyebrows.

'Twenty-six times?'

'Yes, twenty-six times,' replied Sam.

'You should study it and make a list of the places you'd like to visit. Make a wish list.'

I could see Sam thinking hard about making a wish list and what that might entail.

'Making a wish list is writing a list of places you wish you could go but know you never will,' said Sam.

'Well – ,' said Larry.

'I will put the graves cut from rock near the place where St Patrick landed from Ireland on my wish list.'

'Aye – '

'I Googled St Patrick last night,' said Sam. 'St Patrick

had green robes and a halo and a big stick called a staff.'
Larry nodded as Sam continued. 'St Patrick chased all the
snakes out of Ireland when they attacked him up a hill, like
Big Hill. And all with just his stick.'

'Yep,' Larry said. 'That's him.'

'I know. The internet said so.'

I rested on my fork while Larry puffed away.

'When the internet says it, it means it is a true story,'
said Sam.

I stood up straight and frowned. I don't know how
many times I'd told him the internet was choc-a-bloc with
rubbish but before I had time to interrupt Duncan came
rattling back with the power washer.

'We'll do it when it's up,' he said. 'Best get going and
beat the wind.'

Larry stood at one end of the hoops and Duncan at the
other and they started to work the plastic sheet over the
hoops. Duncan yelled at Sam to stand on the opposite
side and to grab the plastic as soon as he could reach it
and pull it over.

It was then I noticed the breeze was sticking my hair to
my lips.

'There is a westerly wind,' said Sam. 'The leaves are
rustling which means the wind is in the range of one to
three on the Beaufort scale.'

Duncan and Larry fought with the huge sheet as the
wind played with it. They struggled on for some minutes.

'There is a leaf blowing along the ground,' said Sam.
'The wind has increased to a four on the Beaufort scale.'

The wind was now getting under the sheet and making
an almighty racket. I rested one foot on my fork to watch.
Sam had his eyes squeezed shut and his hands clamped
over his ears. In slow motion he began to bend double,
looking scared to death.

'Grab it!' shouted Duncan from the other side of the tunnel. 'FOR FUCK'S SAKE, GRAB IT!' The sheet gave a great crack and snapped into the air. 'You're worse than FUCKING USELESS,' yelled Duncan over the wind.

I dropped my fork and ran across the grass and lunged for the sheet. As it came back down I grabbed it and heaved as hard as I could. The three of us struggled for another few minutes until the sheet was firmly on the hoops and had been wedged down at the corners with paving flags.

Sam was curled up on the grass counting aloud to block out the chaos.

Duncan and Larry were both sweating by then and they started to laugh.

'We were nearly blown to Kingdom Fucking Come,' said Duncan.

'Aye, you're no' wrong there. I could have been halfway hame to Scotland by now.'

I squatted down beside Sam. He stayed curled. 'It's okay,' I said. 'It's done. Let's go inside.'

Larry strode over. 'Do you want to help bury the edges of the sheet in the ditch, son? I bet you'll be good at that.'

'No, he's coming inside with me.'

Sam lifted his head. He opened his eyes a chink and whispered:

'I did not know it was a joke. A joke is something that evokes laughter. The wind and the sheet did not evoke my laughter. I did not know it was a joke.'

Larry held his hand out to Sam and I scowled at him. I helped Sam up.

'Come on, son. I'll show you.' Larry looked at me and I nodded. I knew he was right – it would be better for Sam to face the tunnel again straight away or it'd turn into yet another terror on his ever-growing list.

'Come on, Sam.'

Larry showed Sam how to bury the edge of the sheeting to hold it in place.

'Stamp on it, like this, see. Stamp on it.'

'An earthworm,' Sam said, poking among the folded plastic to rescue it. He held it gently then placed it on the grass. 'An earthworm needs to be in the soil or it will dry out and die.' He watched it slither out of sight to safety.

When the sheeting was taut and secured all the way round, Duncan started messing with the washer.

'Okay, time to clean it off.'

'I dinnae think it's a great idea – ' said Larry again. Duncan ignored him and brought the washer closer. 'It's best to use a sheet tied wi' two ropes – '.

'You said Larry was the expert,' I said. 'So why don't you listen to him?'

'Nah, this is quicker,' said Duncan. 'Let's give it a good blast'. He twisted the nozzle then turned the motor on. A hard jet of water shot out. He pointed it at the plastic tunnel and the water battered into it. Sam was backing off, hands on ears, clutching his hat. Larry took a step back too.

'You've got the nozzle too – '

'FOR FUCK'S SAKE, it's effing ripped it!' Duncan kicked the power washer.

I stamped my foot. 'For God's sake, you're ripping the stupid mouldy thing to bits.'

Duncan spun round still holding the power washer and a blast of water got me across the shins soaking my jeans. I screamed and jumped back.

'Don't come interfering here, we don't fucking need your help,' he said. 'You said you wanted nothing to do with it.'

'Well you certainly need somebody's help,' I said,

pulling my wet jeans away from my legs. 'Larry *told* you not to use that washer. And turn the bloody thing off before you do any more damage.'

I kicked the power washer too and a pain shot up my foot. As I rubbed my toe I glanced up to see Sam hurtling towards the house, a look of pure terror and misery on his face.

'Sam?' I pressed my ear harder to his bedroom door and hoped the sound of my beating heart wouldn't drown him out. I could hear him counting, going resolutely up through the four hundreds.

'Four hundred and twenty-four, four hundred and twenty-five, four hundred and . . .'

'Sam?'

His counting was muffled – he must be under his quilt, probably with his fingers in his ears, along with the cotton wool and possibly still with his hat on.

'. . . twenty-six, four hundred and twenty-seven, four hundred and twenty-eight . . .'

'Sam, I'll make you pasta for lunch. Nineteen pieces. How's that?'

'. . . Four hundred and twenty-nine . . .'

'I'll go and do it now . . .'

'Four hundred and thirty, four hundred and thirty-one . . .'

He didn't come down for lunch. I made his pasta plain – how he likes it when he's really stressed and I wasn't even going to nag him to have any pesto on it, or tomato sauce or anything. I shouted upstairs two or three times: 'It's ready now. It's on the table. It's getting cold.' But he didn't come down.

I went upstairs and grabbed his door handle but I

stopped myself. Going in and talking to him, or God forbid trying to wrestle that quilt off him, would only make it worse.

If plain pasta wasn't going to lure him down, nothing would.

Duncan and Larry came inside and made their own lunch; I wasn't volunteering to do it after that shambles. They hacked big lumps of bread, getting crumbs everywhere and taking gouges out of the worktops, and then slapped thick wedges of cheese and pickle on top.

'Larry fixed it with insulation tape,' said Duncan through a mouthful. I ignored him. 'Tunnel's good as new now eh, Larry?'

I went and got the hoover. I turned it on and banged the hose along the bottom of the units and into the top corners and clanged the pans hanging from the rack until they couldn't hear themselves think. It worked. They cleared off.

Duncan went off to his mate's to borrow a rotovator and Larry disappeared outside. I was in the washroom watching him walking round the polytunnel smoothing it down and sticking more and more bits of tape on it. Larry moved slowly as if he had all the time in the world – which maybe he did – and he was very thorough going round and round, checking it over and over.

Then he went and sat in his caravan – I watched him from the landing window – reading and rolling fags and smoking. He took deep drags and tapped off his fag ash without looking up from his book.

What was he reading? What *did* a man like Larry read? An adventure story probably; spies, maybe, or soldiers or something.

Every now and then when he gazed out of the caravan

and across the orchard I stepped away from the window and back into the shadows.

It was heading for teatime and there was still no sound from Sam so I went back and listened at his bedroom door. Not a peep. At least he wasn't still counting. I knocked softly: still nothing.

'Sam?'

I knocked again.

'Sam? There's a cheese butty here. Eat it. You'll feel better.' I put the butty down by the door. I felt like crying.

He was nearly twelve years old. Surely I could talk to him about leaving Backwoods? And not leaving for the day but leaving for good. We needed to get away – but I couldn't break away until he could. I needed him to be brave for both our sakes.

'Sam, please come out or say it's okay for me to come in.'

Still the deafening silence. I wiped my face on my jumper and pushed his door open.

He'd gone again.

The same old images of him panicking and crying somewhere, alone and frightened, probably curled up in a ball, possibly hurting himself reared into my head. Common sense told me he'd be at Jeannie's but it's hard to use common sense when you've as many bad memories as I have.

I once found him under the sink in the washroom, his sweatshirt damp with tears and his arms covered in so many bite marks they looked like cup rings on an old coffee table. That was because he'd got an ink splodge on this favourite soft sweatshirt. Or the time I found him scratching gouges out of his arms when the TV aerial blew away and all we could get was white noise. Or when he was really little and he banged his head against the door and the floor for no reason that I could tell until it was covered in bumps and blackening bruises.

Having those experiences under my belt made it hard not to panic.

I'd taken Sam to the doctors about the head-banging thing – that was in the days when I was still making him go in the car to town. The doctor smiled and asked him some questions: What was his favourite toy? What did he like to eat? What was his favourite television programme? And when Sam looked straight at him and didn't answer the doctor sent him to the nurse for a hearing test. Sam was interested in the little beepers and the headphones and passed the test with flying colours.

Satisfied that Sam was not deaf the doctor said all children went through phases and not to worry about it, he'd ask the health visitor to pop by.

A few days later I found a leaflet shoved through the letterbox, '*Adjusting to Parenthood*'. The health visitor had managed to get the leaflet through the door and leave without my hearing her. She must have tiptoed. Even Bess didn't hear her. Anyway, the leaflet said: 'Some people find parenting easy! Some people don't! Try not to worry if you are finding it hard. Some people take longer than others to adjust!'

I looked on the back of the leaflet for the helpful stuff, but there was no helpful stuff. The message seemed to be: If your child was 'playing up' it was probably a phase but if it wasn't a phase it must be your own fault. 'Change your parenting, change your child,' was the message. 'Is your child playing up because that is the only way he can get attention?'

The health visitor had jotted a note inviting me to join a parenting course. I went. 'Your child is the way they are

77

because you have made them that way,' was the opening gambit from the very pregnant instructor. 'Boundaries!' she said. 'You must set boundaries and make it very plain *what is acceptable.*'

I asked if she already had kids and she stroked her bump and gave a big cheesy smile and said: 'Not yet, but I can assure you that my child will be brought up with *boundaries.*'

When I got home from the course I found Sam, quiet as a mouse, absorbed in rearranging all the tins from the kitchen cupboards in the colours of the rainbow, placing them in a perfect arc across the hearth rug. I knew he'd go berserk when I had to use one, or when I moved one even by an inch. And there'd be no fooling him – he'd remember exactly where each tin went; he had that sort of memory.

But unless we were going to live with the tin rainbow forever I knew with a sinking heart that we'd have to move them sometime and then what would he do? Hide? Throw a day-long tantrum? Stop breathing altogether?

For the time being though he had been absorbed in his own rainbow world. 'Hello Sam', I said, but he didn't hear.

He is what he is, I thought. He does what he does. All the course-leader's waffling about 'boundaries' was like telling me to fight a forest fire with a tea cup. I decided there and then I wasn't going back on that stupid course. He was a weird kid but if I let him be himself maybe he'd grow out of it. Maybe he'd calm down and, left to his own devices, he'd gradually turn into a kid like everyone else's. If I poured enough love into him, surely that would make everything all right, wouldn't it?

That was six years ago and I was still waiting.

When I got to Jeannie's I leant on one of the crosses *(In sweet remembrance of my darling Spoon, buried here until the daybreak)*, while I got my breath back. There were two hard-backed chairs outside in what had probably been a patch of sun, with a view of the cows grazing in the field opposite.

I tapped and went in. Jeannie and Sam were at the kitchen table.

'It's you,' Jeannie said and took a mouthful of cake covered in icing sugar that stuck to her nose and chin and fell off onto her cardi. 'Want some cake?' She took another bite. 'Help yourself.' She nodded towards the dresser. 'Sam, bring me a bit more will you? I'm having cake for my main course and cake for my pudding today.'

There was flour on the floor with animal tracks in it. The cupboard surfaces were covered in cake tins and bags of sugar and mixing bowls and on the dresser was a cake – well, two cakes really, glued together with a thick layer of jam oozing out and dribbling down the sides. The cake was bright pink; Jeannie always put food colouring in her cakes to stop them from being yellow and burning Sam's eyes and throat.

I pulled a chair out and plonked myself down. Sam looked right at home in here, cosied up with all these mangy cats and dogs and Jeannie with her dusty old skirt who was more than likely filling his head with all sorts. He had his pot of green pens out – like the ones he had at home – and was drawing a map.

Sam got up and cut himself and Jeannie a slice of cake each and, balancing them on a hard-backed copy of *Alice in Wonderland*, he took them to the table.

'Here is 45 degrees of cake,' he said.

'Thanks, Chucky-Egg.'

I tried to get a look at Sam's arms to see if he'd been hurting himself but the sleeves were pulled right down. He still hadn't looked at me since I arrived. He took a big bite of cake and munched solemnly

'The Hoover,' he said.

I clapped my hand to my mouth. 'Oh, Sam, I'm so sorry.' I knew the Hoover freaked Sam out if I didn't warn him yet I'd forgotten one of the most basic rules of Living-with-Sam. I must be going mad. How had I done that? He found the Hoover terrifying – the wriggling pipe, the long nozzle, the roaring motor, the way it bashed into everything around it – the whole thing. I always warned him when I was going to switch it on so he could wear his headphones and watch a DVD about outer space or the Amazon jungle or something, but I'd been so angry with Duncan I'd forgotten.

'I flew to Jeannie's,' he said.

'Yes, that was a good idea,' I said. 'I'm so sorry I forgot.'

'Isaac Newton was a genius but, as regards flying, I do not think his laws of motion fully take into account the power of magic.'

'No. Right,' I said

The cake looked soft and sticky and sweet. I cut myself a slice and we ate in silence, but Sam obviously had something on his mind.

He looked at Jeannie. 'Have you got a Wish List?'

'Oh yes,' said Jeannie.

'What's on it?'

'Well, today I wished for cake for my main course and cake for my pudding and now look.'

'Larry has given me a map.' Sam took another bite of cake. 'He says I should make a Wish List of the things on the map that I want to see in real life.'

'Mmm . . .' Jeannie said. She brushed the sugar off her cardi and onto her skirt. 'What's on it so far?'

Sam gazed through the window and over the hedge

opposite at the grazing cows. He frowned. He put his cake down and looked a bit sick.

'A Wish List is only wishes though, isn't it?' said Sam. 'You do not *have* to do the wishes on the Wish List? It is not a binding contract, is it?'

'No,' I said. 'Course you don't – '

'Wishes have a mind of their own,' cut in Jeannie. 'Sometimes they come true and sometimes they don't. Sometimes we wish they would and they don't, or we wish they would and they do and then we wish they hadn't but they won't go away again. Or they do.' Jeannie nodded. 'They're funny things, wishes.'

'Where is your wish list?' asked Sam.

'It's not written on a piece of paper,' said Jeannie.

Sam frowned.

'It's written on my heart,' and, before Sam could give her a lecture on human biology, she added: 'If it was good enough for Queen Mary, it's good enough for me.'

'Don't worry about writing a wish list,' I said, but was interrupted as a cat leapt from the dresser onto the work top and sent a baking tray clattering to the floor.

Jeannie had finished her cake and settled back nicely in her chair.

'On my wish list is visiting outer space,' she said, 'and seeing all the planets in our solar system. Then I want to travel to other galaxies.'

She licked her finger and dabbed some of the sugar off the dust jacket of *Alice in Wonderland*, then licked her finger again.

We all pondered this.

'It takes twenty-three years and a hundred and two days to reach Pluto,' said Sam. 'You would not live long enough to reach it.' Jeannie dipped up more sugar. 'Also,' said Sam, the temperature is minus 375F and the atmosphere is methane and so it would be uninhabitable and you would die upon arrival.'

Jeannie didn't seem to hear these details.

'And after finishing my space travel I would like to do some time travel,' she said. 'I would like to dance at the wedding of Anne Boleyn and Henry VIII.' There was a pause. 'Possibly on the arm of Geoffrey Chaucer.'

'Geoffrey Chaucer died in 1343, ninety years before Henry VIII married Anne Boleyn,' said Sam.

Jeannie waved her hand. 'Geoffrey Chaucer was an alchemist and a time traveller; a mere ninety years wouldn't stop him. I also want to sail on the seven seas in a galleon with purple sails and a poop of beaten gold.' She smacked her lips to catch the last grains of sugar. 'Like Cleopatra.'

'There are in fact five oceans and a hundred and ten seas plus five landlocked seas,' said Sam.

'Yes, that's right,' she said. 'I want to sail on them all. And when I've finished I'll visit both Poles and selected spots around the equator.'

Sam looked excited at that: 'I know the names of all the cities within a hundred miles of the equator.'

I nodded enthusiastically, thinking this might take us onto more predictable territory.

'So which are *you* going to visit?' she said, at which Sam shrank in his chair, the smile crashing from his face.

'Come on, Sam,' I said. 'You'd better come and do some schoolwork, some English or History or something.'

'I want to do Geoffrey Chaucer.'

'Okay – The Canterbury Tales.'

'No. Geoffrey Chaucer.'

'All right, come on then.'

Sam started putting his green felt pens away in the tray, all the lids at the same end and the shades varying from light asparagus at one side to dark forest at the other. His tidying up went slower and slower until it stopped.

'Come on, Sam. We'd better go.'

'Would you like another thirty degrees of cake? Or twenty-five degrees?'

What was he on about? Then I realised.

'The Hoover isn't making that noise anymore,' I said. 'I'm the only person who ever switches it on and I'm here, aren't I?' Sam considered this then got up.

'Bye, Jeannie.'

Jeannie gave him a little wave and her rings sparkled red and blue and gold. I could imagine her waving like that from a galleon as it set sail on the Indian Ocean or from a craft launched into space and heading for the planet Pluto or from a husky-drawn sled setting off for the North Pole.

'Bye, Sam,' she said. 'And don't forget that wish list. Show it to me next time you come. Today I wished for an afternoon snoozing in my chair and dreaming of the time I went to the Bolshoi Ballet. And now look. They're amazing things, wish lists.'

'Thanks, Jeannie,' I said. Sam studied my face, examining my eyes and my mouth and I realised I probably didn't look very thankful. I was still feeling sick about the mistake with the Hoover. I forced a smile.

As we walked back up the lane I said sorry again. He didn't reply. I guessed, if he was listening at all, he was wishing I'd shut up about the damned Hoover, but I needed to apologise. I longed to put my arm around him but I knew I couldn't because he'd shrink away and then I'd be upset.

I wanted him to listen to me, to really take in what I was going to say because it was important. It was always hard to tell if Sam was listening. Sometimes I thought he *was* listening and it turned out he hadn't heard a word, and at other times, when Duncan and I were yelling at each other, he took in a lot more than I hoped.

But I knew how to check.

'It's whatever you want for tea. If you like I'll make you 19 pieces of pasta with nothing on.'

He looked at me; yes, he was listening.

'I'm very proud of you, Sam,' I said. 'You're getting big and you're dead clever, a lot cleverer than me.' He looked straight ahead. 'You're so big and clever that I want you to help me by being really brave as well.' I hesitated. How could I put it? How was I going to say I needed him to be brave enough to help us both escape from Backwoods Farm and from Duncan and the life we were stuck in? How could I explain there was a whole world out there for us to explore and that it was time we took our courage in our hands and went to find it.

But as the words began to form Sam looked at me closely – really studied me for a moment as though he'd never seen me properly before – and then he took off and ran like the wind back towards the house. He was flying again, his trainers skimming the grass as he leapt the puddles. I could hear him counting his steps; counting up to 823 by the time he rounded the corner and vaulted the garden wall.

Chapter 12

Welcome to U Chat

Home   Chat   Message   Rules   Contact   Log in   Sign up
                       Boards   Us

Do wishes come true?

Truestory   Is it safe for me to wish for something I might not
Date: 5 June 2014   want?
Time: 16.00

Re: Do wishes come true?

Fizzy Mascara   Well don't bother praying to some dodgy 'god'. If
Date: 5 June 2014   you want something badly then you're gonna have
Time: 16.06   to work for it. It's all down to you – nobody else.

Re: Do wishes come true?

NoShitSherlock   Wish away, Truestory! Won't make no difference!!!
Date: 5 June 2014
Time: 16.09

Re: Do wishes come true?

Sweet Cheeks I wished for an iPod touch and I just got one for
Date: 5 June 2014 my birthday. WISHES DO COME TRUE!!!!!
Time: 16.15

Re: Do wishes come true?

SpiritLove Believe it, visualise it and it will come to pass,
Date: 5 June 2014 Truestory. At the Spirit&Soul Spiritual Community
Time: 16.22 we use these techniques to help our members
find love, bring back an ex-lover, create wealth,
happiness, passion and success. If you want
on-line 'Wish-Support' our usual rate is $183
but we have a special offer on at the moment of
$3.50. Just click here.

Re: Do wishes come true?

Razzamatazz68 Why u going to wish 4 something u don't want?
Date: 5 June 2014
Time: 16.30

Re: Do wishes come true?

Truestory It has been suggested that I compile a Wish List
Date: 5 June 2014 and I do not know if this is a good idea.
Time: 16.30

Re: Do wishes come true?

Razzamatazz68 Sure, why not?
Date: 5 June 2014
Time: 16.31

Re: Do wishes come true?

FlyAwayBlackbird
Date: 5 June 2014
Time: 16.40

I read about this on a great site. Apparently their are only 1342 wishes left in the world so don't lets waste them!! You've gotta be specific, it said, and spell out your wish in detail. Then youve got to do other things that I can't remember but are something to do with lucky numbers and then your wish will come true. Good luck Truestory!! Hope all your wishes come true. xx

Chapter 13

Duncan came in when Sam was eating his tea – chewing each piece of pasta exactly five times and counting the pieces down from 19. He had got to 8.

'I've borrowed a rotovator from Melville's but we should probably have rotovated it before we put the tunnel up, if we'd thought.'

I didn't say anything but I must have banged the pots in the sink and perhaps I rolled my eyes and sighed.

'You always know everything, don't you?' he said and he grabbed the jacket he'd just taken off and went out, crashing the door so hard the eighth piece of pasta stuck in Sam's throat.

Later I was plating up chips, egg and beans for Larry and Duncan. Sam was parked at the table drawing one of his maps.

'How's you?' Larry asked him, dragging a chair back and plonking himself at the kitchen table, and I realised my heart hadn't clenched with fear over him talking to Sam.

Larry took his plate from me and squashed his egg with a rolled up piece of bread. The yolk burst and Sam squinted as the gooey yellow mixed with the tomato-ey beans and it all dribbled towards Larry's chips.

'Answer him.' Duncan scowled at Sam, who was studying Larry as he shoved half a slice of bread in his mouth.

Sam looked baffled. Answer who?

'How's you today then?' Larry said again as he wiped his mouth with the back of his hand. 'What you been up to?'

'I've been up to Geoffrey Chaucer.'

'Oh, the Canterbury Tales.'

'No, Geoffrey Chaucer.'

Larry put his knife and fork down and grabbed his rucksack that was leaning against the table leg. 'I've got something you might like.' He rummaged around and pulled out a hardback book. *The Canterbury Tales*. He opened the book and unfolded a sheet from the back and laid it on the table.

'See,' said Larry, 'a map of the route the pilgrims took on their journey from Southwark to Canterbury. You like maps, don't you? Come and have a look at this.'

Sam gazed at the map. He could clearly feel the map's lure; its sharp folds and faceted rectangles and he watched it as it tried to fold itself up on the kitchen table.

He edged his chair nearer.

'Come a bit closer, son.'

Sam looked from the map with its black roads and paths and boundaries and red contour lines to the fried egg with its bright yellow yolk and back to the map. He was obviously fascinated by the map and repelled by the egg in equal measure.

'That's interesting, isn't it?' I said, trying to keep his attention on the map. I leant over and flattened the map so he could get a better view.

Larry had scraped all the goo out of the egg and there was only hard yellow left – but it was a hard yellow that was very bright indeed. Larry put his finger on the corner of the map, then with his other hand he took a slice of bread and scooped the remains of the egg yolk up and shoved it in his mouth.

Sam stared at him as you might at a python swallowing an antelope, with a look on his face like the egg yolk was burning his own throat.

'See, they started from Southwark Cathedral,' said Larry, wiping his greasy hand on his trousers, 'and went through Deptford and Greenwich and Dartford, stopping at inns along the way until they got to the shrine of Thomas a Becket at Canterbury Cathedral.'

Larry's finger followed the pilgrims' route east and Sam slid his chair beside him and bent low over the map.

'They told stories to each other as they travelled to pass the time.'

Larry used his last chip to wipe the plate clean and took a big swig of tea.

'Course, it's mainly the A2 nowadays.'

Sam pulled the map closer and studied it.

'Have you been here?'

'Yeah, some of it. There's apple-picking, strawberries, all sorts at the right time of year.'

'Geoffrey Chaucer was an alchemist,' said Sam. 'He used silver and orpiment and burnt bones and iron filings and ground them into a powder to make gold.'

'News to me,' said Larry.

'News to everybody else too, I should think,' said Duncan. 'Is that what you've been teaching him this afternoon? Shame there wasn't another polytunnel to put up.'

I grabbed a couple of plates. 'Geoffrey Chaucer is an important part of Key Stage Two.'

'Orpiment is otherwise known as sulphide of arsenic,' went on Sam. 'It is very poisonous and it is bright yellow.'

90

He smoothed out the map and then looked back at Larry. 'Geoffrey Chaucer was a time traveller too.'

'That's news as well.'

'Jeannie told me. Even Wikipedia does not know that.'

I usually wished Sam would talk. As a rule I was grateful when he said anything at all, but now I wished he'd shut up and keep his ridiculous Geoffrey Chaucer information to himself.

He'd told me he'd learn about Chaucer on his own this afternoon to make up for the work he missed this morning – but it looked like he'd been reading a lot of old rubbish on the internet. With Sam, though, if it was written down it meant it was true – even if it was something as daft as this alchemy nonsense.

Home schooling was a nightmare. Sam would only study what he was interested in, then I couldn't stop him, but anything else and it was a waste of time. I took the easy way out at times and let him read whatever he chose. What else could I do? Constantly fight with him? Do battle day in, day out? I didn't have the energy.

After tea we sat in front of the fire. I was in the armchair and Sam and Larry were on the sofa looking at the Chaucer map. Larry told Sam some of the stories. Sam studied the map and looked up at Larry every minute or two, taking in every word he said.

What was it about Larry that fascinated Sam?

He was scruffy and looked a bit like a gypsy. He had a funny accent – to Sam at any rate. He'd arrived from nowhere and caused a lot of rows since he got here, but none of that seemed to put Sam off. Larry kept producing maps, of course, which wasn't doing any harm.

I plonked a basket of paperwork on my knee. This was the most boring job but it had to be done. Duncan was scared of paperwork so it was left to me – and I only did it when it had built up so much I couldn't stand it anymore and was forced to tackle it.

Sometimes it came in handy that Duncan was frightened of words. That stuff about Chaucer and Key Stage Two was rubbish; I had no idea if Geoffrey Chaucer was anything to do with Key Stage Two and even if he was I didn't think it'd be anything to do with his alchemy and his time travel.

I opened the letters – receipts from the dairy, vet's bills, hardware accounts, bank statements and insurance premiums – for every pound coming in, there seemed to be two going out. As I put the letters into separate piles around the chair and along the chair arms, I listened to Larry's stories.

He was telling Sam the Knight's Tale; about how Arcita and Palamon were two men who loved the same woman, Emilia, and who pined for her through their prison window. Larry said the men fought a great battle for Emilia's hand in marriage but there was a twist and the victor, Arcita, was killed and before he died he said that Emilia should marry Palamon instead, so she did.

I'd half thought Larry had *The Canterbury Tales* in his bag to rip out the pages to make his roll-ups, but he seemed to know what he was on about.

I rested my head back and let the paperwork wait and I listened to the story too.

Larry showed Sam the old language and explained the translations and Sam repeated the phrases out loud.

'I did some of this at school,' I said. 'But I don't think I got it then. It seemed a bit boring at the time.'

'They're great stories,' said Larry. 'Chaucer was a master storyteller.'

Duncan was sitting by the back door mending some

mole traps – I'd told him many a time not to bring those filthy old things inside, but he never listened. He wasn't listening now either and hadn't noticed Sam was having an in-depth conversation about Olde English with a guy who only wandered off the street a couple of days ago.

My eyes were closing with the heat of the fire and the stories. Through half-open eyelids I watched Sam with Larry. Sometimes he looked like a normal boy. He looked like any young lad sitting with his dad in front of the fire listening to stories.

Except who was I kidding? Sam wasn't a normal boy and Larry most certainly wasn't his dad.

The next morning Duncan took Larry to the cattle auction with some bull calves. Larry can't have been at the auction all the time though because when they got back he came straight inside and said he had a surprise, and he unrolled an antique map of Backwoods Farm on the kitchen table. It showed an outline of the house and garden, the buildings such as they were then, and the surrounding fields.

'It's not the original. It's a photocopy; I found it in the library.'

'Oh, that's so kind,' I said.

I was lost for the right words. My first thought was: Duncan's never done anything like this for his son, but then I realised I hadn't done anything like it either. It was Larry, who'd been here three days, who'd thought of it and gone out and done it.

Sam's eyes looked like they were going to pop out of his head. He approached the table slowly like the map was going to bite him. He gazed at it, puzzled, until Larry said:

'It's Backwoods. It's like one of they maps you draw.'
And Sam frowned and stared at it and did not say a word.

'Isn't that lovely, Sam?' I said, by way of a thank you to Larry. 'That is so lovely.'

'Anyway, it's yours, son,' said Larry. 'Though like I say, it's only a photocopy.'

Sam obviously didn't care it was a photocopy; He touched it like it was a precious object, a piece of real-life treasure.

'I will ask Jeannie for a carved treasure box,' he said.

There was some writing on it, all fancy and flowing.

Duncan had arrived inside and bent over to look at the map.

'See the date: 1845,' he said. 'That map must have been drawn up when my great, great grandparents bought the farm. That's six generations, counting Sam.'

Sam carried on staring until Larry pushed it towards him.

'Anyways, it's yours, son. Here's the farmhouse,' he said, pointing, 'and the lane and Jeannie's cottage.'

Sam carried on studying it hard. Eventually he whispered:

'There is Big Hill. But where is the Wildwood?'

Larry pointed to The Wildwood, which was a fairly small wood and not a forest, like Sam drew on his own maps. Sam stared at it and gulped but said nothing.

Wayside Cottage was there and another cottage nearer called Byway Cottage where there was now Sam's Pile of Rubble Covered in Weeds. In the garden at Backwoods there was a big space marked 'Vegetable Garden' and next to it the orchard, where the polytunnel had been put up, and beside that the 'Flower Garden'. At the bottom of the flower garden where there was now overgrown vine and head-high nettles, known by Sam as 'The World of the Jungle at the Bottom of the Garden' it said something we all puzzled over but no one could read.

Sam took one of his own maps from the thick pile of

finished maps beside the range and he laid it beside the antique map. He held on tight to the edge of the kitchen table as he studied both maps side by side.

Larry and I watched him. Larry was delighted he'd brought something that fascinated Sam so much. We looked over Sam's shoulder as he studied both maps. They were very different. The biggest difference was the size of The Wildwood – the forest Sam always drew like an enormous barrier, thick and impenetrable, surrounding Backwoods like a great safety blanket, keeping the world out, was in fact not much bigger than the 'Long Four Acre'. It was a small wood. He traced his finger around it and stared and stared.

'What do you think then, son?' asked Larry, still smiling.

I grinned round at Sam and felt the smile drain from my face. Sam had a look of terror on his face. The size of the Wildwood had obviously come as a terrible shock – as though he'd discovered Backwoods Farm was not a safe place to be after all. He rolled up the map and walked upstairs looking white and stricken.

'Is he all right?' asked Larry.

'Who knows?' said Duncan.

I scowled at Duncan. 'Yes,' I said to Larry. 'New things take a bit of getting used to.'

Larry went to put his boots on to go out and start work in the polytunnel. 'Thanks, Larry,' I said, 'that was really good of you.'

Larry shrugged. 'No bother, I remember being daft about stuff when I was a kid. With me it was stamps.' And he smiled.

I couldn't help it – I smiled back. I'd never done anything but scowl at him since he arrived. He must have thought I was a right miserable cow.

'Do you want a brew before you start?'

'No thanks, I'll crack on.'

I felt my throat constricting. I was going to cry because someone had been kind to my son – done something nice for him – and not acted as though he was a weirdo or a nuisance or looked put out when he didn't speak. The gratitude was nearly choking me.

I turned away so he didn't see the effect his kindness was having and think I was some kind of idiot. I bashed around with the dinner pots until he went outside then I sat at the table with my head in my hands and felt a huge wave of loneliness crash right over me.

Later I stood in the washroom watching Larry messing about with the rotovator. It looked like a huge lawnmower and he was tinkering about with a spanner, squinting through the smoke that was coiling up from the cigarette in the corner of his mouth.

He fired it up and revved it a few times, then he turned it off and tinkered some more.

Larry pushed the rotovator towards the polytunnel. That tunnel was such an eyesore but, let's face it, the whole farm was no oil painting. There'd been another row about the polytunnel yesterday after I'd done the books.

Duncan had told me he'd paid a hundred quid for it, but I'd found £250 withdrawn from the bank. I'd stared at it for a few minutes before I realised what it must be.

'Did you pay two hundred and fifty quid for that bloody monstrosity?' I said.

He rattled his Farmers' Guardian and said nothing.

'I said, DID YOU PAY – '

'Aye!' he cut in. 'I did, and it's gonna be worth every penny – you'll see.'

'Bloody Hell! This gets worse! How stupid do you think

I am? And how daft are *you* for thinking I wouldn't even notice?'

'I'm doing it for everyone, Alice,' he said. 'For you and for Sam and my mum and my dad – '

'You don't need to do it for me!' I said.

He took no notice. ' – and for all the other generations before that. I can't throw everything away – all those years of struggling and working themselves half to death. I can't lose it now, Alice, not when it's my turn to look after it.'

I gawped at him. It wasn't like Duncan to bring his ancestors and his mum and dad into it.

'I have to do something, don't you see?' he said.

'Okay, I can see that,' I said. 'But this cannabis idea's rubbish. We've got to come up with something better than that.'

He stood up and flung his paper down and yelled: 'Shut up about the fuckin' cannabis, Alice – we're doing it,' and he crashed out of the house.

I'd barely spoken to him since. I'd gone to bed before him last night and left him talking to Larry in the kitchen.

I watched Larry push the rotovator into the polytunnel. I didn't blame Larry, I blamed Duncan. This was his responsibility, his decision. This was all Duncan's fault.

Chapter 14

Welcome to U Chat

Home   Chat   Message   Rules   Contact Us   Log in   Sign up
Boards

How do I know what to believe?

Truestory   Do I believe what I can see with my eyes or do I
Date: 5 June 2014   believe what is written down?
Time: 13:37

Re: How do I know what to believe?

ChocolateMoustache Don't take anything on trust, Truestory, always test
Date: 5 June 2014   it out.
Time: 13.49

Re: How do I know what to believe?

Fizzy Mascara   This about god again? *Sigh* Organised religion was
Date: 5 June 2014   created to stop humans from being shit-scared of
Time: 13.55   death. Be brave, Truestory you don't need it.

Re: How do I know what to believe?

JC
Date: 5 June 2014
Time: 14.02

Christianity is based on faith, FizzyMascara. I pray that through GOD'S GRACE you will find it one day.

Re: How do I know what to believe?

AuntieMaud
Date: 5 June 2014
Time: 14.04

Nice to hear from you again Truestory! Maybe another of my mother's pearls of wisdom could help here? She said: 'seeing is believing,' and I don't think there is any use in denying that! Mother did not believe Legoland existed until we stumbled upon it near Windsor when we were searching for Windsor Safari Park. We never did find Windsor Safari Park though, so by the same token I suppose it mustn't exist! It's not your treasure map you don't believe is it? I do hope not.

Re: How do I know what to believe?

Truestory
Date: 5 June 2014
Time: 14.05

It is a map that has come into my possession that does not look like real life. Is this because 1. My eyes are seeing the world wrong or 2. The map is seeing the world wrong or 3. My eyes are seeing the map wrong?

Chapter 15

I hadn't gone into town at the weekend for years; I couldn't even remember the last time, but Larry insisted.

'Go and have a look round. Relax a bit. The lad'll be fine with me.'

Sam was perched by the fire with his old photocopied map of Backwoods open in front of him, examining every detail. He didn't look up when Larry suggested I go out and leave him.

Larry nodded his head towards Duncan who was asleep in his armchair. 'His dad's here anyway.'

We both looked at Duncan. He was flat out which was how he spent every Sunday afternoon and you couldn't really blame him after he'd got up at the crack of dawn all week.

'Sam might get upset.' I felt a bit daft because he looked so peaceful sitting there with his map. 'He's a bit . . .' I hesitated, 'well, complicated. He's a bit complicated. He doesn't like me going out except on a Tuesday at two o'clock and even then he doesn't *really* like it, he sort of puts up with it.' I was gabbling and knew I sounded a bit mad. 'In fact he hates it.' I picked up a cloth and wiped a couple of surfaces. 'He really hates it and often it's a bit of a disaster. Sometimes I think I shouldn't go out at all.'

'Well you know him better than me, obviously, but if I were you I'd go and make the most of it.'

'It's just, no offence or anything, but he hardly knows you.'

We both thought about that for a minute. It was true that Larry had been at the farm less than a week and during that time Sam had said very little to him – but lured by Larry's stories and maps, he'd certainly spent a long time in his company and never shown any fear of him.

Larry shrugged and we both watched Sam.

'Well, I think he'd be okay,' he said.

'What will you do?'

'There's a bit of gardening to do. He can help with that.'

I was a bit thrown by the offer. As a rule Sundays were like every other day – cooking, cleaning, supervising Sam. To be given a Sunday off was totally unexpected and, to be truthful, I didn't really know what to do with a free day. I didn't get this kind of offer every day – in fact any day.

'Go and have a wander round the shops.'

'You really sure about this?'

Larry nodded.

'Right, okay, well, I'll only be an hour then.' I gazed about the kitchen as though I'd find a good excuse not to go lying about on the units or shelves somewhere.

Larry laughed. 'You'll have a job to get to town and back in an hour. Go on.'

I got my carrier bags, bulging with the out-of-date dresses and Duncan's sports jacket. I considered saying something to Sam but decided against it. He'd been there throughout the conversation with Larry; it wasn't like I was sneaking off or anything. Nevertheless I crept out of the kitchen like a thief and held the latch to stop it rattling. I threw the bags in the car, praying Bess wouldn't burst out of her kennel barking like a mad thing.

101

As I drove down the lane and past The Wildwood, a surge of euphoria, a wave of giddy happiness, swept right over me. I tapped the steering wheel and sang along to the radio – except this time I meant it. This time I wasn't pretending to be happy, I was truly, properly happy. I'd forgotten what it was like to feel freedom and I found myself laughing out loud.

Out of blind habit I headed to the council tip. When I got there it was closed, of course, the metal gate slammed shut and locked. But it didn't matter. I drove into town and dumped the stuff at the door of the charity shop. Anyone who wanted it could have it; I didn't care.

I went in the supermarket and got a roast of beef and some veg for tea. It was ages since I'd done the full works but it seemed like a proper family thing to do. In a burst of optimism I bought a couple of bottles of wine too.

Then I mooched about the precinct and gazed at the shop windows – but without money it seemed pointless. I headed to the usual café. It was quieter today with it being a Sunday and there were only one or two lonely-looking old folk staring into space and a mum with a couple of kids who were smearing chocolate cake all over the place. I got my cup of tea and biscuit and sat at my usual place to gaze out at the precinct but ended up watching the chocolatey kids instead.

I caught the mum's eye and she gave me a weary half-smile; she looked knackered. The kids ignored me, with eyes only for the cake. I stirred my tea. So this is what freedom felt like. I could stay out as long as I liked. I could have as many cups of tea and shortbread biscuits as I wanted. I looked at my biscuit. I wasn't even sure I wanted that one.

I had the urge to confide in the other mother, to say how great it was to be away from my own kid for a bit; but the other mum didn't look like she wanted to talk. She was busy wiping her kids' hands and faces and nagging them about the mess they were making.

Motherhood looked no fun at all close up; I'd never noticed before I had my own kid.

I glanced at my watch and was surprised that I'd only been away an hour. Usually the time shot by. I rooted about in my bag and found my mobile. No messages.

What were they up to? Gardening, Larry said. I wondered if he was using the rotovator. A cold anxiety grabbed my stomach.

The rotovator.

It made a deafening racket. What would happen to Sam? Would he have a meltdown? Would Larry even notice if he did or would he be too busy? Oh God.

I crushed my shortbread and ground it into crumbs. I felt sick. This had been a stupid idea. I must have been crazy to think I could leave Sam with a stranger – a bloke who'd wandered off the street not a week since. How bloody daft. And Duncan wouldn't be any help. He wouldn't spot the looming disaster. I couldn't rely on him.

I shoved my tea away and grabbed my bag. I had to get home. Not bothering to nod bye to the other mum, I strode out of the café.

It would take me over half an hour to get back. Anything could have happened by then. I scrabbled about in my bag. I'd have to phone, and hope and pray that someone would hear the phone and tell Larry not to turn the rotovator on.

I stood in the precinct as two shoppers with wheel-along trolleys edged round me, tutting. I could hear it ringing. Come on, come on, answer.

'Hello.'

'Larry? Is Sam okay?'

'Aye, he's right here.'

103

My panic drained away as quickly as it had risen and I felt daft and deflated.

'Oh. I was worried in case you turned on the rotovator and – '

'I wouldnae dae that.'

Larry knew. I hadn't had to tell him. I laughed with relief and surprise.

'Right, well. I'll see you in a bit then.'

'Aye.'

I rang off and dropped my phone in my bag.

I'd told Duncan for years that Sam hated loud noises but he either didn't believe me or he didn't care – or maybe he thought if he ignored it, it would go away. And yet I hadn't even had to spell it out to Larry.

I wandered further up the precinct, but there was nothing up there, unless I wanted over-priced greetings cards, viscose T-shirts or non-brand cleaning stuff. I turned round and went the other way but there was nothing I wanted down there either. There was nothing I wanted in town at all. I'd come here to escape but I didn't want to escape.

I rooted in my bag, found my car keys and headed for the car park. I didn't want to be in town wasting time drinking crap tea and eating biscuits and watching tired mums lose patience with their sticky kids and old folk eking out their pensions in shops full of rubbish. I wanted to be at Backwoods. I wanted to be at Backwoods with Sam and Larry.

Larry's gardening didn't apparently involve the garden.

When I got back he'd put loads of kitchen roll on the utility room floor and the units and he was sprinkling it with water. Sam was helping while Duncan leant against the door frame supping from a bottle.

I went in to see what they were up to and Sam said:

'It is important to get the kitchen roll wet enough, but not too wet. Larry does not want a bloody flood'.

'Oh right,' I said, and I bit back a smile.

Sam sprinkled the paper delicately over and over again. Larry nodded and kept saying:

'That's right, son. Take it easy.'

When the kitchen roll was apparently wet enough but not too wet and certainly not a bloody flood, Larry brought out the seeds.

'What kind of seeds are they?' asked Sam

Duncan gave a little snort. 'Never you mind.'

'They're special plants for the polytunnel,' Larry said.

'What special plants?' asked Sam.

'I said – '

'Grass,' interrupted Larry.

There was a silence.

'You were probably hoping for a beanstalk or a triffid or something, weren't you?' I said.

'This is special grass. It's worth a lot of money and lots of people will want to buy it,' said Larry.

He had the seeds in little plastic tubs and he let Sam look at them.

'Best wash your hands before you touch. We mustn't get germs on them.'

After Sam had scrubbed up like a pre-op surgeon, Larry showed him how to drop the seeds five inches apart all over the kitchen roll.

Duncan watched for a minute then did a big stretch. 'I'd better go and get that cow and calf up,' he said and he wandered off.

'I'll get the roast on.' I went in the kitchen and put the beef in, then peeled some carrots and potatoes. I could hear Larry giving a running commentary on what they were up to with the occasional remark from Sam.

'Now we've got to keep them warm and dark for 24 hours,' Larry was saying, 'so we need to cover each seed with one of these cups.'

'Gardening is usually getting black up your fingernails. This is more like chemistry or biology,' said Sam. 'Or alchemy. But it is better than 16th century alchemy because it does not involve the colour yellow.'

'Aye.' Larry whistled to himself as they messed with the cups.

'Got to make sure they are all pressed down properly.'

I cleared the table for tea and underneath one of Sam's Maps of the World I found a drawing he'd done of what looked like a gypsy, or possibly a pirate or a wizard, but when I looked more closely it was obviously Larry. He had two gold earrings, not one, and they were bigger than in real life. The bandana, rather than being plain blue, had big white stars on it and his beard was long and silky, rather than short and stubbly, but there was a wonky roll-up fag dangling from the corner of his mouth and a little smile on his face. No doubt about it, it was definitely Larry.

'Time for a fag break,' Larry said, and I heard him and Sam go and sit on the back steps.

I put two cups of coffee and a glass of pop on a tray and took it out.

Sam had his antique map unrolled on the path. He was gazing at the map and then at the world in front of him.

'The real world is much messier and rougher round the edges than the world on the map, isn't it?' I said. Sam did not reply but stared at the map then back at the World of the Jungle at the Bottom of the Orchard. I put the tray on the floor and sat down next to Larry who had rolled a fag.

'Enjoy your trip to town?' he asked.

I hesitated, I'd already forgotten it, but that didn't seem very grateful.

'Yes, thanks, it was great.'

'What did you get?'

'Oh, nothing. Just looking.'

He offered me a drag on his fag and I took it even though I knew I shouldn't smoke in front of Sam. It tasted good.

'Well, I got a roast for tea, I suppose'. I took a second drag and passed it back.

'You cannae beat a bit of roast beef,' said Larry. 'Don't you agree, son?'

Sam did not reply. I felt a bit embarrassed because I realised I'd bought the roast in an attempt to play happy families even though Sam didn't like it. He always fretted about the veg touching each other on the plate and hated getting bits of beef stuck between his teeth.

'Aye, it's smelling good already,' said Larry.

'My dad covers roast beef in bright yellow mustard,' said Sam. He was tracing his finger over the map where the World of the Jungle at the Bottom of the Orchard should have been, over the writing that was faint and squiggly. Sam bent close to the map to squint at it.

'Want this, son?'

Larry unhooked a gadget from his belt that had a magnifying glass in it.

Sam peered through the glass and the fancy letters on the map swam and jumped and swirled underneath.

'Can you read it?' asked Larry.

'Yes,' said Sam.

'What does it say?'

'It says,' he hesitated, 'summer house.'

We all stared at the World of the Jungle at the Bottom of the Orchard and Larry blew some smoke rings.

'Summer house?' he said. Then after a pause: 'I think

we should do some exploring. Don't you, son? See if that summer house is still in there somewhere.'

Icy fingers grabbed my stomach at the suggestion of Sam venturing anywhere other than immediately around the farmhouse and the 823 steps down the lane to Jeannie's cottage.

Sam said nothing; he gathered up his map and disappeared inside.

I knew I had to explain stuff to Larry.

Chapter 16

Welcome to U Chat

Home   Chat   **Message Boards**   **Rules**   **Contact Us** **Log in**   **Sign up**

I don't want to be scared. How can I stop?

Truestory
Date: 8 June 2014
Time: 14.00

There is something I want to do but I'm too scared to do it. What should I do?

Re: I don't want to be scared. How can I stop?

Blood Bro
Date: 8 June 2014
Time: 14.06

I get you. I want a ball python but I'm scared to get one in case it bights me.

Re: I don't want to be scared. How can I stop?

Fizzy Mascara
Date: 8 June 2014
Time: 14.12

You should be more scared of it strangling you. And who the hell wants a pet they're scared of?

Re: I don't want to be scared. How can I stop?

NoShitSherlock   Unless you're planning to poke the crap out of it, it
Date: 8 June 2014   won't bite and even if it does, it won't hurt much –
Time: 14.16   tho their teeth are razor sharp and grow backwards.

Re: I don't want to be scared. How can I stop?

Playmeright   What kind of fucking full blown idiot thinks a ball
Date: 8 June 2014   python can bite you? Snakes are shy – specially
Time: 14.19   ball pythons. They are intelligent too and deserve an
                           intelligent owner. Steer well clear.

Re: I don't want to be scared. How can I stop?

Truestory   I do not want to buy a ball python. I am not
Date: 8 June 2014   frightened that my pet will bite me. I am frightened
Time: 14.26   of going to the Summer House in the World of the
                           Jungle.

Re: I don't want to be scared. How can I stop?

MrSoft   That a club?
Date: 8 June 2014
Time: 14.37

Re: I don't want to be scared. How can I stop?

Truestory   No.
Date: 8 June 2014
Time: 14.44

110

Re: I don't want to be scared. How can I stop?

CallmePal
Date: 8 June 2014
Time: 14.45

Well I don't know what kind of a jungle has a summerhouse but if it's the jungle I know then you'd better mind against parasites and pathogens in the water – BOIL IT FIRST. Drinking your own urine will only make dehydration worse. Then there are jaguars, spiders, scorpions, stinging ants, crocs, snakes. Preparation and vigilance are the keys to success.

Re: I don't want to be scared. How can I stop?

Fizzy Mascara
Date: 8 June 2014
Time: 14.51

We all fear what we can't see. Go take a look.

Re: I don't want to be scared. How can I stop?

Truestory
Date: 8 June 2014
Time: 14.55

Thank you for your help.

Chapter 17

'He's never been down there.' I said.

I nodded towards the World of the Jungle at the Bottom of the Orchard, or as I should call it: the bottom of the orchard. That's the thing with Sam, you start to see the world through his eyes. You start to use his words, to think with his brain, to hear with his ears, to feel his fears worming away in your own gut. You scan the world for triggers that might cause meltdowns, hiding, harming, and any number of other kinds of chaos.

Conditioning, I suppose they'd call it. I've been conditioned to live like Sam – trained like Pavlov with his dogs and his meat and his bells to worry and to react to a million different things because of what they might do to Sam.

But how could I explain eleven years of that to Larry?

We were still sitting on the back steps, the two of us. We'd lit up again – he'd rolled me one of my own this time.

'Never in his life has he been down there,' I said. 'He's never managed to get past the last apple tree in the orchard. Not once.'

Larry thought for a minute.

'What's he frightened of?'

I suppose Larry was specifically asking what Sam was frightened of in the World of the Jungle at the Bottom of the Orchard, but the answer to the question suddenly seemed enormous and unanswerable and big enough to smother us. What *was* Sam frightened of? I didn't know where to start: the noises, the colours, the smells, the places, the people.

I took another drag. 'Sometimes I think he's frightened of everything. He's never been happy anywhere but here or Jeannie's cottage – and even then calling him 'happy' might be pushing it. I tried for years to make him normal like other people's kids. But he isn't. He's different and he does things his own way whether the rest of the world likes it or not.'

I dragged on my fag and didn't look at Larry because I didn't want to see judgement in his eyes.

There was silence.

'So, he's *never* been down there?' Larry nodded towards the bottom of the orchard.

'No. But it's not through lack of trying.' I had a strong urge to defend myself. 'I've given him a football to kick towards it – he couldn't have been less interested. I've suggested games of cricket.' I pointed to the bat where he'd leaned it against the back of the house having held it for two seconds and never touched it again. 'I've set up nature walks and treasure hunts. I've tried all kinds of prompts and bribes and I don't know what else but nothing's worked. He'll go round the house, into the workshop, the orchard and 823 steps to Jeannie's cottage and that is that. That's the extent of his world. I've sort of given up anything else as a bad job. I've been left hoping that age and time will eventually sort it out.'

Larry considered this.

'But you don't mind if I suggest something?'

A cold dread gripped my stomach; I felt Sam's disap-pointments and failures as strongly as he did, plus it was my job to get him back on an even keel afterwards.

113

'Well . . .'

There was a rustle and Sam came back still carrying his map. His hair was all ruffled like he'd been hiding under the quilt with his bobble hat on.

Larry took the gadget thing off his belt again and held it out to Sam.

'This is not just a magnifying glass,' he said. Sam looked interested. 'It's a compass as well. Here, have a look.'

Sam took it.

'We can use the compass and your antique map and find places you've never been before. The most important thing is to get your bearings to start with and that means working out where you are right now and where you want to go.' Larry pointed to the map. 'So where are we, Sam?'

Sam blinked at him. 'We are 431 steps from The Pile of Rubble Covered in Weeds and 822 steps from Jeannie's cottage and 1 step from the back door.'

Larry started laughing and then, realising no one else was laughing, he stopped.

'No, I mean on the map. Where are we on the map?'

Sam pointed to the back of the farmhouse, and Larry said 'Right then.'

He gave the compass to Sam who squinted at the quivering needle.

'Let's go find the summer house,' said Larry.

Sam's face was right up to the compass but he said nothing.

My stomach clenched.

'Sam might not want . . .' I said. I stopped myself – I had to see what he'd do.

Larry showed Sam how to set his course using the compass and the map and I listened to him going on about the compass housing and the red needle and the north/south lines and the Earth's magnetic North. Sam took it all in.

'So, Sam,' Larry said, 'we'll have the Direction of Travel Arrow pointing west, because the quickest way to the summer house is to head west past the old apple tree, okay?'

'I've learned to use a compass and a map on the internet,' said Sam. This is not like on the internet.'

'No, this is real life adventure,' said Larry.

Sam gripped the compass but was still glued to the step.

'Some explorers get roped up to keep them safe,' Larry said. 'It can stop them falling into crevasses and chasms and they can be dragged back up when they're dangling over precipices.'

Sam said nothing.

'Lots of good explorers do that,' Larry repeated. 'Maybe we should give it a go, son? Keep us safe.'

Silence.

'Frozen crevasses and yawning chasms?' said Sam.

Larry hesitated a minute; 'Yeah, they're the ones,' he said. 'How about it?'

'And sudden precipices?' said Sam.

'Aye, sudden ones.'

Larry glanced at me to see if he was saying the right thing. I jumped up – there was some new washing line in the washroom that might do for roping up explorers. It gave me something to do as much as anything else, stopped me looking at the fear on Sam's face. I dashed inside and rooted through the junk in the drawers until I came across the washing line and one or two bits of old bailer twine. When I got back Larry was saying: 'Mallory and Irvine were roped together when they tried to reach the summit of Everest.'

I jumped in. 'Maybe we should forget about Mallory and Irvine? What do you think?'

Larry looked at me for a second and then burst out laughing: 'Right enough,' he said.

'Stand up, son,' said Larry and he put his hand under Sam's elbow and pulled him up. He wrapped the washing line round Sam's waist, and through his legs to make a sort of harness. He kept twisting and tying it – Larry was definitely a boy scout when he was a lad. Sam tried to sit down once or twice – he reminded me of a dog not wanting to be groomed – but Larry kept on twisting and tying, twisting and tying and Sam couldn't do a lot about it. After a minute or two he was wearing a harness over his joggers and he stood there clutching his map with a look on his face of abject terror.

There was a lump in my throat nearly choking me. I had to keep swallowing and gulping and forcing myself not to step in and put a stop to the whole thing. The phrase: 'Sam, why not go and draw a map?' was right on the tip of my tongue. I don't know how I kept it back.

'Right,' said Larry. 'We need to prepare. We'll need tools when we get there for slashing through the jungle undergrowth and lots of fresh water and other explorer stuff like that.'

He jogged off to his caravan and came back with two cans of coke and some boiled sweets and his rucksack. Then he went to the garden shed and got some clippers and a saw and he shoved them in the rucksack so the handle was sticking out.

He said: 'Right, comrade, how's you fixed for an adventure?'

It was too painful and I couldn't bite it back any longer: 'It's okay, Sam', I blurted out: 'You don't have to do it if you don't want to.'

Sam thought about it for a minute, with all sorts of wild thoughts flashing across his face.

'Fizzy Mascara says: "We all fear what we can't see. Go take a look."'

116

'Fizzy who?'

'Good idea,' cut in Larry. Then he tied the pieces of baler twine together and Sam let him tie a length to the front of his harness and the back of Larry's own belt. He tied another piece to the back of Sam's harness and gave it me to hold. Larry took a couple of steps towards the World of the Jungle at the Bottom of the Garden and the rope went taut and pulled against the harness which then dug into Sam's back. Sam swayed but stood still.

'Okay, Pal,' said Larry. 'You've got the compass. Look in the direction of travel and find a landmark.'

Sam murmured: 'Last apple tree.'

'Last apple tree it is. Let's go and explore. Any problems, tug on the rope.'

Larry took one or two steps and we set off as ungainly as a car being towed by a learner driver. We inched down the garden with Sam's hesitant steps keeping the rope between him and Larry taut.

I grasped the rope tied to the back of his harness and kept pressure on it to let him know I was there if he needed me. When I started to go dizzy, I realised I was holding my breath.

As we got near the last apple tree before the World of the Jungle at the Bottom of the Orchard, Sam's feet stuck on the grass and Larry looked over his shoulder: 'You all right, son?'

I was holding my breath again. What would happen? I needed him to know we could stop and go back whenever he wanted. But after standing still for a few seconds Sam gave the tiniest of nods and we set off again, creeping at a snail's pace. Sam clutched the compass but his eyes were closed, his feet dragged on the grass and he counted to himself as we inched past the last apple tree. His knees

117

were hardly bending but he allowed the rope to draw him onwards.

Another dozen steps and Larry stopped, the rope slackened and he said: 'Well here it is, son, the world of the jungle,' and Sam very slowly opened his eyes just a chink.

'I have taken eighty-four steps in a direction I had never gone before,' said Sam.

'That's great,' I said. The lump in my throat was aching.

We all stood and stared at the massive tangle of green.

I don't believe in having best stuff. Pots are pots, glasses are glasses. But I wanted to make that night's tea special so I stuck one of the power-cut candles on a saucer and put it in the middle of the table and dug out some old raffia mats and lobbed them round the edge of the table like frisbees.

The roast smelled delicious and the juices bubbled away in the oven as the potatoes turned gold and the batter for the Yorkshires firmed up and crusted over.

I kept going to the washroom and – trying not to knock the kitchen roll and the little black cups flying – I leant over to the window and strained to see what was going on at the bottom of the garden.

I'd left them to it for a bit while I got the tea ready. They were letting rip and making quite an impression on the jungle. There was already a heap of greenery a foot high they'd lopped off. Larry was putting his back into it with the saw while Sam snipped away with the secateurs.

Every time I watched them I felt a bubbling joy. Sam had lived here all his life and he'd never set foot down there before. He might have only travelled twenty yards today but I felt as though he'd scaled a mountain.

I'd thought it was out of my power to help him and yet here was Larry – with his maps and his ropes and his compass and his talk of explorers – who, a week after wandering in off the street, had got Sam further down the garden than he'd gone in his entire life.

I stuck the wine into the freezer to chill. Duncan and Larry might prefer ale but wine was more of a celebration – and we were celebrating.

I poked about in the kitchen cupboards – there must be three matching wine glasses about somewhere, or had I taken them all to the charity shop? I wanted to dig the tape deck out and put some music on but, however quiet it was, I knew it'd send Sam scurrying upstairs for his earphones and bobble hat, so I didn't.

Seeing the Yorkshires rise and crisp, I went out the back door and jogged down the garden.

'You two coming for your tea?'

Larry backed out of the foliage and Sam glanced up.

'Your tea's ready,' I said.

'We're fairly doing some exploring,' said Larry, grinning at me. 'There's definitely something in here, but we've got a lot of cutting down to do to get at it.'

Sam was snipping and flinging bits of greenery over his shoulder.

'Come on, son. Grub's up.'

Larry held his hand out for the secateurs and passed Sam the end of the rope. Sam handed him the secateurs and grabbed the rope and refastened it to the front of his harness. I grabbed the other rope still dangling from the back of the harness.

'You okay, son?'

Sam nodded and closed his eyes and all three of us set off on a slow march up the garden.

When Duncan came in, he stopped at the door and sniffed.

'Beef! Not had that for a while.'

Larry was carving, laying big juicy slices onto a platter.

'Aye,' he said, 'and it's looking good. Done to a tee.'

I filled the wine glasses.

'Wine,' said Duncan, not sounding impressed. 'We celebrating?'

'We certainly are,' I said. 'Sam's been exploring at the bottom of the orchard.'

I paused to let that sink in. 'And we think we've found an old summer house – *in the Jungle at the Bottom of the Orchard.*' I spoke slowly and deliberately. Did Duncan realise what I'd said? Did he appreciate what a break through this was?

He sat down and nodded a bit.

'Oh, bottom of the orchard, eh?' He glanced at Sam, who was examining his photocopied map at the table, his nose a couple of inches away from the swirling images in the magnifying glass. 'See,' Duncan said, 'it's no big deal going down there, is it?' He took a gulp of his wine and grimaced. 'There used to be an old outhouse there when I was a lad – full of junk – dropping to bits years ago as I remember.'

Why couldn't Duncan rise to the occasion? Show a bit of excitement? He might have lived with Sam all his life but he never dredged up an ounce of understanding or empathy for his son. But he wasn't going to spoil it, I wouldn't let him. I cut in before he could pour any more cold water on the project.

'Well, here's to pastures new.' I raised my glass to Larry and Sam.

'Pastures new,' said Larry, chinking my glass. 'Here's to tomorrow and whatever that might bring,' and he smiled at me.

Chapter 18

Over the next few days Sam agreed that, if the rope was tied to the last apple tree, he could hold it as he made his way down to the World of the Jungle at the Bottom of the Orchard and that would be enough to keep him safe. He'd been roped to Larry and me the first ten times he'd gone down there but his bravery had grown with each try.

I could hardly believe it and kept waiting for the crash. When the backlash came from this – if there was one – it would be spectacular.

The bottom of the orchard looked completely different now. There was a pile of branches to burn over six feet high. I'd promised Sam that we'd light it one night and toast marshmallows and maybe cook some potatoes.

When Larry and Sam finally hacked their way to the summer house they found it smothered in vine and ivy. It looked like something out of a fairy story, as if it should have had witches or ogres living in it. Sam seemed part fascinated by it, part terrified.

When he realised it was six-sided, he stood transfixed: 'It is a hexagon,' he whispered, as though this proved once and for all that dreams really do come true.

The roof was hexagonal too and rose to a point with a broken weather vane on top, all bent and twisted. There was wood on the outside in the style of old Tudor houses, except this wood was painted pale blue and was faded and peeling.

The roof was covered with slates and Larry prodded at them with a branch to make sure they wouldn't brain anybody.

We'd been at it three days and Sam hadn't dared go inside the summer house yet but he'd watched Larry dragging out rusty prams and bedsteads, rolls of fencing and coils of barbed wire; all sorts of stuff encrusted and tangled up. Junk, like Duncan had said.

It was dark inside because the windows were smothered with ivy. Sam took one of my butter knives to prise the ivy suckers off the old glass so it would eventually be light enough for him to venture inside. It was a painstaking job as he chipped away at the plant's little fingers that gripped as if they'd been welded there. At the rate he was going it would take weeks to make the summer house light enough for him to go inside, but he didn't seem to mind. He was enjoying peeling off the little ivy tentacles and stood back to admire every square inch he cleared.

I was spending a lot of time outside with him and Larry. As a rule I hated gardening and avoided it like the plague but I was busy dragging branches about and sawing and pruning. I also took out lots of cups of tea and pieces of cake, which tasted much better outside, sitting on a log with Larry and Sam, than they ever had sitting at the kitchen table on my own.

After we'd been hacking away for a full day on the Monday, Duncan sauntered out the back door carrying a cup of tea and wandered down the garden. He saw the slates and said, 'They might be worth a bob or two.' Sam stopped scraping and looked stricken.

'This summer house is the treasure on the map,' he said.

Duncan didn't answer, but he poked his head inside to inspect the black and white terracotta tiles on the floor.

'They might come up too,' he said.

I was glad to see him disappear back in the house to get ready for milking.

Larry and I threw our tools down and took a rest on our log. Sam joined us and pulled his photocopied map out of a plastic bag he'd left hanging on the summer house door. Without a word, Larry passed him the magnifying glass from his pocket.

I slid off the log onto the grass and pressed my back into the knobbly bark. I closed my eyes to let the sunshine warm my face and my eyelids glowed pinkie-orange. I could hear the rustle of the leaves in the apple tree and, much nearer, the soft crackle of tobacco smouldering in Larry's roll-up. I let the sun soak into all the little scratches on my arms where the branches had grabbed and snatched at me. It was so peaceful I jumped when Sam announced:

'The summer house is not the only treasure on the map.'

I opened my eyes, blinking for a second to re-adjust.

'What?' I said.

'I have examined the entire surface of the map with the compass-stroke-magnifying glass and I have discovered a second treasure on the map.'

'What's that then?' asked Larry, squinting through the smoke trickling from his nostrils.

'There is a well behind the workshop,' said Sam. He blinked at us.

'A well?' said Larry. 'Wonder when that was last – '

'There are wells in fairy stories,' Sam said. 'They have roofs on and a bucket and a rope and a handle.' Sam frowned. 'And sometimes a cat.'

'Aye, I've seen – '

'I do not think *this* well can be like that or my mother or father would have said.'

Larry and I waited. Sam looked deep in thought.

'But I cannot say with certainty that such a well does not exist behind the workshop,' he said, 'because I have never been behind the workshop.'

Again we waited; had he finished?

Tentatively Larry said: 'It could be the next – '

'It will be the next adventure,' Sam declared. 'I will put it on my real wish list.'

He scrambled to his feet, rolled up his map and shot inside.

It was Tuesday again and time for my weekly 'escape'. After that last row with Duncan about the two hundred and fifty quid I'd gathered a load of his old football shirts to take to the tip. He hadn't worn them all the time I'd known him; I think they were from school or something. They'd been stuck in a drawer all horrible and nylon-y and getting in the way for years and now they were going.

But on this Tuesday I couldn't be bothered to take them. A trip to the tip and a wander round the shabby shops with the grand finale at the café-with-the-shortbread held zero attraction.

I wasn't the only one acting funny today. Usually at this time on a Tuesday Sam was parked at the kitchen table drawing a *Map of the World* and watching the big hand tick its way to two o'clock. But not today; today he was outside tackling the summer house with Larry.

I cleared away the dishes, gave the table a wipe and then, making my mind up, I grabbed a pair of secateurs and headed outside to join them.

Sam had completely cleaned his first window pane and was onto his second; the first was sparkling in the sunshine, the ivy cut off in a precise line right round the edge. He gave a little frown as I approached but he said nothing.

Larry raised his eyebrows and smiled. He was up a ladder sawing dead branches off an old apple tree behind the summer house. As he sawed, pink and white blossom drifted down from the other branches like confetti. I chose a bush to prune – near Larry but not near enough to get clobbered by a falling branch.

We worked in silence for a minute or two, and then Larry said:

'Therapeutic, gardening, isn't it?'

I was stumped. I would never have described it as therapeutic in a thousand years up until, well, then. If anyone had asked me about gardening last week I'd have described it as pointless, cold, wet, dirty, uncomfortable, never-ending boredom – but, yes, I had to admit that in the last few days messing about out here had made me happy.

'It's good,' I said.

'We'll see if we can get this tree producing decent apples again,' he said. 'It needs sunshine. Nothing can bear fruit if it's trapped without sunshine.'

I nodded. 'The only fruit we've got are gooseberries – but they're all thorny.'

Larry laughed. 'Make a great pie though, eh?'

'Umm.'

I didn't like to admit the only gooseberry pie I'd ever made had been as bitter as Old Harry and ended up in the bottom of the bin.

'Do *you* like gardening?' I yelled over at Sam, to change the subject. I couldn't see him but I could hear the regular scrape, scrape, scrape of the old butter knife. 'Sam!' I shouted again, 'you enjoying the gardening?' The scrape,

scrape, scrape stopped and eventually his voice floated back: 'You are cluttering up the orchard with words.'

Larry and I looked at each other as the scrape, scrape, scrape resumed and we broke into silent laughter.

The next day Duncan asked Larry if he'd go with him to collect a load of compost and sand for the polytunnel.

Sam looked disappointed.

'Are you exploring round the summer house?' he asked Larry.

'No,' said Duncan. 'We've got work to do.'

'We've got to get the food for the magic seeds, son,' Larry said. 'They're going to need lots of nutrients when they're planted out.'

Sam looked bereft. The day before we'd worked on the summer house till dusk and then we'd planted the sprouting seeds into seed trays. Well, Larry and I had planted them while Sam watched, wearing his coat, hat and gloves in case by some miracle he got soil up his nails or in his eyes.

Larry went on: 'Don't forget, Sam, it's your job to keep the seeds watered and the soil moist. But not too wet, mind. We don't want – '

'A bloody flood,' said Sam.

Larry grinned and waved as he shut the kitchen door.

'Are *you* going to explore round the summer house?' Sam asked me.

I watched Duncan and Larry pulling out of the yard gate in the Land Rover. Without Larry the summer house project didn't seem so enticing.

'I'd love to but I've got a ton of ironing to do.' I stared at the empty yard gate picturing them travelling down the lane.

'A ton of ironing,' repeated Sam.

'Well it might not actually be . . .'

I went into the washroom and, avoiding all the seed trays, grabbed the ironing basket.

Sam followed me and, as I set up the ironing board in the kitchen, I watched him watering the seeds one drip at a time. Drip. Drip. Drip. He was concentrating so hard on doing a good job for Larry. Drip. Drip. Drip.

It took Sam more than an hour to water all the seeds but he never seemed to lose patience. Afterwards he stared out of the washroom window at the summer house and I felt bad that he wanted to scrape at the window panes but daren't go out on his own. It was drizzling though, and colder, and I couldn't face it without Larry. Obviously it wasn't gardening that was therapeutic – it was gardening with Larry.

'Let's go to Jeannie's for a bit,' I said. 'Tell her about the summer house and everything.'

Without tearing his gaze from the bottom of the garden he gave a very slight nod.

Jeannie greeted us with a big smile.

'I've not seen you for days,' she said to Sam, 'I *thought* if I baked, you might smell it and come down.' She lifted an upturned bucket on the kitchen table to show us a rich chocolate cake oozing with butter cream.

'I have a good sense of smell,' said Sam, 'but the smell of a baking chocolate cake cannot carry 823 steps.' He bent and examined the cake.

Jeannie grabbed a bread knife and sliced into it.

'I will have forty-five degrees, please,' said Sam.

Jeannie offered him a slab of cake balanced on the knife blade and Sam plopped it onto one of his maps on the kitchen table.

'Yes, forty-five degrees sounds good,' I said to Jeannie.

Sam gazed around the kitchen at all the other maps shoved here and wedged there.

'I will have to remove The World of the Jungle on these maps and put in the summer house. These maps are not currently accurate.'

Jeannie passed me my cake.

'Thanks, Jeannie. Sam's been having an adventure, haven't you?'

We both looked at him but he was lost in his cake. His eyes were closed and the taste sensations were flitting across his face.

When he'd finished and examined his fingers for stray chocolate, Jeannie said: 'Have you started your wish list yet?'

Sam looked wary but nodded.

'That's good,' said Jeannie. 'Let's have more cake to celebrate.' And she cut him another chunk.

'So what's on your wish list?' she asked, settling back in her armchair.

Sam hesitated. 'I drew up the wish list after Larry roped me up and I went past the last apple tree in the orchard for the first time.'

Jeannie nodded as though this was a perfectly sensible statement.

'What's on it then?'

'Well . . .'

'You've not forgotten have you?'

'Is it to go in the summer house?' I said. 'The summer house is fab, isn't it, Sam?'

He shook his head.

'Or is it finding that old well you were on about?'

Another shake.

Then in a tiny voice he said: 'I want to leave Backwoods Farm.'

128

'Oh that's – '

He cut me off. 'But I daren't and I am frightened I will never escape from Backwoods and I will die here without *ever* having left.'

There was a lump in my throat and a burning. I wanted to run round the table, throw my arms round him, hug him for all he was worth and tell him I'd get him away from Backwoods even if it killed me – but I knew none of that would help so I clung onto my chair, my knuckles white.

Jeannie nodded and considered what he'd said.

'You mustn't be frightened, Sam,' she said. 'I'm certain you'll be able to leave Backwoods one day and you'll know when the time is right.' Sam studied her. 'It won't be long before you can leave Backwoods. You're brave, Sam – remember that. Maybe soon we'll leave together.' She nodded her head and thought some more. 'Yes, when the time is right, Sam, you'll know, and we can go together.'

Chapter 19

It wasn't Tuesday, it was Saturday and I was back in town. I was dashing – not because I was worried about Sam, I wasn't; I was dashing because I wanted to zoom round the shops, grab the stuff for the barbecue and get straight back to Larry and Sam.

Potatoes, marshmallows, salad, sausages, bread, wine, beer. That should do it.

I'd left Sam making Jeannie a party invitation. When I saw what he was doing I felt giddy with happiness. Sam had never been to a party in his life – he'd never been invited and wild horses wouldn't have dragged him to one if he had.

Yet there he was with his felt pens out, concentrating on a piece of folded card with a tiny map of Backwoods on it, an arrow pointing to the orchard and the word 'PARTY' in bright red letters.

The barbecue had nearly not happened. Sam had wanted to light the great stack of branches and when Larry said it was too near the polytunnel Sam's face fell a mile; I'd promised him a bonfire and he'd set his heart on it.

So Larry dug what he called a fire pit at the other side of the summer house, away from the polytunnel, and put some kindling in it.

'This'll be easier to cook on anyway,' he said. 'It's better

than a great big bonfire – more like an explorers' fire.'
Sam had squatted down beside it and practised holding
his hands out to the non-existent flames.

When I got back from town, Sam announced, 'Jeannie has
accepted my kind invitation and will be arriving at six.'

I gave him trays of glasses and kitchen roll and plates
to carry to the bottom of the orchard. I watched him go.
Each time he ran to the last apple tree and hesitated before
carrying on – walking like he was on thin ice until he
reached the fire pit. Then he'd put the tray down before
turning round, doing the same slow march back to the tree
and galloping up to the house.

I glanced at the sky. The weather could go either way.
Come on, God, I thought, give the kid a break. Give him
a chance to be normal for once.

Larry lit the fire in plenty of time so the embers would
be perfect for cooking when Jeannie arrived and Duncan
finished milking. He sat on a rickety fold-up chair and
made a few practice sausages for me and Sam before the
party started.

He handed a couple round then took a big bite.
'Delicious,' he said. 'I'd better practise one or two more
before our guests arrive,' and he winked at Sam. They
looked like real mates and it made me smile.

Spotting movement over the hedge, I saw Jeannie
coming down the lane. She was in quite a get-up: a
burgundy velvet cloak and a floppy red hat, and was
carrying what looked like homemade wine in a green glass
bottle. She came through the back gate into the orchard
and waved at Sam who jumped up to greet her.

I was kind of sorry we'd had to invite Jeannie but Sam
had wanted to – and seeing it was the first time he'd ever
asked for any such thing, I couldn't turn him down. But

this summer house project was ours – Larry's and Sam's and mine – and I wished we'd kept it that way.

'Burnt sausages for tea?' Duncan hung his coat up and eyed the pile of buns and bowl of salad on the table.

'Take them out, would you? Jeannie's already here.'

'Oh blimey, we got company? Old Jeannie'll have a cauldron over that fire if we're not careful.' Duncan set off towards the orchard: 'Hubble, bubble, toil and trouble,' he said in a stupid witchy voice, 'eye of frog and toe of newt . . .' I rolled my eyes, '. . . one of Jeannie's cats and a dead dog's ear . . .'

I laughed. 'Get on with it,' I said.

Jeannie sat with her cloak spread out around her as she munched on her hot dog. 'This is a beautiful sausage,' she announced, holding it up and examining it like a jewel to the light. She smiled at Sam. 'You've done a wonderful job.'

'Larry cooked the sausages,' said Sam.

Everyone watched Larry rake the red embers.

'Well, *you* can do the marshmallows,' he said. 'Put one on here, hold it six inches away and keep it turning.

He handed Sam the toasting fork.

'Have you got children?' Jeannie asked.

'No, 'fraid not,' said Larry, topping up Jeannie's glass. 'I don't live the life for children, sorry to say.' Larry ruffled Sam's hair. 'I've got my pal here though. He's keeping me busy.'

I sipped Jeannie's wine, thick and sweet and viscous. It was already going to my head; God knew what kind of a potion it was.

I watched Larry and Sam over the brim of my glass. Sam was concentrating on his marshmallow, twirling it as it melted and bubbled brown. When Larry had ruffled his hair he hadn't dodged or winced or smoothed it down. I took another sip and enjoyed the heat as it trickled down my throat. It warmed me, travelling through my body, making me happy and relaxed – the same sensation I had when I watched Sam and Larry together.

I'd been jealous of Larry when he first arrived and frustrated that he found it easy to say and do the right thing with Sam when I found it so difficult. But however he'd done it – whether it was his maps, his stories, his good humour, his easy-going attitude, or whether it was just because he knew he could walk away at any time – I could not deny he had transformed Sam's life.

'Larry hasn't got kids but he's turned his hand to everything else,' Duncan said. 'He's a bit of a gardener.' Duncan swigged his ale – he'd refused to drink wine, especially Jeannie's. 'When's our new crop ready to plant out?' he asked.

'Pretty soon,' said Larry.

Why did Duncan have to bring that up in front of Jeannie? Maybe he was proud of his daft new venture and wanted to show off.

I shifted on my seat. It was hard and uncomfortable. The wind was getting up and starting to blow the ash about and the clouds were scudding low in the sky.

'We'll have to put this fire out if the wind gets any worse,' said Larry. 'We dinnae want to be mending that tunnel again.'

'More wine?' I said, waving the bottle about and then pouring the dregs into my own glass.

'I'm going to try one of Sam's delicious-looking marshmallows and then I'll have to go,' said Jeannie. She bent forward and pulled the marshmallow from the fork. 'Elvis has a skin infection and gnawed his foot this morning until it was red raw and bleeding.' She put her head back and licked the hot sugary string. 'I've fixed a cone round his neck,' she went on, 'but he keeps getting stuck behind the sofa.'

I bit my lip to hide a smile. 'Oh,' I said, glad I'd finished my sausage. Larry caught my eye, obviously thinking the same thing. A rush of happiness swept over me, fizzing through my body, and it was hard not to laugh out loud.

After Jeannie struggled out of the wicker chair and left in a billow of purple, the sky turned grey and mauve, and dusk arrived within minutes. Duncan stood up and stretched. 'Looks like the party's going to be rained off. I'll go and unpack some ale I got this afternoon.' He looked at Larry: 'Come and try it.'

'Aye,' said Larry.

Sam, Larry and I were dashing about, piling up plates and left-over food, when there was a great clap of thunder and a fat drop of rain hit my cheek. Sam flung down a bag of bread rolls and grabbed his ears. The sky darkened; it was going to heave it down. Before I had a chance to tell Sam to get back to the house, it started – rain coming down in buckets and hard. I screamed and laughed at the same time; it was that kind of rain.

'Come inside,' I yelled, and I dashed for the summer house, trying to cover my head with a plate.

When I turned round, Sam had gone.

Larry was in the summer house next to me. Rain was dribbling through the roof by the door and I shrieked again as a drop slid down my neck. Larry pulled me towards the back of the summer house – it was drier there where the roof was holding. We both laughed and wiped our faces and stared out at the fire spitting and smoking, surrounded by sodden party stuff, Jeannie's chair now soaked and sorry-looking.

I laughed again to see the rain bouncing off the garden. 'That's crazy,' I shouted over the roar of the storm as it buffeted the summer house and Larry laughed too.

Suddenly I gave a great shiver as the rain chilled my skin. I put the plate on the floor and hugged myself and rubbed my arms to warm up.

Larry opened his jacket.

'I'm warm,' he said.

I hesitated, just for a moment, and then moved towards him. He circled me with his jacket and held me tight. He *was* warm and his face was rough against mine.

He wiped a drop of rain off my forehead and twisted his fingers in my hair. His mouth tasted of wine and cigarettes. It was a long time since I'd kissed someone who tasted of wine and cigarettes. A drop of rain slid down either my cheek or his; I didn't know which.

Chapter 20

Welcome to U Chat

Home   Chat   Message   Rules   Contact   Log in   Sign up
                          Boards   Us

Is a thunderbolt Divine intervention?

Truestory   Lightning is caused by negative and positive
Date: 14 June 2014   electrons and thunder is caused by sound waves
Time: 20.15   but is there any other reason?

Re: Is a thunderbolt Divine intervention?

Fizzy Masara   No. But just you wait . . .
Date: 14 June 2014
Time: 20.18

Re: Is a thunderbolt Divine intervention?

JC   Truestory, read the Bible for many examples of
Date: 14 June 2014   God using the weather to show his will. You will
Time: 20.25   find mention of HAIL, FIRE, THUNDER, DROUGHT,
                               RAIN, FLOOD, WHIRLWIND. These are all
                               examples of God, the Supreme Being, showing us
                               his displeasure.

Re: Is a thunderbolt Divine intervention?

Fizzy Mascara   Like I said. No.
Date: 14 June 2014
Time: 20.31

Re: Is a thunderbolt Divine intervention?

ChocolateMoustache   A thunderbolt is the result of natural laws. It is
Date: 14 June 2014   nothing to do with good or evil. Don't worry,
Time: 20.35   Truestory!

Re: Is a thunderbolt Divine intervention?

JC   You must realise that man is not in control of his
Date: 14 June 2014   own life. We exist because God has decided that
Time: 20.37   we will. He sees all. He knows all. He is all.

Re: Is a thunderbolt Divine intervention?

DiamondSky   Why? Wot u been doing, Truestory? LOL
Date: 14 June 2014
Time: 20.45

Re: Is a thunderbolt Divine intervention?

Root Toot   Well I'm in control of my life so speak for yourself
Date: 14 June 2014   JC.
Time: 20.52

Re: Is a thunderbolt Divine intervention?

AuntieMaud   Nice to hear from you Truestory. My mother
Date: 14 June 2014   always said God was all very well in his place –
Time: 20.53   and that place was the back pew at Matins on a
                           Sunday. Hope you are well and that the treasure
                           map is revealing all its riches. x

Re: Is a thunderbolt Divine intervention?

Truestory
Date: 14 June 2014
Time: 20.56

I put the antique map under a magnifying glass and it revealed two things: a summer house and a well. Both have been secret for years. I am worried that meddling with secrets makes frightening things happen. This is not scientific but I have had a bad shock. The noise of a thunderbolt is the loudest noise I have ever heard. It is louder than the rotovator (which I have heard from a distance); it is louder than the Hoover (even when it is right outside my bedroom door), I estimate that it is even louder than a million Finnish scouts all shouting at once (and they have the current world record).

Re: Is a thunderbolt Divine intervention?

AuntieMaud
Date: 14 June 2014
Time: 21.00

Truestory, I'm sorry to hear of your terrible shock but don't worry about disturbing secrets. My mother always said: 'What's for you won't go by you.' You found the map – God must want you to have it! Wishing you many more adventures. xx

Re: Is a thunderbolt Divine intervention?

Truestory
Date: 14 June 2014
Time: 21.04

I know many facts about lightning and thunder from the internet but when I heard the thunderbolt near the summer house I wondered if God was showing he was angry. I have never had that thought before but when you hear a noise as loud as a million Finnish scouts all shouting at once it can change what you believe.

Chapter 21

We stayed in the summer house as the storm turned from a torrential downpour to heavy rain to occasional fat drops seeping through the roof and plopping off the ivy leaves that crept round the door.

'You're beautiful, Alice,' Larry said. He smoothed my frizzy hair and stroked my cheek and kissed my eyelids and said again, 'You are so beautiful.'

He tasted of Jeannie's wine and cigarettes and I couldn't remember anything ever tasting as good. I dreaded him only kissing me once; I dreaded the moment fading away in embarrassment and disappearing forever. I knew with certainty I didn't want that to happen.

I slipped my arms around him, burying my hands inside the back of his jacket, feeling his shoulder blades and the muscles of his back and then I leant up and pulled him towards me and I kissed him again.

In that moment I was totally alive, lost in the taste of him, the smell of him, the feel of his lips on mine. My stomach knotted and tightened and I opened my eyes a fraction. His eyes were shut as he kissed me, he was concentrating only on me.

The intensity of the rain and the rumble of the thunder created a haven in the summer house, a place apart, somewhere without Sam or Duncan or Backwoods or anything.

Only me and Larry, right here, right now. He stroked my face and kissed my neck, brushing his lips against my throat. I closed my eyes and let out a small groan that was lost in the rain battering on the summer house roof and lashing against the windows.

As the minutes passed the rain lessened, the roar of the storm abated and we broke apart. He looked into my eyes and scanned my face and he said again, 'Beautiful.'

My fingers lingered on his shoulders, moved down to the small of his back then, letting my arms fall, I gazed up the orchard at the house which I could see through the clear patches Sam had scraped on the windows. There was no sign of anyone.

One of the wonky garden chairs was collapsed on its back, the cushions were sodden, the abandoned plates brimming with rain water. Through the dusk the farmhouse windows stared back at me blank and black and inscrutable.

'I'd better go,' I said. He took my hand and kissed it; he held it in both his own then let it go. I hesitated. I didn't want to break this spell. I kissed him again urgently, savouring every second before breaking away.

Putting my head down, I dashed through the summer house door, the ivy grabbed at me and cold drops of rain found the bare skin on my hands and face. I ignored them – hardly felt them – and ran up the orchard, past the squandered party stuff towards the house.

On the step I looked back. Larry was beside the summer house, watching me. He raised his hand and I waved back.

I picked my way over the trays of seedlings. With my hand on the kitchen door I stopped and took a deep breath. Where was Sam? What had happened to Sam when the thunder started? I felt sick. I took another breath and slowly released it. I smoothed my hair, straightened my shoulders and walked into the kitchen.

'You get trapped out there?' Duncan was lounging in front of the fire, legs up on the range, swigging from a bottle of ale. 'What's happened to Larry?'

'Where's Sam?' I asked.

'Bolted upstairs like a bat out of hell. Where's Larry? He needs to try some of this ale.'

I kicked off my shoes.

'Drying off, probably, in the caravan.' I avoided Duncan's eye. 'I'm soaked,' I said and I headed upstairs.

I sat on the bed with the door shut and stared into space. How had that happened? Where had it come from? I re-ran the memories. We were probably only in the summer house for fifteen minutes but it was fifteen minutes going round on a loop in my head.

I could still taste him, feel his fingers tangled in my hair, touching my face, his body pressed against mine. I dropped my head into my hands and groaned. What the hell was I doing?

And Sam? His door was shut. I needed to see if he was all right. It was like my life had jumped tracks, raced away, heading to the unknown, out of control. But I couldn't shed my responsibilities as easily as that. For a few minutes I may have felt like a different person living a different life – but I wasn't, I was Sam's mum and he needed me and that was that.

I tapped on his door. There was no reply but I pushed it open. Sam was curled on the bed, the quilt wrapped round his head.

I felt an almost overwhelming urge to hug him.

'Sam,' I whispered, 'you okay?'

He unwrapped half his head. I could only see one eye but I knew he didn't want me to touch him.

141

Occasionally, when he looked like that, I couldn't resist and touched him anyway and he'd shrink away and make me want to cry. Sam didn't like it when I cried, especially if I made a noise – although usually my crying was quiet. Sometimes I could cry making no noise at all, an art I'd perfected since giving birth to Sam.

At times, instead of putting an arm round him, I put a hand on his shoulder or patted his back. Sam didn't react as badly then because these gestures were quicker and not near his face; he could hold his breath and know it would all be over in a few seconds. Afterwards he'd pluck at his sweatshirt or rub his shoulder to smooth away the echo left by my touch.

Very occasionally I'd kiss him, although I hadn't tried to do that for a long time. I used to touch the top of his head with my lips or brush his cheek with my cheek, but he'd wipe away the feeling straight away. He'd see me watching so I'd try not to look hurt and I'd remind myself: he can't help it. It's not his fault; it's just the way he is.

With his one uncovered eye he watched me watching him. Was I going to touch him, to hug him, possibly to kiss him? He pulled his legs closer and curled himself even smaller.

'Sorry about your party getting rained off,' I said. 'Hope you weren't too scared of that thunder.' I perched on the bed in silence.

Slowly he emerged from the quilt and, keeping himself curled tight, he sat up, dropped his chin onto his knees and shrugged his shoulders.

He said: 'I wanted to deaden the thunderbolt in my head but it did not work.'

I forced a smile and, to change the subject, I said, 'I think Jeannie enjoyed her sausages,'

He gazed at his quilt, probably wishing it was still wrapped round his head. 'I know. She said so.'

'Don't worry about that thunder, Sam. It's over now.'

He looked the picture of misery

'You'll be all right. You've had a shock, that's all.'

There was a pause, then he said: 'Now you know I'm okay, why are you still sitting on my bed making it go down at the edge and knocking me off balance?' He hugged his knees even tighter.

Despite knowing better, I put a hand on his shoulder.

'If you're sure you're okay, Sam?'

He started holding his breath so I took my hand away and stood up. He rubbed his shoulder.

I stood for a long moment watching the top of his scruffy head and then I let out a huge sigh. I couldn't help it; the sigh was so enormous I felt myself deflate.

'Okay Sam. I'll leave you in peace. Night, night.'

He didn't look up. I don't suppose he wanted to give me any encouragement to stay or, God forbid, to sit down again. His forehead dropped onto his knees, so I turned and left the room.

I stood on the landing not sure what to do; hide in my room or brave going downstairs? I didn't fancy making conversation with both Duncan and Larry at once, but I couldn't face skulking in my room. I headed downstairs.

Duncan was by the fire on his own. He stood up as I walked into the kitchen.

'I'm going to see if Larry wants any.' He held up his beer bottle. 'It's good stuff.' He shoved his boots on and disappeared outside. I sat by the range, feeling chilled, holding my hands inches from the fire, staring at the flames until my eyes stung and watered. I was shivery; the cold had got into my bones and the fire could not warm me up.

'He says he's beat.' Duncan was back, knocking his boots off. He had a look on his face like a kid not invited to the party. 'He says he's going to get his head down.'

I felt a kick of disappointment, followed by a wave of relief. It was probably for the best Larry staying outside, I couldn't have acted normal anyway.

'I'm getting an early night myself,' I said. 'I've caught my death out there.'

I went upstairs leaving Duncan with his feet on the range and a canned-laughter sitcom on the telly.

On my way up I stared out of the landing window at Larry's caravan. The lights were on but the curtains were drawn. I could see the faint shadow of him sitting at the table. What was he doing? Was he reading? Was he smoking? Was he thinking about me? I watched for ages, the low glow of the caravan light shining across the orchard, so close I could shout his name and be heard and yet so far away.

Next morning I was down early. I'd barely slept all night. Duncan was still milking and Larry was nowhere to be seen. I felt shaky, embarrassed and self-conscious and nervous but excited too.

I'd dug out a T-shirt from the back of the wardrobe. It was a bit on the small side but I thought I could get away with it. I breathed in and felt my breasts strain against my top. I still looked all right if I gave myself half a chance. I'd put a skirt on too – my legs were good, I knew that. I was only forty-two, even if some days I felt more like a hundred and forty-two.

It was eight o'clock. Duncan would be in any time and Sam would be down at half past as usual. I caught sight of myself in Duncan's shaving mirror propped up behind the kitchen sink. I'd put mascara on. I hadn't bothered with mascara in a long time. I'd brushed my hair too – though you couldn't tell. I looked glassy-eyed and wary – furtive even – or was that my imagination? I flicked the kettle on and gazed unseeing across the yard. Bess yelped and wagged her tail. Larry must be coming across from his caravan. My heart leapt and I felt myself holding my breath.

There was a tap on the door. I didn't answer. I glanced at myself in the mirror and pulled in my stomach just in time for the door to open.

Larry stuck his head round and half-smiled. 'Is it okay?' he said, nodding towards the kitchen table.

'Hi, course,' I forced a smile and grabbed the coffee jar. 'Coffee?'

Larry glanced at the clock and walked towards me. 'Alice, I'm sorry, I was . . .'

I interrupted him: 'Don't be. Don't be sorry.'

Larry touched my arm 'No.'

We looked at each other for a second and then his hands were holding my waist and my arms were round his neck. Somehow we side-stepped the kitchen window, getting out of sight of the yard and I could feel him pressing me against the kitchen wall, his hands moving down my body, pulling me even closer.

Bess yelped again and we broke apart, listening for the trudge of Duncan's boots coming up the yard. We heard him call to the dog, telling her to be quiet and go to bed. I spun round, coffee jar still in hand and faced the boiling kettle, getting my breath back, trying to wipe the desire off my face.

Duncan strode in and nudged his boots off.

'Anyone fancy scrambled egg?' He was grinning at me and Larry. 'They're laying well.' He had six eggs from the hen cabin.

'Aye, good idea,' said Larry. He took the eggs from Duncan and crossed to the kitchen unit beside me. 'I'll do it,' he said. 'It's a speciality of mine,' and he smiled at me.

145

I tried to smile back and say something normal but I couldn't remember what normal was. I put coffee granules in three mugs and poured boiling water on top.

This was excruciating. Larry was so *close;* I could feel his closeness when he passed me the milk carton and when he leant in front of me to get a glass bowl. I took ages to make the coffees. I didn't want to turn round in case what I was thinking was written across my face. It had to be; it was too strong not to be.

After stirring the coffee till I nearly wore out the spoon, I handed a mug to Duncan. 'Ta, Love,' he said sitting at the kitchen table with his feet on another chair. 'So,' he took a big swig and wiped his mouth with the back of his hand, 'what's happening today?'

'Erm . . .' I couldn't think; in fact it took me a minute to work out it was Sunday – everything had been thrown in the air.

'I'm digging in some compost in the tunnel,' said Larry.

Duncan seemed interested. 'Need any help?'

Larry was beating the eggs. 'Aye, could do,' he said, and Duncan nodded.

'It's not a bad day,' Duncan said. 'That storm changed everything. We needed it.'

Larry carried on beating the eggs and I fiddled with some pots and pans.

'Aye,' said Larry after a few seconds, 'I reckon we did.'

Chapter 22

After breakfast we went outside. Duncan and Larry disappeared into the polytunnel and Sam and I messed about in the garden. Sam scraped away with his butter knife. Scrape, scrape, scrape.

I gazed past him into the summer house to where Larry and I had sheltered, hidden together last night.

'You all right, Sam?' I asked but I didn't wait for an answer. I wandered off and picked up the sodden cushions. I carried them at arm's length and pegged them on the line. I couldn't settle to anything so I brewed some tea and took it outside with a plate of cake.

Duncan and Larry came out of the polytunnel.

'I'm glad of this,' said Duncan. 'It's as hot as a whore's arse in there with the sun on it.'

I scowled. I didn't think there was any need for *that*.

Duncan laughed but Larry didn't so Duncan stopped.

'You want to help in the polytunnel?' Larry asked, but Sam shook his head.

'I am never going in the polytunnel. It is full of black soil and it smells funny. Also it is as hot as a whore's arse in there with the sun on it.'

I raised my eyebrows and Duncan avoided my eye and took a big bite of his cake.

★

I chopped an onion. I wasn't concentrating; I'd be lucky if I didn't chop my finger-ends off. I brushed a strand of hair from my face and my eyes prickled and stung. I hated onions. I hated cooking full stop but I was making Spaghetti Bolognese because it was the one thing I was good at and Larry might like it.

My eyes welled up with onion tears and I wiped them away then noticed the mascara streaks across the back of my hand. Damn, I'd forgotten about that. I glanced in Duncan's shaving mirror. Bugger it; black eyes and a red nose. Bet he wouldn't think I was beautiful now.

I smiled and then couldn't stop. It was mad. *I* was mad. But I didn't need to feel bad because nothing had happened. Not really. Nothing had happened except a kiss, and what was a kiss?

I watched Bess zig-zag on her chain, to and fro, to and fro, rounding up an invisible herd. My hands rested on the chopping board. I'd done nothing wrong because almost nothing had happened. *Almost* nothing. I drove the knife through the onion.

And yet everything had happened.

The way he'd pressed me against the kitchen wall and kissed me. The way he'd stroked my face and run his hands down my body and told me I was beautiful. The way he'd pulled my head back and kissed my throat and my neck and whispered my name.

I thought I'd got too weary to feel excited and alive, but I hadn't.

I attacked the rest of the onion before swiping it off the board and into the frying pan where it hissed in the hot oil. I stopped myself wiping my hands down my T-shirt, as I would if I'd been wearing one of my old sack-jumpers.

I stirred the onions and wondered what Larry and Sam were up to.

I tipped the mince on top of the onions and bashed it around. I'd stick a bit of wine in as well; there was a half-drunk bottle of red somewhere.

I closed my eyes and imagined uncorking the wine and pouring a glass and sipping it and offering it to Larry and tasting it on his lips.

The mince was spitting and burning on the bottom of the pan. My eyes flew open and I grabbed the handle and knocked it off the heat. I'd lost interest in Spaghetti Bolognese. I wanted to go and find Larry and Sam.

I jogged down the garden feeling shot-through with energy.

Larry and Duncan had finished in the polytunnel and Duncan had gone to check on a calving cow. Larry and Sam were clearing round the summer house.

'Why don't we do some more exploring?' I said. 'We could look for that old well.' Sam's butter knife slowed in its scraping. 'What do you think?'

'Aye,' said Larry. 'We could do.'

We both watched Sam who was focusing on the window pane and scraping with glacial slowness.

'I've had a brainwave,' Larry said and winked at me. 'Why don't you take your divining rods? They find water, don't they?'

'Wikipedia says a brainwave is a "rhythmic or repetitive neural activity in the central nervous system",' said Sam. He stopped scraping. 'I do not think you have had a brainwave. I think you have had a good idea.'

'It is, isn't it?' said Larry. 'Go and get them.'

Sam put down his scraper and slow-marched towards the house.

Larry strode over and stroked my upper arm with the back of his hand.

'I've wanted to touch you all day.'

'I know,' I said.

His hand slid down my arm and briefly our fingers linked.

We followed Sam towards the house.

'We'll talk later,' Larry said, and I nodded.

Sam was in the kitchen with his photocopied map spread on the table and his water diviners beside it.

Larry gave him the magnifying glass. 'Okay, let's check the exact location of this well.' They bent over the map and Sam pointed. 'Right. Do you want to get roped up again, Sam? Keep you safe?'

Sam nodded.

'No!' I said. 'He doesn't need that, do you, Sam? You've already cracked The World of the Jungle at the Bottom of the Orchard. Going behind the workshop's nothing, is it? You've been in the workshop before – this isn't much different.'

I felt euphoric. With Larry's help we'd achieved so much with Sam and today we were going to take another step towards leaving Backwoods for good.

'Come on!' I said, heading to the door. 'Let's do it.'

Larry hesitated for a moment then followed.

'Come on, Sam,' he said. 'I'll grab the spade on the way.'

Sam clung to the kitchen table. He was counting to himself under his breath. I willed him to move.

'Come on,' I said again. I felt as though I had enough energy to get all three of us behind the workshop and digging for a well.

I went back for Sam but I didn't touch him, I kind of herded him, urging him ever closer to the door.

150

He gripped his divining rods and inched away from the table.

It was a stop-start journey and Sam's face never lost the look of stark terror but eventually we turned the corner behind the workshop. It had taken so much energy to get him there, I was beginning to feel drained. We scanned the area for signs of a well.

Larry prodded about with his spade and examined the ground.

'It should be round here, son.'

Sam hovered by the corner of the workshop, clinging onto his divining rods and counting to himself under his breath.

'Aye, this'll be it,' said Larry and he pointed with his spade to where the ground had sunk.

'I think we've found it already,' I said to Sam, and grinned at him.

'There is no slate roof or brick surround or bucket on a rope with a handle.'

I laughed but Sam did not crack a smile. 'Or a cat,' he whispered. His divining rods were out in front of him, clacking around, and he was gripping them so hard his knuckles were white.

Larry hacked at the ground to break the grass. Then he slammed the spade in and started digging. It was impressive. I wondered if he was putting on a show for me and I hoped he was. If he was it was working.

Within a few minutes he'd cleared the grass and his spade hit something hard.

'Here we go,' he said.

After another few minutes we could see it was something wooden. Slowly he cleared more and more soil.

Larry said: 'It's the well cover. Looks like it's slipped.'

'It has slipped to an angle of 45 degrees,' whispered Sam.

Larry carried on scraping and digging, with sweat beading on his face, until we could see the whole of it, black and rotten.

'It's had it; I reckon I can put my spade right through it,' he said, and he whacked it. The wood cracked and splintered and he hauled it out bit by bit.

Sam's eyes were screwed shut.

'You okay, Sam?' I said, grabbing his shoulder. He shrank away.

'Larry must have dug through the top soil and some sub soil,' he whispered. 'The well may go right through the bedrock and on to the centre of the earth.'

'I don't think – '

'The internet says you need a diamond pickaxe to dig that far.' He was starting to bend at the waist. 'But that might not be a true story.'

He fell to his knees, dropped his divining rods and clapped his hands to his ears.

He wailed: 'Larry has opened a bottomless pit to the centre of the earth.'

'No, Sam.' I was appalled. I could see where this was going. 'Larry will stop now, he'll stop.'

'I should be roped up,' said Sam, bent double. 'There is a yawning chasm. A sudden precipice.' He collapsed onto the grass and curled up, wrapping his arms round his head.

'Sam', I said, kneeling beside him. 'It's okay, it's just the well. Larry won't dig anymore.'

But it was too late. Sam let out a scream; a terrible high-pitched shriek that brought me out in a sweat.

'Sam,' I begged, 'Sam, it's okay. You're all right. Forget the well. We'll leave it. Sam!' I took him by the shoulders, trying to get him to stand. Larry nudged me aside and attempted to pick up Sam. His screams went up an octave.

'Don't drop me down the well! Don't!'

'Leave him, Larry.' I grabbed Larry's wrists. 'Don't lift him, you're making it worse.'

'Take some deep breaths, son,' he said, 'You're safe. Take some breaths.'

But Sam's screams got more hysterical. I held my hands over my ears. 'I'm sorry, Sam,' I sobbed, 'I'm sorry. This is my fault. I'm sorry.'

Larry was saying: 'Breathe, son, breathe.'

I knelt beside him. He hadn't been this bad for ages and it felt worse because he'd been so great since Larry arrived. And this was all my fault for trying to make him run before he could walk. He'd wanted to get roped up and I hadn't listened to him. I'd been stupid.

His screams were ripping right through me. I'd have given anything to make him stop. Then the screams turned to sobs and I wiped my eyes to look closer only to see he was biting his arm so hard he was shaking.

'No! Stop it, Sam!' I grabbed his arm to force it from his mouth. 'Stop biting. Stop it!' I yanked his arm from between his teeth and he screamed again so loud it shook my brain.

'I'll get him inside,' Larry said.

'No,' I grabbed Larry. 'Don't pick him up. Leave him.' There was blood trickling down Sam's arm.

Larry took no notice and put his arms under Sam's armpits. Sam's shrieks went up a pitch and his arm swung round. He must have grabbed his water diviner because the wire whipped round and caught my face with a great sting. I screamed and felt the warm wet blood on my cheek.

153

'No,' Larry shouted, but the wire thrashed again and hit Larry as he held Sam.

'Shit,' he said, letting Sam crash to the ground.

'What the fuck is going on?'

Duncan was striding round the workshop corner. 'What in holy fuck is going on?'

He took in the scene with a look of fury.

He marched up to Sam who was lying on his side, purple in the face, covered in snot and tears with bloody streaks down his arm and he picked him up, pinioning Sam's arms by his sides and crushing him to his chest, much as he would have picked up a calf, and strode off with him.

I ran behind. 'We were doing some exploring. He got frightened.'

Duncan did not answer. He took Sam inside and straight upstairs and laid him on the bed and covered him with his quilt.

'Are you all right, Sam?' I wiped my eyes.

'Well he doesn't look all right, does he?'

I stroked Sam's head and he shot further down the bed until he was completely covered.

'Leave him,' Duncan said and he turned and went downstairs.

I knew it was pointless trying to talk to Sam or to touch him so I pulled the door to and followed Duncan downstairs.

He'd poured himself some water and was taking a long swallow.

'Leave the lad in peace,' he said and marched out past Larry who was having a fag by the open door.

Larry stubbed his fag and came in.

'Is he all right and are you all right?'

We were both far from all right, but I nodded.

154

'Is Sam like that a lot?' he said.

'Not as often as he was.'

I walked over to the abandoned cooking and examined the burnt mince. 'Thanks for your help,' I said. 'Sorry if he got you with that wire.'

Larry shrugged. 'The lad was scared. We're all scared of something. Anyway, he didn't get me as bad as he got you.' Larry examined my face. 'Got any TCP?'

I pointed to the dusty first aid kit stuck on the wall and he took some cotton wool and antiseptic out and dabbed my cheek.

'Thanks, anyway,' I said. 'You were trying to help.'

'I'm sorry it worked out like that. I'm fond of the lad.'

'It was my fault. I wasn't thinking straight. It was a stupid idea. I got carried away.'

'I took a photo on my phone down the hole to show the lad it's only a foot or two deep and full of rocks and soil. He'll see there's nothing to be frightened of.'

'Thanks,' I said. I fought my bottom lip to stop it wobbling. 'It's not usually that simple though. What he's frightened of – I don't know – it doesn't make sense half the time. That's why it's so hard to help him.'

I picked up the pan, scraped some mince off the bottom and flicked one or two burnt bits into the sink.

There was silence during which I could still hear Sam's shrieks echoing round my head.

'I thought I'd make some Bolognese sauce . . .'

Larry was standing close behind me. He slipped his arms round my waist and kissed the back of my neck.

'. . . only it got a bit burnt . . .'

His hands slid to my hips and he pulled me against him.

'Alice, you're lovely,' he said, and I could feel the heat of his breath in my hair. 'So fucking lovely.'

I put down the pan and was about to turn to him when

155

we heard Duncan's footsteps heading back to the kitchen door.

Larry stepped away.

'I'll be in the polytunnel at milking time,' he said, and I nodded.

Chapter 23

Welcome to U Chat

Home   Chat   Message   Rules   Contact Us   Log in   Sign up
                   Boards

Why am I frightened of something that cannot happen?

Truestory
Date: 15 June 2014
Time: 16.20

I am afraid of something that cannot happen but my stomach hurts and my legs are shaking and I cannot stop thinking about it.

Re: Why am I frightened of something that cannot happen?

SpiritLove
Date: 15 June 2014
Time: 16.24

Hi Truestory, I think we've talked about the power of the mind before. My booklet on this and other visualisation techniques is still available on our Spirit&Soul website, or purchased here for only $2.50. Plus p&p. Truestory, use affirmations. Say every day: 'I am fearless' and mean it. Put your shoulders back, look yourself in the eye and say 'I am fearless'. We are here at the Spirit&Soul Spiritual Community to help you on your spiritual journey!

Re: Why am I frightened of something that cannot happen?

NoShitSherlock
Date: 15 June 2014
Time: 16.28

I can guarantee the minute you let your guard down some bastard'll bite you on the arse. Stay scared Truestory!!

Re: Why am I frightened of something that cannot happen?

Fizzy Mascara
Date: 15 June 2014
Time: 16.30

It's common sense to be scared. It's only the idiots who aren't scared.

Re: Why am I frightened of something that cannot happen?

JC
Date: 15 June 2014
Time: 16.33

The devil is making you fearful. Offer your fear to God. If He is with you you can come to no harm.

Re: Why am I frightened of something that cannot happen?

NoShitSherlock
Date: 15 June 2014
Time: 16.37

Joking apart, Truestory, you've gotta face that fear! Fear is always worse than the reality.Go face it now!!

Re: Why am I frightened of something that cannot happen?

Truestory
Date: 15 June 2014
Time: 16.38

I have faced it – Larry took a picture down the well with his smart phone and it is full of soil and rubble and I could not fall into the burning centre of the earth but it has not stopped me shaking when I think about it.

Re: Why am I frightened of something that cannot happen?

NoShitSherlock
Date: 15 June 2014
Time: 16.41

Okkkaaaaayyy!! wot else you scared of?

Re: Why am I frightened of something that cannot happen?

Truestory
Date: 15 June 2014
Time: 16.44

Going in the poly tunnel because it is as hot as a whore's arse in there and it's dirty and it smells funny.

Re: Why am I frightened of something that cannot happen?

NoShitSherlock
Date: 15 June 2014
Time: 16.44

You kill me Truestory!!!!

Re: Why am I frightened of something that cannot happen?

ChocolateMoustache
Date: 15 June 2014
Time: 16.50

I've heard of people writing their fears down and burying them or burning them. Watching your fears disappearing into the ground or going up in smoke can help you overcome them.Good luck, Truestory!!

U Chat
Private Message to NoShitSherlock
15 June 2014 Time: 17.48

Truestory

Dear NoShitSherlock, Thank you for your advice about facing my fears. However, I am concerned that you say I 'kill' you. I am checking with you that your use of the word 'kill' is a 'Figure of Speech' – possibly hyperbole. I believe you are using the word in a way that departs from its customary meaning. Am I correct?

U Chat
Private Message to Truestory
15 June 2014 Time: 17:57

NoShitSherlock

There you go again! You're a funny guy Truestory.

You been in that place that's hot as a whore's arse yet!! Get in there Truestory. Go for it!!!

U Chat
Private Message to NoShitSherlock
15 June 2014 Time: 17.58

Truestory

My heart rate has been more than 120 beats a minute for several hours today and my palms have been sticky. The internet calls this the 'fight or flight response', but I did not fight anything or fly anywhere. I got under my quilt.

Experiencing the 'fight or flight response' under your quilt does not feel good. I think you are right. It is better to face your fears.

Ps.
SpiritLove recommended 'Affirmations'. Wikipedia says: 'Affirmations are carefully formatted statements to be repeated.' I repeated 'I am fearless' twenty times, but it is not a truestory. I am not fearless which means 'Affirmations' are lies.

Chapter 24

Duncan was milking; I could hear the hum of the milking parlour. Larry was waiting in the polytunnel and I was going out to meet him.

We hadn't spelled it out, it seemed too mean, but we both knew Larry had suggested the polytunnel because Sam was too frightened to go in. I felt bad about using Sam's fears against him, but Sam didn't usually come down at this time anyway. He'd be happy in his room drawing maps or going on the internet. He'd be fine, absolutely fine.

I'd been married to Duncan for twenty-four years and been faithful all that time – pretty miserable for a lot of it – but faithful all the same. And now I was going to do something that would change everything with someone I'd known a fortnight. I was risking the lot: my marriage, my home, my relationship with my son, but that wasn't going to stop me. Nothing was going to stop me.

I stood still listening at the bottom of the stairs. Not a sound. Sam was busy doing his thing. He had been down for a few pieces of pasta for his tea and then he'd disappeared back up to his room. He'd calmed down. He was fine.

In the downstairs loo I brushed my teeth. I inspected my face close up: lines, wrinkles, yes a few, but my eyes were bright and I looked alive – sexy even. As I opened the bathroom door I heard the hum of the milking parlour again, loud and insistent. I looked at my watch: six o'clock – Duncan would be milking for another half hour. I listened again at the bottom of the stairs and then walked out of the back door.

I jogged across the orchard towards the polytunnel. I couldn't help glancing back at the landing window for any sign of Sam, but there was just a blank, black window staring back at me.

At the tunnel I pushed aside the plastic sheeting that served as a door and felt the humidity and the heat hit me.

Larry was sitting on a stack of compost sacks and he stood up as I went in.

Neither of us said anything. I put my arms around him and he held me tight and kissed me.

'You sure about this?'

I kissed him again; I didn't want to talk. I wanted to taste him, to hold him, to be alone with him and make every second count.

Larry slid his hands under my T-shirt and I shivered. I opened my eyes to see him watching me. I smiled, stretched up and kissed him – biting his lip just enough to hurt. Larry pushed my bra up and took the weight of my breasts. He leant me backwards and the compost sacks pressed against my legs and I sat down and then edging up the sacks I lay down.

The sacks had soaked up the sun and were warm against the bare skin on my back. Larry lay beside me and pushed my T-shirt further up and I closed my eyes. His face was rough against my skin as his tongue traced around my breast and sucked my nipple which was so hard it hurt.

The white plastic of the polytunnel was right above my head; it was like being encased in a weird bubble, as if Backwoods, Duncan, Sam and everything had disappeared. It was a place apart: hot and sticky, smelling of soil and surrounded by the breeze rustling the plastic sheeting.

I pulled Larry's shirt and slid my hands underneath to feel the skin on his back, smooth and taut.

The breeze dropped and I heard a noise by my head. I froze. What was that? Was somebody there? I strained to hear but the breeze blew on the tunnel again and it rattled. Was it only the wind? Larry didn't look like he'd noticed anything.

I felt him pulling my skirt up and his hand moving up my thigh. I listened again, but there was nothing except the wind. I pressed myself against him and fumbled with his belt.

He pulled my knickers aside and I realised I'd put a skirt on this morning to make it easier for him to do this. I didn't feel ashamed either, not a bit.

I felt his weight on me and I held my breath.

'Alice, oh God, Alice,' he said and I bit my hand and buried my face in his shoulder to stop myself making a noise.

I mustn't make a noise; it seemed vital not to make a noise – like we were doing this in another life, in another world, somewhere that was ours, and it didn't count as long as I made no noise at all.

Afterwards I pulled my skirt down as Larry sorted his clothes.

'You okay?' he said.

I nodded. It must be nearly half six. My back was sticking to the plastic sack and I held my hand out for Larry to pull me up. I leant against the plastic wall, my head spinning. It was bloody hot in here. Larry bent over and kissed me full on the mouth.

'You are beautiful and gorgeous,' he said and he stroked my face.

I wiped around my eyes. Was mascara smeared everywhere? I smoothed my hair down. I needed to get myself cleaned up and looking normal before Duncan came in. I hutched myself off the sacks and stood up. Larry put his arms around me.

'It's probably best I don't come in the house tonight,' he said.

My throat constricted. I didn't want to be on my own with Duncan. 'I want you to,' I said.

Larry shrugged. 'I don't want to make it awkward, that's all.'

'Come inside,' I said. 'It'll look funny if you don't.'

Larry nodded. 'Okay. If you're sure.'

He put his arm round my shoulders and walked with me to the doorway. Before I pushed the sheeting aside he took my hand and pulled me to him and kissed me. I wound my arms around his neck and took in the taste and the smell of him to last me until I was with him again.

We broke apart. After a moment Larry let go of my hand and I slipped through the plastic sheet and ran back across the orchard.

Chapter 25

Welcome to U Chat

Home   Chat   Message   Rules   Contact Us   Log in   Sign up
               Boards

Should I trust the evidence of my own senses?

Truestory   I saw it but I do not know whether to believe it.
Date: 15 June 2014
Time: 18.35

Re: Should I trust the evidence of my own senses?

Blood Bro   Love Duck Soup! Best Marx Bros film ever!!
Date: 15 June 2014
Time: 18.38

Re: Should I trust the evidence of my own senses?

JC   Doubting Thomas asked for evidence of sight and
Date: 15 June 2014   touch. So there is nothing wrong with using rational,
Time: 18.40   scientific reason – but as Jesus told him: 'Stop
                         Doubting and Believe.'

Re: Should I trust the evidence of my own senses?

Mr Soft
Date: 15 June 2014
Time: 18.44

Fooling yourself into believing is the easiest thing. Don't trust your own eyes. Observations have got to be scientifically tested otherwise we fall victim to illusions, & False perceptions. A good place to start with scientific inquiry is to take Field Notes. Make careful records of your observations, and quantify things and attach a number to whatever you can.

Re: Should I trust the evidence of my own senses?

JC
Date: 15 June 2014
Time: 18.45

Ultimately we have faith.

Re: Should I trust the evidence of my own senses?

Sweet Cheeks
Date: 15 June 2014
Time: 18.47

Seeing is Believing, Truestory. What have you seen anyways?

Re: Should I trust the evidence of my own senses?

Truestory
Date: 15 June 2014
Time: 18.48

I know about tricks of the eye and optical illusions I know about Chinese Shadow Theatre and shadow puppets. But today I did not see any of those things – I saw the shadow of two people kissing through the plastic door of the poly tunnel.

Re: Should I trust the evidence of my own senses?

Sweet Cheeks
Date: 15 June 2014
Time: 18.55

?? Well perhaps that's cos there were two people kissing behind the plastic door of the poly tunnel. Wotever that is!!

Re: Should I trust the evidence of my own senses?

Playmeright
Date: 15 June 2014
Time: 19.00

Yep, I've always put great faith in the evidence of my own senses. Sooner trust my own than anybody else's that's for sure.

Re: Should I trust the evidence of my own senses?

Truestory
Date: 15 June 2014
Time: 19.02

I can still see the shadow-people kissing in my head. I can see a shadow-man putting his arms around the shadow-woman's waist and the shadow-woman putting her arms around the shadow-man's neck and the shadow-man bending down and kissing the shadow-woman on the lips and the shadow-woman kissing him back.

Re: Should I trust the evidence of my own senses?

Mr Soft
Date: 15 June 2014
Time: 19.10

To improve your powers of observation you need to learn to observe. Observing is more than just looking and is the way great discoveries are made. Start on those Field Notes, Truestory. It can make the world more predictable and less worrying.

Re: Should I trust the evidence of my own senses?

Truestory
Date: 15 June 2014
Time: 19.15

My on-line dictionary says 'predictable' means 'possible to foresee what is going to happen'. That would be helpful. I will go and observe what is happening downstairs. I will start my Field Notes. Thank you for your help.

Chapter 26

I knocked back the rest of the red wine while I stirred the Bolognese sauce so my head was swimming and I was humming The Lambada by the time Duncan came in from milking. Larry tapped on the door and came in a few minutes later.

I concentrated on dishing up dinner and said nothing. I left them to talk about the weather and some fencing that needed doing and other farming stuff. I probably looked lost in my own thoughts but I was aware of every word they were saying and every gesture they were making.

Then Sam turned up as I was dangling the spaghetti over the bowls.

He slid into his place at the kitchen table. I was glad to see him. His sleeves were pulled right down to cover the bite marks on his arms but I was relieved he'd come downstairs because sometimes he stayed in his room for twenty-four hours after a meltdown like the one he'd had before.

'Hi Sam, do you want some spaghetti?' He didn't answer.

Larry said: 'You okay, son?' But there was no answer there, either.

Duncan said: 'He's not speaking tonight.'

Sam opened his notebook and ran his fist over it until it was flat. He was holding a pencil and he stared round the table, from person to person, studying them up and down like he was about to do an artist's sketch . Duncan and Larry didn't notice and tucked into their spaghetti like they hadn't eaten all week.

'How's things in the polytunnel?' said Duncan, and I froze.

I poked my spaghetti around my bowl and Larry carried on eating for five seconds until he said: 'Yeah, good. I'll plant out some seedlings over the next few days.'

My skull prickled. I was casting about for something to say, anything, just to change the subject.

'Great scran, Alice,' said Larry.

I gave him a watery smile. Then I noticed that Sam had written 'SCRAN' in his notebook.

'What you doing?' I asked.

'Field Notes.'

'Oh,' I said. 'Field Notes.' I wrapped spaghetti round my fork. 'Is that the first time you've heard the word scran?'

He nodded.

'Can you guess what it is?'

Sam blinked.

'Perhaps Larry is referring to the spaghetti in the brown lumpy sauce,' he said. 'Or maybe he is referring to your separate and noticeable chests in your blue T-shirt.'

The spaghetti unravelled from my fork. We all looked at Sam, and Duncan gave a snort of laughter.

'Scran is food, Sam,' said Larry. 'Your mum has made some great food.'

'My mother is wearing a T-shirt that I have not seen for four years. That is an observation,' he said. 'It is stretched tight over her chests and makes them poke out and look

169

like separate things – not like her baggy jumpers that make them look like one Big Hill. That is another observation.'

'That's too personal, Sam,' I said. Duncan laughed, still cramming spaghetti into his mouth. I don't think Larry was laughing but I daren't look.

'She also has a skirt on,' went on Sam, relentlessly. 'I have not seen my mother in a skirt for, I estimate, five years. The skirt does not reach her knees by one and a half inches. That is – '

'Yes, don't tell me: an observation. That's enough,' I said. I could feel my face burning.

'I have not seen her legs for five years either.'

'Does anyone want any more?' I stood up, yanking my skirt down an inch or two. I grabbed the pan and dumped more spaghetti in Duncan and Larry's bowls without waiting for an answer. Larry gave me a little smile. He felt sorry for me, I could tell, which made me even more embarrassed.

'Thanks, Alice,' he said. 'It's a good recipe you've got there.'

'Observation is one of my skills,' said Sam. 'But I aim to improve those skills. With honed observational skills it may be possible to foresee more and to cut down on the unpredictability of life.'

'Right,' I said. I didn't want to encourage him. I didn't trust what he'd come out with next. 'Bread?' I pushed the plate towards Larry.

'No, I'm perfect, Alice,' Larry said. 'That was great. I'll give you a hand clearing up.'

We cleared the table as Sam went back upstairs and Duncan chose some bottles from his beer cupboard.

'You okay?' asked Larry in an undertone. He was standing very close to me at the sink.

I nodded, and mouthed 'fine'.

'You've got to try some of this "Proper Job",' said Duncan, coming back in and waving a bottle at Larry. 'Taste the finish on this.'

Larry said: 'Aye, okay, Pal,' and carried on drying the pots.

We took a long time over it. I was washing up in slow motion so I could stay feeling the warmth of Larry right down my left-hand side.

Duncan had his back to us and I glanced round once or twice to see him tipping his head back and necking from his beer bottle in front of the fire. The telly was on and there was a Formula One roar and whine.

When we'd finished Larry went over and Duncan opened a bottle and handed it to him. He took a swig, wiped his mouth with the back of his hand and said: 'Aye.' Duncan grinned and plonked his feet up on the range.

I went across and squeezed between them both to reach my magazine on the mantelpiece. I shrieked when I felt a slap sting across my bottom, so hard it made me wobble inside this stupid skirt.

Duncan laughed and said: 'Well don't go sticking it in my face then.'

I smoothed my skirt down.

'Stop it, Duncan.'

But Duncan didn't stop. He grabbed me by the hips and pulled me backwards onto his knees. He wrapped his arms around my waist and rubbed his face in the back of my neck and tried to kiss the side of my face, making stupid noises like he was trying to eat me.

I was so furious it nearly choked me. What the hell was wrong with him?

'I told you to stop it!' I yelled and I wrenched at his arms to get him off.

Knocking his hands away, I struggled up and marched

off, putting the kitchen table between me and him. Duncan laughed.

'I'm only having a joke,' he said and looked at Larry but Larry was staring into the fire with a closed look on his face. Duncan swigged some beer.

'Forecast's good for later in the week,' he said. 'Happen we'll get everything planted out sooner than we thought?'

'We'll keep an eye on it,' said Larry.

'Aye,' said Duncan, and they lapsed into silence, staring at the telly.

I'd had enough. Without saying a word I went upstairs.

Chapter 27

Next morning I put a platter of eggs and fried bread in the middle of the table. I didn't squeeze between Larry and Duncan but walked round the table and leant between Larry and Sam on the other side.

I hadn't put a skirt on today; the last thing I wanted was Duncan acting like he had yesterday. Duncan and I had lived in a sexual desert for ages – or if not a desert then a pretty dried up and withered garden. We were lucky if we had sex once a fortnight. Although I don't know why I use the word 'lucky', it didn't feel lucky, more like part of the day-to-day routine of Backwoods.

It hadn't always been like that – we'd been pretty good together for years before Sam came along. We'd kept the whole thing going longer than you'd expect afterwards, too, considering the pressures we were under. But eventually every aspect of our lives got ground down and tired and it became easier not to bother most of the time. I didn't want him taking a renewed interest in me now. That would be too complicated, much, much too complicated.

I had my jeans on but I'd worn a T-shirt again. I was going to chuck my baggy old jumpers. I should have done it years ago. I had two – one with Monet's poppies on the front and another with Van Gogh's bright yellow sunflowers. I hardly wore the sunflower one anyway; I only put it on when I really needed Sam to leave me alone. I'd always felt mean about that, but I was so exhilarated at the moment I couldn't imagine ever feeling the need to put it on again.

I had the urge to go into town and buy myself something new, something flattering, something that made me look as good as I felt.

First though I had to tear myself back to reality. It had been a life-changing weekend, unforgettable, one I'd like to relive again and again but now it was Monday morning and I had to pull myself together and do some real-life stuff, like sorting out schoolwork for Sam.

He was wearing those great big sunglasses and had his notebook and pen at the table again. He had finished his Weetabix and was staring at everyone and making more notes – or observations as he called them. What was he observing now?

Larry was munching through his fried bread and egg and he kept casting me the odd glance and a smile. I watched his fingers wrap around his mug and my stomach flipped. I hadn't thought about sex for years – not over the breakfast table anyway – but now I could hardly think about anything else.

'I'm taking a couple of bull calves to the auction, do you want to come?' Duncan was looking at Larry. He polished his plate with a half slice of fried bread and shoved it all in his mouth at once.

Larry shook his head. 'Nah, Pal.'

'Might nip in the Dragon after,' said Duncan, raising his eyebrows – obviously thinking he was making an offer no man could refuse.

'Nah,' said Larry, 'I'd better get more sorting done outside so I can plant out later in the week.'

Duncan nodded and I caught Larry's eye. I knew we

were both thinking the same thing; this was a chance to be on our own.

Larry asked Sam: 'What yous up to today?'

It was difficult to see Sam's expression behind his glasses but he said: 'I am working on my "Field Notes". They will sharpen my observational skills, cut down on the unpredictability of life and help me make a discovery.'

Larry nodded.

'And what have you observed today exactly?' cut in Duncan.

Sam consulted his notebook.

'I have made four observations about three people over one meal that lasted twenty-three minutes and involved six eggs, twelve halves of fried bread, two mugs of tea and one cup of coffee.'

Duncan swilled his dregs round his cup. 'Aye? Like what?'

'Number one: my mother has a different T-shirt on today.'

I froze, but thank God, he sailed straight on.

'Number two, Larry can eat three fried eggs and six halves of fried bread without being sick or burning his throat.'

Larry nodded. 'Yep, that sounds about right.'

'Number three, my dad takes ten gulps of tea to finish his mug. Number four, my mother has eaten no breakfast at all. Number five, Larry is one inch taller than my dad. Number six, my dad's shoulders are two inches wider than Larry's and his hands are one and a half times as big.'

There was an awkward pause as Sam consulted his pad then laid his pencil down. 'Unfortunately I do not think these observations are sufficient to make a significant discovery, like it said on the internet.'

'No, I think you've got a bit of work to do yet, lad,' said Duncan.

Sam shut his notebook, slipped off his chair and went upstairs.

'Can you give us a hand getting them calves in the back of the Land Rover?' said Duncan.

'Aye,' Larry said, 'no bother.' He finished his tea and stood up. 'Thanks, Alice.'

They vanished outside and I was left with the usual pile of greasy pots, but I didn't mind. Today I could scrape cold food into the bin and wash pots and stack plates without bothering. I could do anything because Duncan was going out and Sam was doing his schoolwork and I was going to be on my own with Larry. I cleared up, singing The Lambada again.

I trotted upstairs to make sure Sam was busy and likely to stay busy. I tapped on his door and pushed it open six inches.

'You busy, Sam?'

'Yes.'

'What you doing?'

'Field Notes.'

'Oh, right.' I hesitated. 'Still?'

Sam did not reply.

'It's like doing research, I suppose?' I said.

'It's Field Notes.'

I waited. 'Okay then.'

'I must practise very hard,' he said, looking up from his laptop, 'because seeing is not observing.'

'Okay. Right, so you've got lots to do then,' I said.

'Observing is much more than seeing and I need more observations for my Field Notes. Then I can make a significant discovery.'

'Well, you work on that till lunchtime, all right?' I was

176

backing out of the room. 'I'll have lunch ready at half twelve as usual. Okay?'

Sam nodded. His eyes fixed on his notebook.

'Right, well, you keep yourself busy.'

I was already out on the landing and I quickly pulled his door closed.

I flew round the kitchen putting the rest of the stuff away. When Duncan went out he'd be gone for about three hours – and if he ended up in the pub it'd be even longer – and Sam wouldn't come down until half twelve for his lunch. I looked at my watch: that was three hours with Larry all to myself.

Out of the kitchen window I watched Larry and Duncan at the bottom of the yard driving a couple of calves towards the back of the Land Rover. Duncan was saying something and they were both laughing.

Duncan wasn't a bad person even though he did some daft things. I felt bad watching him being friendly with Larry but he wasn't going to find out. He'd never know. I'd lived a pretty lonely and miserable life here for the past few years and it was about time something good happened to me.

Larry and Duncan lifted a calf each and put them in the back of the Land Rover, then Larry grabbed Bess's collar to stop her jumping in and he slammed the Land Rover door. He rubbed Bess's ears and she sat at his feet and wagged her tail.

They stood talking another minute – it must have been about the polytunnel because I could see Duncan pointing and gesticulating. Larry leant against the barn wall and took out a fag and lit it. There was something sexy about the way he dragged on his cigarette, half closing his eyes. I liked to watch him smoking. I liked to watch him doing

177

anything really. I thought about yesterday and my stomach tightened. Was Duncan never going to leave?

After another couple of minutes Duncan climbed in the Land Rover and pulled out of the yard. Larry watched him drive out of the gate and down the lane, and then he dropped his fag, ground it out and walked towards the farmhouse.

I listened at the foot of the stairs. There was no sound from Sam; he must be doing his foot notes or his case studies or whatever they were.

I was usually pretty good with his schooling but I'd been slacking this past week or two. I'd been distracted; I admitted it, but I'd got years of dedication in the bank. They must count for something. At least he'd decided about these field note things himself so it must be something he was really interested in. They'd keep him busy and out of trouble till lunchtime. Bound to.

I heard the latch and spun round. Larry poked his head round the door and smiled at me.

'You busy?'

I laughed and ran to the door. Larry grabbed my hand and we walked outside. A leaf quivered on the yard then caught by the breeze it cartwheeled ahead. Taking care not to let the latch rattle, I closed the door silently behind us.

Chapter 28

Welcome to U Chat

Home   **Chat**   **Message Boards**   **Rules**   **Contact Us**   **Log in**   **Sign up**

Is it possible to learn everything I need to know on the computer?

Truestory
Date: 16 June 2014
Time: 9.36

Can I observe everything I need in my bedroom?

Re: Is it possible to learn everything I need to know on the computer?

DiamondSky
Date: 16 June 2014
Time: 9.38

Play computer games – you learn everything! I learned what a mortar and pestle was by playing Jade Cocoon when I had to make potions. The Sims taught me the Importance of fire alarms and burglar alarms – plus how to use the 24 hour clock. It's all these little random things you learn by gaming.

Re: Is it possible to learn everything I need to know on the computer?

Fizzy Mascara
Date: 16 June 2014
Time: 9.42

This is a difficult question because the internet is full of real people – you are interacting with them not actually with computers.

Re: Is it possible to learn everything I need to know on the computer?

Sweet Cheeks
Date: 16 June 2014
Time: 9.45

I learned everything I know about cars from my boyfriends Gran Turismo. Which is not much!!

Re: Is it possible to learn everything I need to know on the computer?

DiamondSky
Date: 16 June 2014
Time: 9.48

Too right, Sweet Cheeks, I learned how to wield a sword, how to concoct a spell and how to fly a dragon on Skyrim. Cool!!

Re: Is it possible to learn everything I need to know on the computer?

Root Toot
Date: 16 June 2014
Time: 9.50

Computer games are just for fun – life is for living. Get out of your bedroom and live it, Truestory.

Re: Is it possible to learn everything I need to know on the computer?

Razzamatazz68
Date: 16 June 2014
Time: 9.51

Time spent on the computer can be useful but it can be highly addictive. People get addicted mostly to cybersex and online gambling. Consider if this is you, Truestory, and if it is back away now and go for a dose of real life. You know – somewhere outside your bedroom!

Re: Is it possible to learn everything I need to know on the computer?

Truestory
Date: 16 June 2014
Time: 9.52

I have considered it and I am not addicted to cybersex or online gambling. But observing the world from my bedroom is not a good way to make Field Notes. I may have to go for a dose of real life even though I told my mum I would be in my bedroom doing Field Notes until lunchtime.

Re: Is it possible to learn everything I need to know on the computer?

Razzamatazz68
Date: 16 June 2014
Time: 9.53

That's good Truestory. Online stuff is fine but there's nothing like interaction with the REAL WORLD. Your mum will be delighted to get you away from the computer. Give her a nice surprise!

Chapter 29

We were back in our white plastic bubble. The sacks were already warmed by the morning sun, and the breeze, which was picking up around the tunnel, created a wall of sound – a barrier against the world. Although we had well over two hours and weren't in a hurry there was a sense of urgency.

Larry kissed me and pulled my T-shirt out of my jeans.

'Slow down,' I said. 'We've got ages.'

But he didn't slow down; he slid the T-shirt over my head and we lay back on the sacks. He undid my jeans and I wriggled side to side to help him get them off. He kissed me hard and I wound my arms around his neck and, despite the plastic sacks sticking to my back and the white tunnel stretching over my head and the incessant clattering of the wind, I didn't want to be anywhere else.

He stroked my face.

'I'm falling for you, Alice,' he said.

I kissed his neck. 'I know,' I said.

'Close your eyes.'

I closed them and felt his stubbly face kissing between my breasts and his tongue running down to my belly button. I was trying to be serious – a serious, proper lover – but it tickled and I laughed and opened my eyes. I gazed upward and saw, inches from my face, the shadow of a hand pressing on the outside of the polytunnel. It was white and ghostly, with spread fingers, as though it was reaching down for me.

For a split second I thought of people in prison touching opposite sides of the glass when they weren't allowed to hold hands. I stared and held my breath. Then the hand disappeared. I stifled a scream and pushed Larry off and scrabbled around for my clothes, hissing:

'. . . there's somebody . . . for God's sake . . . there's somebody . . .'

Larry wrenched his trousers up and staggered to the door. I grabbed my jeans in a blind panic and thrust my legs in. I hadn't time to bother about my knickers – I'd find them when I was decent. I tried to drag my T-shirt on before Larry opened the door. It was inside out and for a second I was shoving my head down an armhole; I twisted the T-shirt this way and that. Shit. What a mess.

With a clatter Larry opened the plastic flap and I heard a weird yelp of surprise that was obviously Sam. I was facing away from the door dragging up the zip on my jeans. I glanced over my shoulder and saw Sam stumble backwards from the polytunnel door.

Larry was out of breath and red in the face. Was it obvious to a child what we'd been doing? Larry tried to yank the plastic sheeting shut behind him but it was bent and folded and Sam peered at me past Larry's shoulder as I sat on the pile of sacks with my back to him.

'What's the problem, son?' I could tell Larry was trying to make his voice sound normal. He tugged on the plastic sheet and straightened it out and the glimpse of Sam disappeared.

I don't think Sam answered, or if he did it was in a whisper.

'You okay?' Larry said.

183

Still there was silence from Sam

'I'll find your mother, son, you go in the house.'

'My mother is not lost.'

'She'll be inside in a minute. Go on.'

After a minute, Larry pulled the plastic aside and came back in.

'He's run inside,' he said.

I dropped my head into my hands; I was going to throw up.

'S'okay, Alice. He didnae see anything.' Larry rubbed my shoulder. 'He was only standing outside.'

I slumped forward on the sacks. I put my hand on my stomach and bent right over. I was going to heave. I needed fresh air but my heart thundered and my legs shook and all I could do was bury my head in my hands and groan with the horror of it. Could I ever act normal in front of my son again?

What had he seen? I broke out in a sweat picturing how much worse it could have been. Thank God I'd seen that ghost of a hand pressing on the side of the tunnel.

Larry sat beside me. 'You best go see the lad's okay,' he said.

He took my hand and stroked it. 'Bad timing eh?' He smiled. 'You okay?'

Tears welled up in my eyes. How stupid had I been treating this place like a bubble separate from reality? It was only a bit of plastic offering no privacy or protection at all.

I squeezed Larry's hand. If only we could wish ourselves away from here, away from Backwoods and Duncan and Sam and everything. I imagined cutting a cord and me and Larry floating higher and higher, looking down at Backwoods as it got smaller and smaller until it vanished altogether.

184

Larry wiped away a tear that slipped down my face.

'It'll be okay,' he said. 'Honestly, he didnae see anything.'

'I'd better go,' I thrust my shoes on and stood up. My legs were weak. I grabbed my knickers and shoved them in my pocket. I was a woman old enough to know better who was taking stupid risks for the sake of having sex with this man.

'Come into town with me tomorrow,' I said.

Larry was still sitting. He nodded:

'Aye,' he said. He put his hands on my waist, slid them onto my bottom and squeezed me to him. 'We've got unfinished business,' he said.

I bent and kissed him and for a split second imagined tearing my clothes off again and pushing him backwards onto the sacks. It felt good to want him so much.

But I needed to see Sam. Breaking away from Larry I said, 'Tomorrow.'

I paced around Sam's bedroom for what must have been ten minutes before I started to pull the quilt off.

'Come out, Sam,' I begged. 'Everything's okay, come out. Please. You can show me your Field Note things.' At first I tugged gently on the quilt but Sam held on underneath with fingers as strong and determined as those ivy suckers and he refused to let go.

I kept pleading with him: 'Sam? Come on, Sam. Are you all right? Please come out.'

Then I gave a big tug. This time I was determined not to let go and eventually Sam's fingers slipped off the inside of the quilt. I flung it aside. He was curled in a ball, his notebook and pen beside him. I sat on the edge of the bed and I felt him stop himself rolling towards me as the mattress sagged. I put my hand on his side and he flinched and curled up smaller.

185

'Why don't you go on the computer?' I said. 'Or draw a map?' I kept rubbing his arm but he couldn't shrink away any further because there was nowhere left to shrink to. 'Everything's all right,' I said over and over. Silent tears ran down my face.

I'd never pulled the quilt right off before when he was hiding underneath. Usually I gave it a couple of tugs then I'd leave him to come round on his own, but today I needed to see him – I needed to make sure he hadn't seen anything. I'd been in his room for fifteen minutes and he was still hiding his face and refusing to talk and lying there like a dead person. I could see the livid teeth marks on his arms from yesterday. I stroked them. He recoiled and tucked his arms tighter up under his armpits.

'Larry could work on the summer house with you after lunch,' I said, more in hope than expectation. There was no reply. I sighed and wiped my face.

'I'll call you when your lunch is ready – all nineteen pieces. How's that?'

I stood up. It was as though his curled body had the power to force me off the bed, to physically repel me and eject me from the room.

Chapter 30

Welcome to U Chat

Home   Chat   Message   Rules   Contact Us   Log in   Sign up
                        Boards

Is it better to keep a secret or to tell the truth?

Truestory   Is it even a secret if no one has said it is a secret?
Date: 16 June 2014
Time: 11.44

Re: Is it better to keep a secret or to tell the truth?

Fizzy Mascara   If it looks like a secret and quacks like a secret, it's
Date: 16 June 2014   a secret.
Time: 11.48

Re: Is it better to keep a secret or to tell the truth?

FlyAwayBlackbird   I love a secret!! Tell me what it is!! Pleeeese
Date: 16 June 2014   Truestory!!!
Time: 11.51

Re: Is it better to keep a secret or to tell the truth?

Boody Queen
Date: 16 June 2014
Time: 11.57

Secrets cause division, guilt and fear – they take control – so avoid them, is my advice.

Re: Is it better to keep a secret or to tell the truth?

Root Toot
Date: 16 June 2014
Time: 12.00

Depends what the secret is. If it's trivial ignore it. If it's serious tell it. And the sooner the better – a big secret can rot you from the inside out.

Re: Is it better to keep a secret or to tell the truth?

Truestory
Date: 16 June 2014
Time: 12.01

Yes, Boody Queen and Root Toot, this secret is creating fear and could be rotting me from the inside out. On the internet it says if I live until I am 73 years of age my heart will beat three billion times but my heart has been racing at one hundred and twenty beats a minute since I saw this secret and I am worried that I will get through my three billion beats too soon. I tried to work out how many beats I had left but my calculator flashed a big 'E' and turned itself off. Running out of heartbeats is a new fear since I discovered the secret. My heart is still beating like it has been turned up to SUPERFAST speed. Each heartbeat is one beat nearer to my three-billionth heartbeat, which is the last heartbeat I will ever have.

Re: Is it better to keep a secret or to tell the truth?

Boody Queen
Date: 16 June 2014
Time: 12.05

This secret is causing you great anxiety. Either share it or if that is really impossible, find a way to deal with your fear before it takes over.

188

Re: Is it better to keep a secret or to tell the truth?

Truestory
Date: 16 June 2014
Time: 12.07

Yesterday Chocolate Moustache told me to deal with my fears by burying them or burning them. I have decided to follow that advice because despite drawing up a Wish List and going exploring, saying Affirmations and taking Field Notes to make the world a more predictable place, I have more fears today than I did yesterday, and even more than I had the day before.

Re: Is it better to keep a secret or to tell the truth?

Boody Queen
Date: 16 June 2014
Time: 12.08

Okay, Truestory. If you think that will help. Good luck.

Re: Is it better to keep a secret or to tell the truth?

Truestory
Date: 16 June 2014
Time: 12.21

I have written my fears on a piece of paper and cut round each fear and folded it into a square, the fear-squares are now in my pocket and I am going to bury them and burn them. There are 6 fear squares. They are: 1. I am using heartbeats up too fast and will run out. 2. I will fall down the well to the burning centre of the earth. 3. I will give Larry's magic grass too much water and it will die. 4. I will burn my eyes with yellow and go blind. 5. I will never be able to leave Backwoods and will be here until I die. 6. My mother and Larry will continue to have sexual intercourse in the poly tunnel.

189

Re: Is it better to keep a secret or to tell the truth?

Boody Queen   Okay, Truestory. Like I said: Good luck.
Date: 16 June 2014
Time: 12.22

Re: Is it better to keep a secret or to tell the truth?

Fizzy Mascara   Whoa . . . Big secrets are mad, bad and dangerous
Date: 16 June 2014   to keep – they breed, take over and fight to get out.
Time: 12.28   And they will get out – no doubt about that. Anyway,
                         you've answered your own question – that's why
                         you're called Truestory isn't it?

Chapter 31

Despite him refusing to talk to me this morning he turned up dead on time for his nineteen pieces of pasta with nothing on. I watched him from the corner of my eye. Was he okay? What had he seen? I could feel myself sweating. He was certainly agitated.

He forked up a piece of pasta and chewed it determinedly; five chews no more, no less.

'I want to burn and to bury something.'

'What?'

He stuck his hand in his pocket and took out these folded scraps of paper. He dropped them on the table picking off the last few that stuck to his sweaty palm.

'I need to bury and burn these.'

'What are they?'

'Secret.'

Sometimes it was better not to question but to go with it.

'Okay, well, you could put them on the fire tonight when it's lit.'

'No, that is not the perfect place.'

Larry and Duncan came in then and before Larry could get his boots off Sam turned to him: 'I want to go back to the old well.'

'Oh no, Sam,' I said. 'I don't think you should go near that well again. We had enough stress with that thing yesterday. Why not use the fire pit? That made a great fire for the sausages didn't it?'

Larry frowned: 'Better listen to your mother, I reckon.'

Duncan strode over to the table. 'Better keep away from that well – the bloody state you were in yesterday.' He reached out for the scraps of paper. 'What are these?' He was about to pick them up but Sam lunged across and grabbed them.

'They're secret,' I said.

Sam shoved them back in his pocket.

'I am going to put them down the old well. They can fall onto the rocks and the rubble and work their way through the gaps and down into the burning centre of the earth.'

'Right,' I said. 'But the fire pit would burn them just as well.'

'It is 7,000 degrees Celsius in the burning centre of the earth,' said Sam. 'Not in the fire pit . . .'

'But – '

'. . . and that is 4,800 degrees hotter than lava.'

'Yes, but – '

'. . . which is 6,990 degrees hotter than Backwoods Farm. Even in the fire pit.'

Larry looked at me. I shrugged, and he refastened the lace on his boot.

'Now? Okay, let's go.'

Larry, Sam and I walked slowly across to the workshop and turned down the back.

Sam slowed to a shuffle as we got nearer to the well, which Duncan had covered with an old outhouse door. Larry didn't say anything but walked in front. When Sam was ten feet from the hole he stopped and Larry turned round.

Sam held out both hands, palms open, to reveal the squares.

'Throw them in,' he whispered.

192

'What are they?'

'Bad things.'

Larry picked the squares off Sam's sticky palms and walked to the hole.

'You want me to throw them down?'

Sam nodded. Larry squatted beside the well, shunted the old door aside, and dropped the squares in. He looked at Sam to see if he was satisfied.

'Okay?'

Sam nodded again and backed away his eyes fixed on the hole.

'Do you want a picture, son?'

Sam managed a single nod and kept backing away in slow motion, like he didn't want the hole to notice and jump up and bite him. Larry rooted in his pocket for his phone and took a snap down the hole then came to show him. Sam held his breath and stared at the photo.

'What is on the paper is a secret,' he said.

'Ok, son,' Larry said. 'Whatever's on them is your secret. No problem with having a secret is there, Alice?' He looked at me. Feeling terrible but elated, I shook my head. 'Want to explore anywhere else?' he asked Sam. But Sam shook his head. 'I am going to sit in my bedroom and wait for my fears to disappear one by one,' he said.

As soon as Duncan and Larry sat down for supper that night I screwed up the courage to go through a little charade about tomorrow's trip to town.

'I'm off to town tomorrow. Anybody need anything?'

Larry pretended to think. 'Yeah, matter of fact I do.'

'Feel free to jump in the car if you want.'

'Aye. I'll probably hitch a ride if it's all the same to you.'

'No problem,' I said, glancing at Duncan to see if he'd noticed anything.

193

I leant against the kitchen unit to pick up the shepherd's pie and I felt a bump in my pocket digging into my hip bone. I remembered it was my knickers stuffed in there from earlier. I wasn't embarrassed. On the contrary I stopped myself from smiling remembering Larry sliding them off, his hand running down my thigh. I put my face straight before turning round.

I sat at the table toying with my supper and trying not to watch Larry who was tucking in like he was starving.

I knew people would judge and sneer and say it was undignified if they had any idea what I was planning. But I didn't care. Dignity was neither here nor there. I wanted to be on my own with Larry and if it took pretending to go to town and sneaking off in the car and having sex on the back seat or in a field somewhere or up against a tree – so be it.

'Bloody terrible trade at the auction,' said Duncan.

'Getting worse?' asked Larry.

'Practically had to give 'em away,' said Duncan. 'Carry on like that and we're as good as working this bloody farm for nowt.'

'Well if we can get the polytunnel planted up this week – '

'Aye,' replied Duncan, looking a bit more cheerful.

I gazed at the table, replaying the scene from the polytunnel over and over again. Not the horrible scene when Sam turned up but the scene before that – me and Larry lying on those sun-warmed sacks as the wind blew a cacophony all around.

Duncan and Larry were still discussing the farm and the auction and stock prices, but I wasn't listening.

Chapter 32

Welcome to U Chat

Home   Chat   Message   Rules   Contact Us   Log in   Sign up
                        Boards

How do you know when to stop waiting?

Truestory   Burying and burning my fears has not worked. I have
Date: 17 June 2014   been awake for 25 hours and 14 minutes waiting for
Time: 13.15   my fears to disappear but they have not.

Re: How do you know when to stop waiting?

Root Toot   I've got to say – I never thought that was much of a
Date: 17 June 2014   plan.
Time: 13.22

Re: How do you know when to stop waiting?

Truestory   I expected my fears to float away or dissolve or burn
Date: 17 June 2014   up and disappear. They did not. Now I will have to
Time: 13.47   stay at Backwoods Farm for ever. I will die here and
                       will never see the graves cut from rock where St
                       Patrick landed, or anything else. I will never travel
                       down Hell Fire Pass and out into the Rest of the
                       World. Never.

Re: How do you know when to stop waiting?

JC
Date: 17 June 2014
Time: 13.52

Do not despair, Truestory. '*We are afflicted in every way but not crushed; perplexed, but not driven to despair; persecuted, but not forsaken; struck down, but not destroyed.*' 2 Corinthians 4: 8-9. Maybe one day you will go on a pilgrimage to St Patrick all the way to County Mayo. Bless you, Truestory.

Re: How do you know when to stop waiting?

Fizzy Mascara
Date: 17 June 2014
Time: 13.56

Well blow me (so to speak).That's quite a cool quote from JC.

Re: How do you know when to stop waiting?

Truestory
Date: 17 June 2014
Time: 13.59

I have used up more than 188,640 heart beats since I buried my fears. I feel sick thinking about all those heart beats I will never get back.

Re: How do you know when to stop waiting?

Fizzy Mascara
Date: 17 June 2014
Time: 14.00

Nil Desperandum. Truestory.
NOW GET ON WITH LIFE

Chapter 33

I used to look forward to a Tuesday afternoon thinking it was an escape – a treat – but it wasn't. A cold cup of tea and a tasteless biscuit could never be a big enough treat to make up for life trapped here.

Now it was Tuesday again but today was going to be different. Today was for me and Larry; away from Backwoods, just me and him together, alone.

Sam was being no trouble. He obviously hadn't seen anything yesterday in the polytunnel. Although why he'd left his bedroom in the first place I didn't know – as a rule he was so reliable and predictable in his movements. But who knew? Maybe even Sam didn't know.

He'd had breakfast this morning and lunch at his usual time and now he'd vanished back upstairs to do some Maths. I'd given him Maths because Maths was his favourite and that made me feel better. Calculus would keep him busy until I came back.

I'd stuffed my old sack-jumpers into carrier bags and brought them downstairs. Going to the tip was the last thing on my mind today, but I thought I'd better act normal.

Larry was leaning on the car having a fag.

'Ready?' I said.

He blew smoke into the sky.

'Never more so.'

'Where's Duncan?'

'Fencing behind the barn, this side of the Long Four Acre. '

I laughed, a laugh that bubbled up and escaped without warning and I knew then it was possible to get drunk on freedom.

'Well, what you waiting for?' I jumped in the driver's seat.

Larry climbed in and I turned on the radio. I wanted music-enhanced euphoria, a real-life sound track to my film-like life.

George Harrison sang '*Got My Mind Set on You*', and I rammed the car into reverse and backed down the yard. Larry opened his window, put his arm out and tapped in time to the music on the car body.

We sang along, me doing the high lines and Larry the low ones.

'He wasn't daft, was he, George Harrison?' said Larry, shouting over the radio. 'Time and money – they'd both be good, eh?'

'Well we've got today,' I said. 'Or at least we've got *right now, right this minute*,' and I tapped his leg with each word. I shoved the car into first gear and bounced across the potholes and through the gate. I sang another line at the top of my voice, and was about to put my foot down and zoom up the lane when something flashed into my line of vision and I screamed and slammed on the brake. The wheels skidded to a stop with a loud crunch of stones.

There, out of breath and with his hair all over the place, tumbling in front of the car was Sam.

He must have come out of the washroom door and hurtled over the wall before almost bouncing off the bonnet. For God's sake, my heart was going to crash through my ribs and burst out of my body. What the hell was he playing at?

His hands were splayed on the bonnet and he stared at us through the windscreen with terror in his eyes.

I couldn't move and gaped at him as he gazed from me to Larry and back. Larry jumped out of the car and grabbed Sam's arm.

'You okay?'

Sam looked confused, and gasped for breath.

I let my head fall forward onto the steering wheel and rested it there. He'd done it again; he'd dragged me, kicking and screaming, from another world back to this one.

'What is it, son?' Larry said. 'Do you need your mum?'

I got out of the car, strode round to him and grabbed his shoulders much more forcefully than usual. I glared at him.

'I always go out on a Tuesday,' I said. 'Come on Sam, what's all this about?' I closed my eyes. 'You nearly got yourself bloody killed then.'

Sam squirmed under my grip and winced. I let go and gave a sharp sigh. I could feel my temper rising.

'Sam, be fair. I only go out once a week.'

Larry put his hands on his knees, his face level with Sam's.

'What is it, son?'

Sam tried to speak but only managed a gasp.

'It might be a panic attack, Alice,' Larry said.

'Come on, Sam,' I grabbed his arm and turned him back towards the house. 'We'll get you a map set up.'

I tried to propel him back through the garden gate but he resisted.

'LANCASTER.' He gasped.

199

'I'll be back in two hours,' I snapped. 'I'll be back before you know it.'

'LANCASTER,' Sam said again over his shoulder at Larry.

'Does he want to go to Lancaster?' said Larry. 'Is that what you want, son – to come to Lancaster?'

Sam nodded once. I let go of his arm and put my hands on my hips.

'Since when?' I said.

'Maybe he fancies exploring a bit further afield,' said Larry.

'You want to come to Lancaster?' My voice rose in disbelief. 'Really?'

Sam gave a kind of a nod and he looked at the car.

Larry shrugged. 'I'll get him in,' he said, glancing down at Sam's bare feet. 'You get him some shoes.'

I didn't move. 'Really?' I said.

'Come on, son.' Larry put his hand in the small of Sam's back to nudge him towards the car. Sam took a stumbling step and stopped. Larry opened the car door and waited for him to climb in.

'He'll not manage it,' I said, feeling the panic rise. 'It'll not work.'

Sam gazed into the car. The floor had two aerosol cans and three tattered magazines cluttering it up and the seats were covered in bits of straw and crumbs and the two lolling carrier bags with the old jumpers spilling out. The one with the yellow sunflowers gaped from the bag; Sam clapped his hand over his face.

'He won't go,' I said. 'It'll be a disaster.'

Sam steadied himself with the car door.

'It's okay, son, jump in,' said Larry.

Sam kept his hand clamped over his eyes.

'It'll be a bloody disaster,' I said again.

Sam let go of the car door.

'She is correct,' he whispered. 'I can never get in the car.'

'I didn't mean that, Sam,' I said, 'I was only – '

'Sam, we can help – ' Larry spoke in a low tone. 'We can – '

Sam took a great gulping breath and gabbled: 'I am only two steps from the car and ten miles from Lancaster but it is not possible.'

Shrugging off Larry's hand, Sam spun round, jumped the wall and ran like the wind back to the house.

Without speaking to Larry, I turned the car round and parked it back in the yard. There was no trip to Lancaster today, not for Sam, not for me, not for anybody.

I felt sick.

I could fool myself that life was fun and exciting or even just normal from time to time; but it wasn't. I was trapped at Backwoods and I might as well be being kept here under lock and key.

Larry was in the kitchen.

'Are you going up to him?' he asked.

I shook my head. 'What can I do that'll help?' I slumped on a kitchen chair. 'There's *nothing* I can do. I'm useless.' I put my face in my hands. Larry stroked my hair.

'You're not useless, Alice. Far from it.' He kissed the top of my head.

'Come on,' he said. 'Let's sit in the sun.'

He took my hand, tugged me out of the chair, and led me outside.

I sat cross-legged in the orchard and Larry lay next to me and squinted up at the sky. He was chewing a long piece of grass with seeds on the end and he kept touching my face with it. I couldn't even smile; I wiped it away.

201

I felt like I had the day Sam stopped breathing on the way to town; today I'd heard the portcullis come crashing down for a second time.

I told Larry about Sam's early years, about my fear that he was too different to survive in the real world, about the isolation of not being like other families, about the loneliness of asking for help from doctors but not getting it, about the pain of seeing Sam shunned and judged by the world, about how Duncan couldn't face the reality of Sam and blamed me, about the terror of thinking I'd be trapped at Backwoods forever and never be able to leave.

I poured out everything about Sam's tantrums and his silences and his obsessions and the stopping breathing. About my struggles to home-school and about the friends who gradually dropped away and about weeks going by when I hardly spoke to anyone and only escaped for a cup of tea on a Tuesday afternoon.

About how I'd tried to make myself feel better by secretly emptying the house of all the stuff that was choking it and in the process trying to loosen my ties to Backwoods Farm – even though I knew that the ties were getting tighter not looser. About how I cried for a week when a mad old woman buying biscuits in a supermarket said I wasn't fit to be a mother.

It sounded pathetic. But I couldn't stop talking, and Larry listened without interrupting.

As the sun sank in the sky he turned onto his stomach. He carried on chewing the grass but did not tickle my face with it. It was such a relief that he didn't judge me. He didn't roll his eyes or say I must be exaggerating, or worse still, laugh. He listened, really listened, nodding every now and then and letting me talk.

The words poured out. I rarely talked to Duncan about

Sam because it would only start a row. He'd criticise Sam and get mad and rant about how it was time Sam started acting his age or how he should pull himself together and bloody well grow up.

Then he'd hint that it was all *my* fault. Or sometimes he wouldn't hint, but come right out with it: What had I done to make him like that? What the hell was wrong? If I wasn't so soft with him perhaps he'd be a bit more bloody normal.

Once I'd been so furious when he said such a thing I flung my fork across the breakfast table, hitting Duncan's plate which broke clean in two. Sam had slid onto the floor curled into a little ball, moaning, as I sat with my face in my hands and Duncan knocked his chair backwards and stormed outside.

I could feel the sun warming my shoulders and I wanted to lie down beside Larry and feel his arms around me, strong and comforting. I longed to rest my head on his chest, listen to his heartbeat, feel his voice rumble in his chest when he spoke, telling me everything was fine; Sam was fine, I was fine, every single thing was fine, because if Larry said it, I might believe it.

I didn't lie on the grass because if I did the temptation to rest against him would be too great. I'd have to bury my face in his neck and breathe him in and feel his warmth seep right into me.

'I admire you for sticking by Sam and doing your best for him,' Larry said. 'Not everybody could have done it, Alice. No way.' He thought for a minute. 'I've never been tested like that. I've had a free life, a selfish life really, drifting here and there as the fancy takes me, never staying anywhere long enough to grow roots or get bored.' He looked at me intently. 'The two weeks I've spent here have been the best I've ever had, I love being with Sam. He's

203

a great kid. He's imaginative and creative and intelligent.' He touched my arm. 'You've done a fantastic job with him, Alice.'

My eyes welled up. No one had ever told me I'd done a fantastic job with Sam. Never. On the contrary, my husband, the health visitors, crazy old ladies at the shops – everyone had said the opposite.

'You've done a great job.'

I swallowed hard. 'Thanks. That means a lot.'

'Well, it's true.'

Confiding in Larry had opened a huge well of loneliness in me and made me realise how sad and empty I felt about Sam and our isolated life here. It was a sadness so vast I could sink and drown in it.

Larry smiled at me; I tried to smile back but my mouth wouldn't let me.

'You're a strong woman, Alice,' he said. 'A fighter. That's one of the things I love about you.'

My heart flipped.

Warmth flooded through me. I realised that since Larry came to Backwoods I'd felt transformed. I'd felt younger, years younger and attractive for the first time in a decade. I felt alive and excited about every day. Sam had been getting braver too; possibilities had been opening up. Even his idea to go into Lancaster today – although crazy without proper planning – was a leap in the right direction. And it was all down to Larry. He'd come into our lives like a gypsy and worked his magic like a wizard. He couldn't leave. How could I go back to my old life? It was unthinkable.

I touched his fingers, stroking the rough skin, the cuts and the gnarls, and the nails, broken and discoloured from digging and planting.

'I love you being here,' I said.

I wanted to kiss him. I wanted to eat him up.

I smiled and went to stroke his hair, then noticed Duncan standing by the back door staring at us, arms folded. I ran my fingers through my own hair instead. How long had he been watching?

'Duncan's there.' I muttered. Larry didn't jump up or do anything suspicious; he stayed where he was, eyes fixed on the summer house, and said nothing.

Knowing I'd seen him, Duncan turned and went inside. I made a show of looking at my watch – Duncan was probably still spying on us from the washhouse window – and I stood up and dusted off the legs of my jeans.

'I'd better go inside,' I said. 'Thanks for listening. It means a lot.'

'Don't thank me. I'm always here,' he said.

I walked towards the door and glimpsed Duncan backing away from the window.

Sam was watering the plants in the washroom, putting the water on drip by drip.

'Are you all right?' He didn't reply. 'Sam?'

He shook his head. 'I will lose count of the drips on the magic grass.'

In the kitchen I glimpsed Duncan leaning so far back on his chair he was as good as lying down. Usually I told him off for that but today I didn't bother.

'You were back early,' he said.

'We never went out,' I whispered. 'Sam was upset.'

'Oh,' he said. 'Where's Larry?'

I filled the kettle. 'Don't know,' I said. 'Gone to his caravan, I suppose.'

I knew full well he wasn't in his caravan. I knew he was still sitting in the orchard smoking one of his roll-ups, staring at the house and thinking about me, and I wished with all my heart I was out there with him.

Chapter 34

Welcome to U Chat

Home   Chat   Message   Rules   Contact Us   Log in   Sign up
Boards

What is the strongest magic in the world?

Truestory   What is the strongest Magic in the world? All the
Date: 17 June 2014   other magic does not work for me.
Time: 16.02

Re: What is the strongest magic in the world?

Root Toot   Alcohol. Best magic ever. Can make anything
Date: 17 June 2014   happen!
Time: 16.05

Re: What is the strongest magic in the world?

Fizzy Mascara   For god's sake – here you go again, Truestory. Stop
Date: 17 June 2014   expecting god or magic or spells or whatever it is to
Time: 16.08   sort stuff out. Do it yourself. Then there's no one to
                      blame when the shit hits the fan.

Re: What is the strongest magic in the world?

ChocolateMoustache
Date: 17 June 2014
Time: 16.11

Not very compassionately put, Fizzy Mascara, but I see where you're coming from. Truestory. I repeat: Face your fears. Get help with this. What about a teacher? parents? priest? best friend? There are many people out there who can help. Go find them.

Re: What is the strongest magic in the world?

Truestory
Date: 17 June 2014
Time: 16.12

That is the problem. I cannot get out to find them.

Re: What is the strongest magic in the world?

ChocolateMoustache
Date: 17 June 2014
Time: 16.13

There will be help on-line too.

Re: What is the strongest magic in the world?

Truestory
Date: 17 June 2014
Time: 16.14

That is what I am asking for.

Re: What is the strongest magic in the world?

Sweet Cheeks
Date: 17 June 2014
Time: 16.16

On You Tube there's someone called Lionel making a Quality Street disappear! It's good magic!! Have a look!

Re: What is the strongest magic in the world?

My Name is Magic I am fully qualified in the use of magic and can
Date: 17 June 2014 provide the most powerful spells you will find on-line.
Time: 16.22 Check out my web site here or private message
me for all the information you will need. Terms and
Conditions apply.

Re: What is the strongest magic in the world?

Psychic Rabbit Magic is a way of life and not just a bit of fun. Take
Date: 17 June 2014 care with it. It may be stronger than you think.
Time: 16.26

U Chat
Private Message to My Name Is Magic
17 June 2014 Time: 16:35

Truestory
Dear My Name Is Magic

Thank you for inviting me to private message. I need your magic because I am
trapped and want to escape. I have tried different ways to escape, but nothing
has worked and now I need something stronger. As you have access to the
most powerful spells on-line I think you may be able to help.

What magic do you suggest?

Thank you very much
Truestory

My Name is Magic

Dear Truestory

You are right; I have all the information you need and I can assure you that if you follow my advice you will break the terrible fear that is currently keeping you prisoner. My spells have been tried and tested over many years and have never let my clients down.

I deal with clients struggling with all sorts of problems including addiction, love troubles, money worries, weight loss issues and every other challenging situation you can think of. I offer a one-year unconditional guarantee of success. That's how confident I am I can solve your problems.

For glowing testimonials from just some of my satisfied clients please click here.

I have a free introductory offer running currently which you can take advantage of straight away. This will help prepare you to respond to the magic of the universe. After that to shore up your success you simply click on **Buy Now** and for $30 I cast a personalised spell designed especially for you and your particular problem. You can apply for as many personalised spells as you choose, for all different areas of your life.

To use your special offer introductory spell you will need
To be outdoors at an elevated situation
To have cleared your mind
When you are prepared and ready to invoke the magic simply close your eyes and repeat the following incantation:

> Spirits in the Universe
> Come to me with help
> To make me brave
> To make me strong.
> To fill me with your power.

Say these magic words confidently out loud several times (at least ten times) and you will begin to feel the power flowing into you. The strength to attain your wishes will grow stronger and stronger and you will know that anything and everything on this earth is within your grasp. At that stage come back to me and get the first personalised spell. To enable me to tailor it correctly please complete the following questionnaire:

What is your problem (please state main features)?
What is the ideal solution to the problem?
What is stopping you attaining this solution?
I accept payment by all major credit cards and Paypal.

Regards
My Name Is Magic Psychic Dhp, Phrs

U Chat
Private Message to My Name Is Magic
17 June 2014 Time: 17:05

Truestory
Dear My Name Is Magic Psychic Dhp, Phrs

Thank you for the special offer introductory spell.

I will find an elevated situation and clear my mind and then I will use it.

The special offer introductory spell does not sound very much. However, My Name is Magic Psychic Dhp, Phrs, you have 52 satisfied clients on your website. I have read all the testimonials. I have read about spells that help people get lovers back, lose weight, turn brown eyes blue, blue eyes green, wreak revenge, have sex changes and win $8,000 at the Black Jack table.

This is my favourite testimonial: 'My Name is Magic you are a spell caster of genius. Thanks to you my life has been transformed overnight. That is the best $240 dollars I have ever spent.'

The testimonials make leaving Backwoods Farm and travelling down Hell Fire Pass to the graves hewn from rock look simple and I believe your 'special offer introductory spell' will help.

There will be a delay in getting back to you for the personalised spell/spells because I do not have a major credit card or a Paypal.

Thank you for your help and for explaining your 'special offer introductory spell' and sharing your website.

With best wishes
Truestory.

U Chat
Private Message to My Name Is Magic
17 June 2014 Time: 17.11

Truestory
Dear My Name is Magic Psychic Dhp, Phrs

I have examined my Ordnance Survey map: No 296 in the Explorer Range to find an elevated situation

There are not many contour lines on the map around Backwoods (which in case you are not a cartographer indicates a flat terrain). The only place with contour lines is The Pile of Rubble Covered in Weeds so this will be my elevated situation.

I do not want to consult you to confirm this is acceptable as I do not have a major credit card or a Paypal. I do not have $240 dollars. I do not have any dollars. I have £2.36 I found at the back of the cutlery drawer.

With best wishes
Truestory

Truestory

Dear My Name is Magic Psychic Dhp, Phrs

This is not a consultation.

I wanted to let you know that clearing my mind may not be possible. Clearing my mind is harder than locating an elevated position on the map.

I do not think I understand how to clear my mind. Is it possible to have a mind that is clear? Can I empty my brain? I do not think so. I have never experienced an empty brain. My thoughts fight each other and make frightening pictures out of nothing.

Sometimes my brain is like a firework display, which is something I have never experienced in real life. My mind is full and noisy and makes me jump.

I thought I should tell you this.
This is not a consultation.
With best wishes
Truestory.

Truestory

Dear My Name is Magic Psychic Dhp, Phrs

Your magic is very strong.

Even though I did not consult you regarding difficulties with clearing my mind (due to my not having a major credit card or a Paypal or $240 dollars) your magic has worked.

I was listening to the hum of the milking parlour and when I repeated the incantation thirty times the humming faded away and my mind became filled with the words: *Spirits in the Universe Come to me with help To make me brave To make me strong To fill me with your power*, and there was no room for anything else.

To empty my mind I have to fill my mind with something else.

Dear My Name is Magic Psychic Dhp, Phrs, you promised that your spells were the strongest available on-line and I have experienced their power.
It will now be possible to escape Backwoods Farm with your 'special offer fully-guaranteed introductory spell'.

I will then write a testimonial for you.

This is not a consultation.
With best wishes
Truestory

Chapter 35

Sam was difficult to get through to at teatime, which was nothing new. He was muttering to himself under his breath, between spoonfuls. I couldn't catch it but it sounded like a prayer. He didn't appear to be counting his spoonfuls of soup or the number of times he chewed each piece of bread either.

And for Sam that was weird.

Any changes in his behaviour put me on edge. You never knew what was going to loom up next, what crazy ideas were going to emerge fully-formed to disrupt our lives for the next few weeks or months or years.

Something that started small – a comment about a plughole or a drain for instance – could, within a couple of days, become a full-blown phobia of sinks and baths, or a nettle sting could become a terror of the colour green that kept him housebound for weeks and unable to eat salad for the rest of his life.

I was paranoid, I knew that. But who wouldn't be? Life with Sam had the habit of pulling the rug from under your feet just when you thought you'd found your balance and then everything would suddenly change, and usually for the worse. Oh yes, however you looked at it, life could be rubbish when it came to being Sam's mum. Complacency was a luxury I couldn't afford.

Constant vigilance was required – but constant vigilance was depressing and over years could grind you down into a million little pieces.

He ate his soup – reluctantly, he'd wanted pasta – and kind of muttered and sang to himself in this weird way the whole time. Yes, this was something new.

Earlier on, of course, he'd nearly got himself killed saying he wanted to go to Lancaster. That was *definitely* new. Something was up. Could these changes be good for him – for all of us – or did they spell disaster as usual?

I should be delighted he wanted to go to Lancaster. That's what I'd always hoped would happen, after all; that he'd grow out of his self-imposed exile and want to break away from this prison. So why was I filled with dread that it meant nothing but trauma and misery for us all? I'd had too many bad experiences and dealt with too much disappointment to take it in my stride.

Anyway, my mind was buzzing with other things – I had no head room left to make sense of Sam. Sam's wants and needs and demands had dominated my life for years, pushing everything else out of sight, but not today.

Today I wanted to dwell on Larry and what he'd said in the orchard. He'd as good as told me he loved me. If Duncan hadn't appeared I think the conversation would have headed that way. I felt a warm rush through my body when I imagined him saying it.

It was a long time, a very long time, since I'd pushed Sam's needs to one side, but that's exactly what I was going to do now.

I poured myself a glass of wine. It wasn't even six thirty but so what? I wasn't living in the real world today. Larry was giving Duncan a hand with the milking – there were four newborn calves to be fed. I sat down, put my feet up on another chair, closed my eyes and let the wine slip down.

Duncan and Larry would both be inside in a minute and I'd have to eat soup and drink tea and make conversation as if everything was normal. I wasn't sure how I'd manage that, but this glass of wine would help.

The latch rattled and I twisted round. Larry walked in and over to the table, then he bent over and kissed me. I heard Duncan's boots tramping up the yard but I didn't push Larry away. As Bess started barking Larry broke away and briefly stroked my face.

'Stay there. I'll set the table.'

He opened the cupboard and grabbed some bowls and a handful of cutlery from the drawer.

'There's bread warming in the oven,' I said.

'I'll get it. You sit down.'

The door opened again and Duncan came in. He took his boots off and saw me with my feet up, drinking wine.

'We celebrating again?'

'Nah,' said Larry, 'No excuse needed for relaxing for a few minutes.'

Duncan looked at him and frowned. I took my feet off the chair and put the glass down. Larry topped it up an inch and grabbed another couple of glasses.

'Drop of wine?' he said to Duncan. Duncan shook his head.

'A cup of tea'll do me,' he said, plonking himself down at the table.

I watched Duncan from the corner of my eye. Was he acting funny? Or was it Duncan being Duncan? He didn't have the dog-with-two-tails air about him that he usually had when he was with Larry. Did he suspect something? I didn't see how – we'd only been sitting in the orchard. We hadn't been touching each other or anything. For

216

goodness sake, intuition had never been Duncan's strong point. Surely it wasn't Larry setting the table that was pissing him off?

'How's the seedlings coming on?' Duncan asked.

'Aye, no bad.' Larry had taken the bread out of the oven and was slicing it on the board. 'Should be ready to plant out soon.'

I couldn't stand watching Larry do the work and I got up.

'I'll rig up some supports to use for when they're a bit bigger,' said Larry.

Duncan nodded.

'So is that you nearly done then, getting it all set up?' Duncan said. Larry looked at him.

'Aye, well, after they're planted out it's a case of keeping an eye out for pests and checking the temperature and ventilation and that.'

'If they're ready you might as well get them out tomorrow. The sooner they're out the sooner we get a crop.'

'Well they're coming to no harm where they are,' Larry said. 'We might get a night frost or two yet.' Larry carried on slicing the bread and I grabbed the butter knife and slapped thick smears of butter on it.

'We'll manage fine when the plantings done and the tunnel's set up.' Duncan looked at me. 'Won't we, Alice?'

I piled the bread into a wobbling heap.

'I'm no expert,' I said, 'never claimed to be.'

'We'll manage fine,' repeated Duncan. 'You'll be wanting to move on, I expect,' he said to Larry. 'I know you never stay in a place for too long.'

Larry shrugged. 'No plans.'

'You'll need to be heading south for the early harvests,' said Duncan. 'You'll not want to miss them.'

Larry sat down. I took the plate of bread to the table and went back for the soup. I ladled it out in silence.

Later that night when I was in bed and the light was out Duncan said, 'I think it's time Larry went.'

I pretended I was asleep.

'He's been here a while. I think he's stringing it out because he's onto a good thing.'

He nudged me. 'Alice. Are you listening? It's time he went.'

'Why? *You've* changed your tune.' I said.

'The cannabis is ready really. He's using the weather as an excuse. There won't be any night frosts now.'

'He'd be as well taking his time and getting it right, wouldn't he?'

'Well, I'm only suggesting doing what *you* wanted and getting him gone as soon as possible.'

My heart was thumping. 'That was before he started helping with Sam.'

'Yes, and I think that's a bit weird as well. Why's he so interested in Sam?'

I hutched myself up onto one shoulder and looked at him. 'What do you mean?'

'He seems to want to spend a lot of time with Sam. I think it's weird.'

'Why? Just because you don't want to spend any time with him? He's helping me out. First help I've ever had with him.' I fell back onto my pillow. 'You begrudge me a bit of help with him. That's pathetic. And it's horrible to call Larry weird because he wants to spend time with Sam. Frankly I think that says more about you than him.'

I turned over onto my side facing away from him, dragging acres of quilt with me. I stared out into the dark and pretended to be going to sleep, hoping he couldn't hear the crash of my heart against my ribs.

Next morning at breakfast Duncan was at it again, trying to push things along.

'Best get those seedlings planted out today,' he said to Larry.

'It's maybe a bit soon,' said Larry. 'Weather's unpredictable. It's a rookie mistake. A frost'll finish them off.'

'Nah, we need to get on with it,' said Duncan. 'It's daft to hang about.'

'I can give you a hand,' I said to Larry. 'I've got Sam set up with some History so I've got time.'

'No you won't,' said Duncan. '*I'll* do it.'

I took a gulp of my coffee.

Duncan looked at me. 'Well, *you're* not interested in growing this stuff are you? You've made that plain enough right from the start.'

Chapter 36

U Chat
Private Message to My Name Is Magic
18 June 2014 Time: 10.15

Truestory
Dear My Name is Magic Psychic Dhp, Phrs

This is not a consultation.

Tomorrow is the 19th of June. My internet research suggests this is a good date to try your special offer fully-guaranteed introductory spell. The number 19 is a prime number and in Mathematical Theory it is a Fortunate Number and a Lucky Number, also the on-line Talismanic Calendar says the 19th of the month is a lucky day.

A Feng Shui site does not say tomorrow is a lucky day, but Feng Shui is a different kind of magic, to do with houses and rooms, which may not mix with your kind of magic, so I do not think that matters.

I wish 18 was a prime number and a fortunate number and a lucky day because I want to try the strongest magic on the internet as soon as possible. But it is not, so as soon as possible is tomorrow which is still 13 hours and 45 minutes away.

This is not a consultation.
With best wishes
Truestory

Chapter 37

Sam came downstairs mid-morning; from the corner of my eye I could see him hovering about from foot to foot.

'What's up, Sam?'

He looked from his watch to the kitchen clock and back to his watch.

'What is it?'

'Time has slowed down.' He looked at the clock again. 'I have been reading the questions about the formation of the 19th century toll roads but I keep looking at my watch and time is not moving on.'

I was sitting at the table wondering how to persuade Duncan that Larry should stay, while making it look like Duncan's idea.

I became aware that Sam was talking again.

'What?' I said.

'Einstein said time is relative. It depends on what you are doing. I am going to Jeannie's because it might make time speed up. Plus she is old and might know about the formation of the 19th century toll roads.' He peered at me. 'Are your ears working?'

'Sorry,' I said. 'My mind's full of other stuff.' He was looking at his watch again then scrutinising the kitchen clock. 'Er, anyway, yeah, let's both go to Jeannie's,' I said.

We wandered down the lane and I watched the poly-tunnel as we passed. I wondered what was going on in there. Was Duncan still being funny with Larry? Or were they working side by side like mates? If I knew Larry, I was sure he'd be able to win Duncan round and get him to trust him again.

Sam was counting his steps aloud and as usual we got to 432 steps as we reached the 'Pile of Rubble Covered in Weeds'. Sam stopped and studied it.

'That is an elevated position,' he said.

'Umm,' I said and I nodded. It was difficult to show a lot of interest in a pile of stones, but I did my best. He studied it for another few seconds and then he shot off.

When we arrived at Jeannie's Sam didn't bother with a hello or a how are you? He launched straight in.

'Jeannie, you are old. What do you know about the 19th century toll roads?'

'Not a thing,' said Jeannie, 'but I know I've got some tarts filled with red jam,' and, still sitting in her armchair, she shoved the plate across the table at him.

Sam examined the tarts up close, presumably looking for 'bits' – strawberry seeds and skin, and the like – and as he did so I saw Jeannie put a plate of tarts filled with yellow jam on the floor and cover it with a newspaper.

Jeannie wasn't her usual self; her face had a grey tinge and she looked exhausted.

'You all right, Jeannie?' I asked.

'Yes,' she said. 'I'm fine. I'm old, is all.'

She seemed out of breath and still didn't get up.

'Help yourselves to lemonade,' she said, and waved her hand towards the dresser.

There was stuff piled all over the table – even more than usual – and yet more stuff on the floor which the dogs were scattering about. They'd knocked over their sack of feed and were eating it off the floor, their tails thudding on the carpet. The cats had obviously got inside their sack of feed; there were two tails curving elegantly out of the top. A couple of other cats were lapping at dirty pots in the sink.

I shooed at them, but Jeannie waved me away.

'Leave them, love. It's not important.' She gazed at the chaos and said: 'I lost my tablets. Had to have a good search.'

She sounded even more out of breath and leant her head back.

'Did you find them?' I asked, and she nodded.

She'd obviously been raking around everywhere because half the cupboard doors and drawers were gaping open.

'Are you sure you're okay, Jeannie?' I said.

She barely opened one eye and said: 'I was up half the night with Elvis. He was stuck under the bed.'

Sam took one of his many maps off the wall and pushed piles of letters and envelopes and newspapers and boxes and knitting needles aside on the table to make a space to draw some adjustments.

'What you doing, Sam?' I thought I'd make conversation with him because it didn't look like Jeannie wanted to chat today.

'I am drawing contour lines,' he said. 'But it is difficult with the table so full. The pen keeps going in the wrong direction. Perhaps Jeannie should clear up?'

I frowned. 'Sssh!'

'Have a tart,' she wheezed, peering at us both before putting her head back again and closing her eyes.

'Jeannie?' said Sam, and he waited for her to open her eyes. 'Jeannie, do you think tomorrow will be a lucky day?'

'Why?'

223

'I think it will be lucky. I think it will be a fortunate day. I have something important to do.'

Jeannie did a thin, almost invisible smile and said: 'Maybe you and me both.'

'What have you got to do that's important?' asked Sam, but Jeannie did not answer. 'Are *you* planning to do some magic?' he said. There was a long pause.

'Take care, Sam,' she said. 'I'm sure everything will work out for you. You take care.' Then she closed her eyes again.

'Are you going to tell me stories about your adventures in the Orient or in the olden times or with the space aliens?' he said.

'Ssh, Sam,' I said. 'I don't think Jeannie's up to it today, and don't have any more tarts – that's your fifth.'

Sam munched on his tart and gazed at the dozing Jeannie. 'Perhaps she is trying to empty her mind,' he said, reaching for a sixth.

'No, Sam. That's enough. We need to leave Jeannie in peace. She's worn out by all these animals keeping her up half the night.'

'Have you put anything else on your wish list, Jeannie?' Sam said in an extra loud voice and he studied her to see if she responded.

'I think she smiled,' he said.

'Yes,' I said. 'I think she did.'

We looked back through the window as we walked away and saw that two cats had jumped on her knee and were kneading her chest trying to turn her into a great big bed.

'It is good that Jeannie has cats to keep her warm,' said Sam. Then he broke into a trot, loudly counting his steps as he went. He waited at the Pile of Stones Covered in Weeds.

'The small trees in leaf have begun to sway which means the wind is at number five on the Beaufort scale.'

I pulled an 'impressed' face. 'You've been doing your Geography.'

'If the wind gets any stronger it will make the electricity wires whistle,' he said, 'and be number six on the Beaufort scale.' He clapped his hands over his ears and set off at a gallop to race home.

There was no pasta left for lunch and when I told him he looked stricken.

'I'll make ham butties,' I said. 'No mustard.'

He considered the offer.

'I hope tomorrow is luckier than today,' he said. 'Today I will have to have ham sandwiches but they must be cut into equilateral triangles and not squares because they taste better as equilateral triangles. Not squares.'

I nodded, managing not to roll my eyes.

'Or if the bread is rectangular rather than square you can cut them into right-angled triangles.'

'So what's this important thing you've got to do tomorrow?' I was rooting in the fridge searching for ham. He didn't answer. I glanced round but he was wrapped in his own thoughts, staring into the middle distance, and for the moment I'd lost him.

I gave him his butties and he took the top off one triangle to examine it.

I sighed, a loud bad-tempered sigh.

'These are right-angled triangles but they are not ham. These are corned beef.' He looked at me like I'd committed a terrible crime against sandwiches. 'Corned beef is bits of meat mashed up and squashed. It is not ham.'

'It's nearly ham!'

'Corned beef is cow meat not pig meat. It could never be ham.'

'For Goodness sake, get it eaten. Think yourself lucky you've got some lunch.'

Larry had arrived inside as this was going on.

'Do you like cooking, Alice?' he said, knocking off his boots.

'It comes somewhere on my list of favourite things after washing the car and trimming the holly hedge – neither of which I'd dream of doing in a month of Sundays. So what do you think?' And we both laughed.

'I did not know you had a list of favourite things,' said Sam. 'What is a month of Sundays?'

'Oh, nothing.'

'I'll throw together one of my world-famous pasta sauces later if you like,' Larry said. 'Would that be good?'

'It certainly would,' I said. 'You're a guy with many talents.'

'I will Google your world-famous pasta sauce,' Sam said, and we laughed again.

Duncan wandered in and we stopped laughing. Larry talked to him about soil testing in the polytunnel and keeping mice from eating the plants and the dangers of spider mites and aphid attacks. He made it sound as if there would be an all-action movie going on in there when the plants were growing.

Duncan was quiet and listened, chewing hard on his butties. I didn't know if growing cannabis was really as complicated as Larry was making out or if he was exaggerating, to stop Duncan pressing him to leave.

Anyway Duncan was obviously taking it all on board because he said they should pick up some pest repellent and chicken wire and other things to protect the plants they'd just planted out. Larry said yes, good idea; so, after lunch when Sam went upstairs, Duncan and Larry disappeared in the Land Rover.

I decided to make a cheese and onion pie while they were out. I worked on it in a trance, nearly grating my finger-ends off. I found some orange cheese in the freezer, hoping that Sam would eat the pie if it wasn't too yellow.

When I'd finished, it looked rubbish – sort of mottled and flat with hard brown bits round the edge. Well, I'd never claimed to be a cook.

I knew I should go and check on Sam's schoolwork but I couldn't be bothered. Sam was quiet; I might as well let sleeping dogs lie.

My mind was packed with Larry; I couldn't get enough of him. Yet it was only two and a half weeks since I'd first set eyes on him and thought he looked like something the cat had dragged in. What if Duncan hadn't gone to the pub that night? What if he'd done what I said and got rid of Larry first thing the next morning?

Life before Larry seemed far away, distant and lonely; it was like looking at a life through the wrong end of a telescope. And it was a life I did not want to go back to.

There was the rumble of the Land Rover as it pulled into the yard and my heart lurched. I filled the kettle and stood with my back to the door as they came in.

I grabbed the tea bags and tried to look busy, plopping three in the pot and getting the milk out of the fridge. They were talking about the best way to put up plant supports and I could tell right away that the afternoon spent with Larry had given Duncan his enthusiasm back.

'What you been up to?' Duncan grinned at me as he flung his jacket over a chair back.

'Bit of cooking . . .'

Everybody looked at the greasy pie sitting on the table and there was a heavy silence.

'What?' I said, even though I knew it looked like a pile of ingredients that had died a sad death at the hands of a terrible cook.

'Anybody got any shoes that need mending?' said Duncan, prodding it and laughing. Then he turned to me and ruffled my hair.

'I'm only pulling your leg, love.' He plonked himself down at the table.

Larry grinned at me and winked and I smiled back. At least Duncan wasn't sulking any more.

'I'll knock together a sauce for tomorrow's tea,' said Larry. 'See what you think of that.'

'Summat else you're good at?' asked Duncan.

Larry laughed. 'I'm no bad, though I say it as shouldn't.'

'What stuff do you need for it?' I asked.

'Whatever you've got.'

We drank our tea. They'd brought back chicken wire and a load of powders and pellets to keep the pests away. Larry told Duncan how you knew when the flowers were ripe and ready to harvest and the drying and preserving that would need to be done after that. It all started sounding a bit complicated again.

When Duncan went out to milk, Larry said: 'So where do you keep your herbs?'

I looked at him. Herbs?

'For the sauce. I might as well do it now.'

I thought about it; there were some sticky jars in the pantry left behind by Duncan's mother.

Larry followed me to the pantry and I flicked the light on. It was a narrow room with long shelves down either side covered in sticky half-empty jars of unusable stuff like 'baking glaze' and packets of angelica and gelatine

228

and faded hundreds-and-thousands alongside bun cases and icing bags and doilies and other mysterious things abandoned donkey's years ago and belonging to someone else's life. It smelled sweet – of generations of Christmas puddings and birthday cakes and sherry trifles. There was no window in the pantry – only a tiny aperture high up, covered in mesh. I heard Larry click the door shut behind us.

'Come here,' he said.

He had his back to the door with his weight against it and he held his arms out. I walked to him, pressed myself against him and kissed him as though I hadn't kissed anyone for a lifetime.

Chapter 38

Welcome to U Chat

Home   Chat   Message   Rules   Contact Us   Log in   Sign up
Boards

How can I make my lucky day even luckier?

Truestory   Tomorrow is my lucky day and I am doing the most
Date: 18 June 2014   important thing I have ever done. How can I make
Time: 14.20   my lucky day even luckier?

Re: How can I make my lucky day even luckier?

Root Toot   You can avoid cracks and black cats and touch wood
Date: 18 June 2014   all day long and it won't make any darned difference
Time: 14.23   – but if you believe it's going to be a lucky day then
                        that's what it will be.

Re: How can I make my lucky day even luckier?

DiamondSky   Hey if it's your Lucky Day try some on-line roulette –
Date: 18 June 2014   Here's crossing my fingers for you man.
Time: 14.27

Re: How can I make my lucky day even luckier?

NoShitSherlock
Date: 18 June 2014
Time: 14.33

We create our own luck. The secret is to grab the good opportunities that crop up every day. Keep your eyes open, Truestory, and FIND the luck that's right there in front of you.

Re: How can I make my lucky day even luckier?

Fizzy Mascara
Date: 18 June 2014
Time: 14.39

Lucky charms and all those kinds of bollocks are just placebo effects. In other words if you believe in them they might work for you but don't rely too much on the Good Luck Fairy. It was either Prince Philip or Confucius or some other old bloke who said: 'the harder I work the luckier I get'. It's all in the planning.

Re: How can I make my lucky day even luckier?

Sweet Cheeks
Date: 18 June 2014
Time: 14.44

Hey Truestory I just checked on line and the luckiest hours tomorrow are between 9 and 11. The unluckiest are 2 til 5 in the afternoon, so whatever you are doing (asking someone out?!!) do it between 9 and 11. Hope it all works out for you Truestory. xxx

Re: How can I make my lucky day even luckier?

ChocolateMoustache
Date: 18 June 2014
Time: 14.46

Hi Truestory Some good points made above. People say it's lucky to be in the right place at the right time – but it's really about being in the right place at the right time in the right frame of mind. Be positive, Truestory, and all will be well! I hope your venture is a great success.

Re: How can I make my lucky day even luckier?

xxLove wordsxx
Date: 18 June 2014
Time: 14.49

If you need cute passion words for girlfriend visit my site www.cutepassionwordsforboyfriend.com by clicking on link. Words will suit boyfriend or girlfriend.

Re: How can I make my lucky day even luckier?

Truestory
Date: 18 June 2014
Time: 14.53

Thank you Sweet Cheeks. That is useful information for flying down Hell Fire Pass.

Re: How can I make my lucky day even luckier?

Sweet Cheeks
Date: 18 June 2014
Time: 14.57

Glad to help, Truestory!
Wow!! Flying down Hell Fire Pass! That sounds like a theme park or something. Have fun and hope It all works out on your travels.

Re: How can I make my lucky day even luckier?

Earn $$$$$$
Date: 18 June 2014
Time: 15.05

Earn $$$$$$$$ from the comfort of your own home. Interested? Who wouldn't be? Contact me by clicking here

Re: How can I make my lucky day even luckier?

Truestory
Date: 18 June 2014
Time: 15.10

Dear Earn $$$$$$, I do not want to earn $$$$$$$$ from the comfort of my own home. I want to get away from my home. That is the problem. But thank you for the offer.

232

Chapter 39

I came out of the pantry and only just stopped myself shrieking when the first thing I saw was Sam parked at the kitchen table, eyes fixed on the pantry door, holding his fork and spoon in his fists.

It was heading towards five thirty and he looked worried about the lack of tea-making going on. It was a wonder he wasn't wearing a big white hankie knotted round his neck.

'We were looking for ingredients,' I said, before realising I wasn't carrying any. 'Er, we need some ingredients for Larry's sauce.' I about-turned and went back into the pantry. Larry followed. 'For God's sake,' I hissed, 'he haunts me. I can't do any-bloody-thing without him *being there.*'

'Well, you can't say you haven't been warned that he likes to eat at half five.' Larry smoothed a wisp of my hair back and kissed my forehead. 'Let's cook,' he said, scanning a dusty spice rack of jars of what looked like faded grass cuttings.

'Oregano. Basil. Yep, we'll have these. Onion Salt?' He shook the jar but the stuff stayed solid. 'Nah,' he said, and he put it back. 'Garlic Salt? You cannae do it without garlic,' he said, grabbing that one. He had another quick squint round. 'Okay, these'll do.' He dumped them into the veg tray with its onions, tomatoes and odd bulb of garlic then, picking up the tray, he headed back into the kitchen.

As I followed him out I saw a dusty old pasta packet lurking behind some rusty tins. I grabbed it and hid it behind my back.

'Do you fancy some cheese and onion pie?' Sam responded with a mutinous stare. 'I could do it with baked beans . . .'

There was still no reply so I produced the pasta packet from behind my back.

'Good job I've found this then,' and I waved it above my head like a maraca and sang a couple of bars of Lambada.

Sam stared at me deadpan. Having pasta for tea was clearly no laughing matter, so I gave up trying to make him smile and put the kettle on.

Larry grabbed the chopping board. He turned to face Sam and started juggling with three of the onions. It looked tricky and I felt a childish surge of happiness as his hands, barely moving, kept the onions circling in the air. I laughed and wondered – was it possible to watch a juggler without smiling?

Yes, it was, because Sam was staring at Larry with a face as straight as Duncan's draining rods, then he swivelled on his seat and very obviously consulted the clock.

'We'd best get on with it,' said Larry, catching the onions and grinning at me.

He chopped them while I counted Sam's pasta pieces into the pot and gave it a stir. It was still only 5.24pm. The pasta was quick-cook so I had time to get it on the table by 5.30. It mattered. I wanted to keep Sam calm and I wanted to make him as happy as I could. It mattered even more to me now I was involved with Larry – as though I could wipe out some of the guilt of deceiving Sam by being a mum who got the pasta on the table dead on half past five. I reached up for his favourite bowl and put it in front of him.

'Anyway, not too much onion,' said Larry, stirring it. 'I'm only using one. The others were for showing off my circus skills.' He looked at me. 'Not that they did me much good.'

'No. When it's time to eat, it's time to eat. Not juggle,' I said, and I poked him in the ribs. I looked sidelong at Sam – he was still staring at us like a starving cat watching a tin of Whiskas.

'Then when the onion's soft, add the garlic.' Larry sliced the garlic and I watched. Larry was good at cooking and I liked watching him doing something he was good at.

'Okay, so we need to liquidise these tomatoes,' Larry looked at me. 'If you've got a liquidiser.'

I sort of heard what he said, but I was remembering the sex we'd just had in the pantry. It was distracting. Sex grabbed in the nooks and crannies of life is hard to beat.

It reminded me of when me and Duncan were teenagers and had sex all over the place, trying to avoid his parents: in the barn, in the car, once against the door of the outside loo. We'd had to be quite inventive – back then I lived with my mother and it was hopeless, there was no privacy or opportunity there, it was tiny and my mother hardly went out. She spent her life watching telly, waiting for my stepdad to come home so she could dance attendance on him. I bet they never had stand-up sex in the pantry.

Larry was looking at me.

'What?' I said.

'A liquidiser?'

'Oh yes, sorry.' I pointed under the sink. 'I was a bit distracted.'

I drained Sam's pasta and dumped it back in the pan, before slapping on a big dollop of butter.

235

'Okay, there we are,' I glanced at the clock as I emptied the pan into his bowl, 'dead on time.'

Sam looked back at the clock.

'It is five thirty-three – '

'Clock's fast,' I said. 'Now eat it before it goes cold.'

The sauce was made and needed to simmer but we stayed by the cooker stirring it and tasting it. Larry put his hand over mine on the wooden spoon and said: 'No, that's not how you stir it. It's like this,' and he stirred it the other way, as though there was a science to it. I burst out laughing.

'So that's where I've been going wrong.'

'And now for your next lesson you're going to learn to juggle.'

Grabbing three onions out of the tray he stood behind me with his arms either side of me and juggled so I could watch the action of his hands. Then he threw one onion back in the tray.

'You're going to start with two. Okay, throw from left hand to right and just before it gets there throw the one in your right to your left.'

'Eh?'

'Come on,' he said. 'You're a talented woman, aren't you?'

Sam was watching and looking interested; he could relax now his stomach was full.

'But I haven't got a clue.'

'Like I said; throw the one in your left hand and before it arrives throw the one in your right.

'Well that sounds easy but – '

I tried and the onions shot in different directions.

'It's impossible!'

It cannot be impossible,' Sam said. 'Larry just did it.'

'True, son. Very, very true!' Larry gathered the onions

236

and put his arms around me again and demonstrated in front of my face.

'I bet I can do it with my eyes shut,' he said.

He started but one of the onions caught my nose. I brought my hands up to my face and accidentally knocked the onions all over the kitchen, leaving Larry momentarily juggling with thin air.

We both laughed and then realised Sam was giggling. This was a rare sound, a rare and wonderful sound. It was remarkable enough getting a smile from Sam.

We watched him as he rocked back on his chair laughing a big belly laugh at the sight of his mother getting hit on the nose by an onion and Larry juggling with thin air. His laugh was infectious and within seconds Larry and I were laughing too and the more we laughed the more Sam laughed.

We were making such a racket we didn't hear Duncan come in and I wasn't aware of him until I saw him watching the three of us laughing our heads off all together. I moved away from Larry and felt his hands slide quickly off my hips.

'Larry was teaching me to juggle,' I said.

There was silence from the adults and the sound of Sam laughing loud and all alone.

I felt sorry for Duncan. For a split second I felt really sorry for him because he looked gutted standing there by the kitchen door as we all laughed together.

'What's so funny?' he said.

'I was trying to juggle. I wasn't very good.'

He nodded and looked from me, to Larry, to Sam and back to me.

'Well, it's tickled Sam, anyway,' he said.

Larry turned to the cooker and stirred his sauce.

'Do it again,' said Sam. 'Juggling with nothing. Do it again.'

I unfroze: 'No, not now. We've got to get Dad's tea sorted.'

'I haven't finished,' said Duncan. 'I came in to ask Larry to give me a hand with the calves. There are a quite a few need feeding.' Duncan stared at Larry. 'If you're not too busy.'

'No bother,' said Larry heading for the door. 'I'll be right there.'

Without waiting for Larry to get his boots on, Duncan gave us all one last look and headed outside.

Chapter 40

Welcome to U Chat

Home   Chat   **Message   Rules   Contact Us   Log in   Sign up
                    Boards**

Re: How can I make my lucky day even luckier?

Truestory   Escaping at 9:00hrs means I might miss the world
Date: 18 June 2014   famous pasta sauce Larry has made for tomorrow.
Time: 19.00   It smells funny and I would like to miss it. I looked
                      on-line to see if it was a true story about Larry's
                      sauce being world famous but could only find 'Lonzo
                      Larry's Soon-to-be-Famous Cooking Sauces'. There
                      was a photograph of Lonzo Larry who was wearing
                      a cowboy hat and sunglasses and he had a white
                      beard. Lonzo Larry was definitely not the Larry who
                      lives here.

Re: How can I make my lucky day even luckier?

Truestory   I feel sick. The smell of Larry's not world famous
Date: 18 June 2014   pasta sauce has crept under my bedroom door and
Time: 19.05   filled my room. I am breathing through my nose so
                      the smell particles do not get into my mouth.

Truestory

Dear My Name is Magic Psychic Dhp, Phrs

I am 11 years 10 months and 21 days old. I have been alive 4312 days but unfortunately 4312 is not a prime number. If I had been born 15 days earlier or 15 days later I would have been alive for 4297 days or 4327 days tomorrow, both of which are prime numbers and would feel luckier for leaving Backwoods Farm.

I will leave at the luckiest hour which is 9.00 hours so there are only 13 hours and 45 minutes to wait until I can leave Backwoods Farm and be free for the first time in living memory.

That is not a true story. I do have a living memory of leaving Backwoods Farm when I was aged four but I was always fastened down in a buggy or a car with my hat pulled over my eyes and most of the time I was screaming so I may have been down Hell Fire Pass and out into The Rest of the World but I have not seen it, or heard it, or felt it. I have never been free in it. Tomorrow I will see it and I will hear it and I will feel it. Tomorrow I will be free in it.

There are now 13 hours and 40 minutes until I can leave Backwoods Farm.

Thank you very much
Truestory

Chapter 41

'What's going on?' Duncan was standing at the bottom of the bed with his arms folded.

'What?' I hugged my book to my chest. 'What you on about?'

I'd come upstairs because I didn't want to sit downstairs with them both, feeling self-conscious. Dinner had been uncomfortable. We'd made conversation – the usual stuff about the weather and jobs that needed doing and that sort of thing, but it had been stilted. After we'd finished, Larry tried to tempt Duncan to watch telly – some documentary about the SAS – but Duncan didn't show much interest. I disappeared upstairs with my book. I'd been staring at the same page for the past half hour, unable to concentrate even before Duncan burst in.

'You're always laughing and giggling with Larry. What's going on?' he said.

'Giggling and laughing?' I said. 'Just because we were having a joke about the juggling? Don't be pathetic.'

My heart was thudding and I could feel my face heating up. I knew it was best to stay on the defensive. Or maybe it wasn't, maybe it was better to smile and sweet-talk him, charm him a bit. But I didn't feel like charming him. I felt embarrassed and mad at being put on the spot and at a definite disadvantage lying in bed with nothing on but my knickers and an old T-shirt.

'You watch him all the time. I've seen you,' said Duncan.

'Watch him!? That's crap! I do not. What do you mean watch him?' I swept on, not giving him chance to speak. 'And even if I do watch him it's because he's so good with Sam and I can't believe my eyes. Maybe that's why I'm watching him. Had you thought of that?'

I could feel myself blushing hot. I hoped I didn't watch Larry all the time – or if I did I hoped he hadn't noticed.

'There's something different about you and it's to do with Larry. What's going on? Has he been trying it on?'

'Trying it on! No, he has not. He's been looking after our son, telling him stories, buying him maps, taking him exploring – all the things his own dad has never done.'

'That's not fair. You know I've tried my best.'

'No, you haven't. Not at all.' I knelt up in bed and pointed my finger at him. 'You've never tried to understand Sam. You blame him for being who he is. Larry doesn't. Larry *likes* Sam for who he is. Maybe that's why I'm different with Larry. Maybe that's it!'

'So you admit you're different?'

'Oh, for God's sake, it's Sam who's different. Haven't you noticed? He's daring to spread his wings a bit. Going behind the workshop, investigating the summer house, having a party, lots of stuff – God, he's even talking about leaving the farm – imagine that! But all you're interested in is whether there's something going on with me and Larry.' I put a stupid voice on, mimicking him: 'Has Larry been trying it on?' I slammed my book onto the duvet. 'Do you realise how pathetic that sounds? Give Sam a break for once and give me a break too.'

I folded my arms, wishing I had a bra on because my boobs got in the way and spoiled the effect a bit when I couldn't decide whether they should go above or below my folded arms. I glowered at him, daring him to carry on.

'And I saw you in the back garden.'

'Saw us doing what?'

'Talking and laughing.'

'Oh, call the bloody fun police, why don't you? God forbid that I, Alice McCabe, prisoner of this parish, should be allowed to laugh and talk with a man.'

'It wasn't just normal talking.'

'What the hell was it then?'

'You were looking at each other.'

'God, listen to yourself. Just because I've been stuck out here looking after Sam for nearly twelve years doesn't mean I'm not allowed to talk to anyone else.'

'You looked guilty when I saw you. You know you did.'

'Maybe I was looking guilty because I'd nearly knocked down our son when he jumped in front of the car like a lunatic. Maybe I looked guilty because I was taking a few minutes to calm down rather than running around fussing over him. Maybe that was it.'

I blinked at him. I could feel tears not far away and thought they might be no bad thing. I dropped my gaze and encouraged the tears to come.

'I'm just trying to help Sam,' I said, 'like I always am.' I covered my face with my hands and gave a big sniff. 'And you go mad because I'm actually daring to laugh.'

There was a silence. Then Duncan said: 'I'm not going mad, I'm asking, that's all. I'm allowed to ask.'

I heard him walk around the side of the bed and felt his hand on my hair. 'I do want you to laugh, Alice, I do.' He stroked my hair; something I don't remember him ever doing before. 'I know you've been lonely and I know I don't tell you often enough that you're doing a good job with Sam.' I heard him sigh. 'I can't manage him like you do. You do a good job. I can't do it and I don't know what I'd do without you.'

I felt my throat constrict; he'd never said anything like that before either.

'I think it's time Larry moved on, that's all,' went on Duncan. 'He says himself he doesn't stay places long. We'll be fine on our own without him – Sam's growing up a bit, it's not Larry that's changing him, it would have happened anyway.'

'That's not true! Sam's coming out of his shell and if you're jealous of Larry because of it then you need to grow up a bit and put Sam first.'

'I just want us to be together again as a family, the three of us,' he said. I kept my face hidden and did another loud sniff. There was a long pause.

'All right, I'll leave you in peace,' he said. 'Let you get that early night.' He slowly walked away, pulling the door to behind him.

I lay down and snuggled under the duvet pulling it right up and wiping my eyes with it. I felt terrible. I didn't like lying and now I was lying about lying.

I knew I wouldn't stop though, however guilty I felt I'd carry on seeing Larry. My head was full of him; every day was full of him and I wanted my life to be full of him. I turned the bedside light off and curled up tight and gazed blindly into the dark.

I put a load of toast on the table and huddled behind my laptop.

'What are you up to this morning?' asked Duncan.

'Sam's schoolwork.'

'What's it today then?'

Duncan hardly ever asked about Sam's schoolwork; he was making an effort after last night.

'Geography. Maps.'

'You like maps. Don't you, Sam?' He smiled at Sam.

Sam shovelled his Weetabix in and said nothing. He looked distracted – even more so than usual.

Finding his smile blanked by Sam, Duncan said, 'Anyway . . .' He smothered jam on a slice of toast and turned to Larry instead. 'Forecast's bad. Wind's getting up later so I reckon we need to check the fastenings on the tunnel.'

Larry nodded. 'Aye, I'll do it.'

'I've got to meet a bloke from the council about some blocked drains down the lane so I won't be here to give you a hand.'

'No bother. I'll sort it.'

Having been accused of looking at Larry too much, I daren't glance at him and kept my eyes fixed on my computer screen.

'Sam,' I said, 'I'll send you a link about your schoolwork for this morning. Okay?' He didn't answer and I looked up. Had he heard? He rose from the table and mooched across the kitchen without acknowledging I'd said a word.

'Sam?' I said, but without a backward glance he disappeared upstairs.

Despite having his hearing checked years ago, I still sometimes wondered if he was deaf – but then I knew he wasn't because when he wanted to, he could hear fine. It made me want to yell in his face 'CAN YOU HEAR ME?' It was so frustrating the way he thought answering was not necessary – even when I asked him a direct question.

Sometimes he did reply and that was worse. When I'd handed him his Weetabix bowl this morning I said – half to myself – 'Well, I think I'll have a cup of coffee,' and really deadpan he said, 'Why should I care?' And he wasn't even joking – he was making an observation and I suppose, in a way, a reasonable one. Why *should* he care? It was a small thing but it made me feel lonely, really lonely. It was like him saying 'you're boring, I'm not interested in what you say or what you do, now leave me alone'. But I knew that was how he was; I couldn't take it personally or it would break me into little bits.

I let out a sigh that sounded louder in the silence than I'd realised it would.

'You okay?' Duncan said, at the same time as Larry asked: 'You all right?'

'Yep, yep, I'm fine,' I said. I closed the laptop and went to the bathroom because for the moment I wanted to get away from everyone.

A couple of hours later I was sitting at the kitchen table with my feet in Larry's lap. Larry squeezed and rubbed my toes and I closed my eyes. He was supposed to be re-fastening the polytunnel down with paving slabs but somehow he hadn't got any further than this.

He slipped his hand up the leg of my jeans and stroked my calf. What I'd give for an evening on our own, but Duncan wouldn't clear off to the pub tonight. Not unless Larry went with him at any rate. He certainly wasn't going to leave us on our own.

I gave a little groan.

'That good?' asked Larry.

I opened my eyes. 'Yep.'

I watched him bending over my foot; his stubbly chin, his long eyelashes casting shadows on his cheeks.

'What about the polytunnel,' I said. 'Doesn't it need fastening?'

'Nah, he's panicking. It'll take no harm.'

'Good. Stay here.' I put my head back and enjoyed his thumbs pressing hard against the sole of my foot. I hadn't told Larry about the confrontation with Duncan; perhaps now was the time.

'Last night Duncan asked if there was something going on between us.'

Larry's head snapped up.

'What did you say?'

'I told him he was being stupid. And I said you were good for Sam.'

'And then what did he say?'

'Well, he'd like you to be gone but I probably stopped him going on about it for a bit. He definitely believed there was nothing going on.'

Larry looked distracted and I wiggled my toes to remind him of the job in hand.

'You sure?'

'Yeah, well the only evidence he had was that we were always laughing and joking. Oh, and that we looked at each other.'

Larry laughed, and said: 'Okay, well no looking then.' And he leant over and kissed me hard on the lips. He opened his eyes and caught me watching. 'I said no looking.'

'He wants you to go, but you're not leaving, are you?' I said.

'No.'

'Where were you this time last year?'

Larry thought about it. 'Norfolk, on a big arable farm. Nothing like here. Not a family farm or anything.'

'I know you said you grew up in the countryside, and your dad was a labourer, but what are they like, your family.'

He looked like he didn't want to tell me but I was curious so I waited and after a minute he started talking.

'My dad was useless. He drank too much. Sometimes he was around, usually he wasn't – and it was better when he wasn't. My mam was a bitter woman. Her life had been shit and she took it out on everybody else. I escaped soon as I could. I was sixteen. Left my wee sister to fend for herself.'

He stopped stroking my feet and held them between his warm hands. 'I feel bad about that. That was twenty-five years ago, I've never been back. Been on the road ever since. It suits me, no ties, no plans, just seeing what crops up.'

'Do you phone them?'

'I've not spoken to any of them since – at first it was in case Julie begged me to go back. I felt bad about leaving her. She was only fourteen. After a bit, well, I dunno, you feel you've missed the opportunity.'

'That's a shame.'

'Aye, but it's better being away than back there fighting with my dad and hating my mum. If they're still alive, that is.'

'You could contact your sister.'

'Why should she forgive me for leaving her? I haven't forgiven myself.'

'Do you never want to belong anywhere? To feel somewhere's home?'

'Having a home was nothing but trouble. I was glad to be done with it.' He touched my face. 'Until I came here. I feel closer to you and Sam than I have to anyone since my wee sister.'

I squeezed his arm.

'He's a great kid is Sam,' he said.

'He *is* a great kid,' I said. 'I know he is, but I don't think many other folk would see it.' I put my feet on the floor, leant forward and rested my forehead against his shoulder, pushing my face into his neck.

'I can't remember not knowing you,' said Larry, stroking my hair. 'Perhaps I was meant to come here to find you. That's why I've been on my own travelling for so long. I've been searching for you and Sam.'

I slid my arms round his waist. I couldn't let him leave; he made me feel safe. I relaxed against him.

That was a mistake because a second later the kitchen door crashed open, bashing against the wall with a great clatter-bang that made me shriek and Larry leap to his feet.

'What the hell – '

'For fuck's sake – '

'Sam!'

Sam dashed into the kitchen out of breath and wild-eyed.

'Why aren't you – ?'

'You all right, son? What's happened?'

'Sam, where have you been?'

He gazed about the kitchen as though he'd never seen it before then ran across the room and pelted up the stairs.

'I didn't even know he was outside,' I said. 'I'll go and find out – '

As I bounded up the stairs I heard his door slam.

I knocked. 'Sam, what's happened?'

No reply.

'Sam, I need to know. Answer me.'

Still no reply.

I was filled with a fury – some kind of hangover from this morning when he'd ignored me – and I flung the door open: 'Sam, you *will* answer me! What's going on?'

His computer was powering up and he was clinging to the edge of his desk for grim death. His eyes were shut and he was counting to himself: 'Forty-five, forty-six, forty-seven . . .'

'What's happened, for God's sake? Tell me!'

'Forty-nine, fifty, fifty-one . . .'

'TALK TO ME! FOR GOD'S SAKE, TALK TO

249

ME!' The fury had swelled and taken hold of me and I swiped at his desk sending a pile of maps skidding and fluttering to the floor. 'You've got to talk to me. You're driving me mad.'

'I . . .' Sam stared at the maps settling on the floor, then up at me and back at the desk. 'I . . . I . . . It was supposed to be lucky.'

'What was? Where have you been?'

'It was the strongest on the internet. It was supposed to be lucky.'

I took a deep breath. I had to calm down; shouting and storming about might feel good for a few seconds – although this didn't feel *that* good – but there was always a price to pay.

'Okay, Sam. Sorry for shouting.' I took another deep breath. 'I will not shout. You are not in trouble. I just need to know.'

Sam gave a gasp then lunged over to the bed to grab his bobble hat. He plopped back in his seat, wrenching the hat over his head and pulling it past his eyes. 'Sixty-one, sixty-two, sixty-three . . .'

'I am calm,' I said, feeling a throb in my temple. 'I am *really* calm. Now tell me.'

I sat on the bed to give him the message that I was prepared to wait all day if necessary.

'Sixty-seven, sixty-eight, sixty-nine . . .'

Sam's counting was going fainter; I think he was listening to see if I'd gone. I gave a little cough.

'What happened, Sam?'

His counting ceased and there was silence.

'Tell me.'

He was sitting bolt upright clutching the desk.

'I killed it.' The words were so faint I thought I'd heard him wrong.

'You . . . what?'

'I killed it.'

'What?! What did you kill?'

There was a pause, followed by a sob.

'A goose flying free down Hell Fire Pass. I killed it.'

It took me a second to make any sense of what he'd said.

'No. What do you mean you killed it? How could you have killed a goose?'

'It fell from the sky.'

'Well, that's not your fault, is it? You didn't kill it.'

He was rigid and tense; the picture of unhappiness.

'Come on, Sam. How can you have killed a goose? That doesn't make sense; maybe it had a heart attack or something?'

Most of his face was covered by the hat and he rubbed his eyes through it.

'Are you crying, Sam? Listen, don't worry about this goose. It's not your fault – you couldn't harm a goose, honestly, not even if you tried. Were you off to Jeannie's?'

Sam gave a great sob and slumped his head onto the desk banging it hard. Then he lifted it and banged it down harder. Fortunately the hat was taking some of the impact but I jumped up as he lifted his head for a third time.

'Right, that's it! I'll call the doctor if you do that one more time.'

He brought his head down again, whacking it hard.

It was an empty threat; there was no way the doctor would drive out here because my son was bashing his head on his desk.

'I'll take your computer away if you do that ONE MORE TIME.' I grabbed the lid of the laptop. He crashed his head onto the desk again then stayed slumped forward.

'Is there anything else, Sam?'

251

He didn't respond.

'Can I do anything to make you feel better?'

He stayed stock still and silent.

'If I can, you'll tell me, won't you?' Fat chance, I thought. 'Okay, I'll go away now. And don't you worry about that goose. There's no way you could possibly have harmed a goose. I'm going now.' As I backed out of the room I saw him push the hat up above his eyes and start tapping at his keyboard with a feverish look on his face. Christ Almighty, there was always *something* with that lad – but a dead goose was a new one. I pulled the door to and plodded downstairs. Larry was waiting for me.

'What was it?'

I shrugged and raised my eyebrows. 'He thinks he killed a goose. He says it fell out of the sky and that somehow it was his fault and he killed it.'

I slumped onto a kitchen chair. 'Where he gets these ideas, God knows.'

'A goose? He'll have forgotten about that by teatime, won't he?'

I looked at Larry. Forgotten? Perhaps he didn't understand Sam as well as I thought. Forget? Sam? Never.

Chapter 42

Welcome to U Chat

Home   Chat   Message   Rules   Contact Us   Log in   Sign up
Boards

Is it possible to die because of a secret?

Truestory   I have a terrible secret. I am worried this secret is so
Date: 19 June 2014   bad it will kill me.
Time: 10.00

Re: Is it possible to die because of a secret?

FlyAwayBlackbird   There you go again, Truestory! Teasing us about
Date: 19 June 2014   your secrets!!! You know I love a secret. Tell me!!!!
Time: 10.05

Re: Is it possible to die because of a secret?

Boody Queen   No offence FlyAwayBlackbird but Truestory needs to
Date: 19 June 2014   find someone trustworthy to confide in.
Time: 10.08

Re: Is it possible to die because of a secret?

FlyAwayBlackbird
Date: 19 June 2014
Time: 10.11

I am trustworthy!!!!! Perhaps he could post his secret on this great site I found especially for secrets. There are some fab ones. Mainly about sex!!!!

Re: Is it possible to die because of a secret?

JC
Date: 19 June 2014
Time: 10.14

Truestory, there are no secrets. Remember the Collect prayer: *Almighty God unto whom all hearts be open, all desires known and from whom no secrets are hid*. Remember John 8:32 '*The truth will set you free*'. Speak to God Almighty. He is listening.

Re: Is it possible to die because of a secret?

Root Toot
Date: 19 June 2014
Time: 10.18

Don't worry! If a secret's that good it'll always get out anyways.

U Chat
Private Message to My Name Is Magic
19 June 2014 Time: 10.15

Truestory
It has gone wrong. I used your Special Offer incantation to break free but now everything is much worse than it was before.

The magic got out of control. I do not know how, but it did.

I left the house at the luckiest hour of 9 o'clock and went to the elevated position. I emptied my mind and used the Special Offer incantation ten times as you instructed.

I heard a horrible sound which was a goose flying over the cow meadow.

I watched the goose and I repeated the incantation an eleventh time but then the goose crashed into some electricity wires and dropped into the field. It lay on the ground with its neck twisted the wrong way.

I ran to Jeannie's because I wanted to tell her I had used strong magic – the strongest on the internet – and that it had gone wrong and I had killed a goose. But Jeannie could not help because my magic had ruined everything. I am cursed and must stay at Backwoods for ever and never plan to leave again.

Jeannie once promised she would help me leave Backwoods when the time was right, but I do not think the time will ever be right now.

Today was supposed to be a lucky day but it has not been lucky. Psychic Rabbit told me to take care because magic was not a bit of fun. Psychic Rabbit was right. Magic was no fun at all.

You may use the above words as a testimonial for your website.

With regards
Truestory

Welcome to U Chat

Home   Chat   Message   Rules   Contact Us   Log in   Sign up
**   Boards**

Can a dead body be brought back to life?

Truestory   Can something dead be brought back to life?
Date: 19 June 2014
Time: 14.10

Re: Can a dead body be brought back to life?

NoShitSherlock
Date: 19 June 2014
Time: 14.15

Soon medicine will be able to bring folk back from the dead. We'll be able to cool bodies down, pump them with oxygen and revive them. Heart attacks will be curable. Good eh?

Re: Can a dead body be brought back to life?

CallmePal
Date: 19 June 2014
Time: 14.18

Depends on what you mean by 'dead'. People who 'drown' can be revived using what we currently know. CPR in effect brings people back from the dead. This happens every day – as we know from 'near death experiences'.

Re: Can a dead body be brought back to life?

ChocolateMoustache
Date: 19 June 2014
Time: 14.23

Actually it is not that easy to say when someone is dead. Death usually happens gradually. And, Call Me Pal, CPR keeps people alive whilst the defibrillator arrives.

Re: Can a dead body be brought back to life?

Fizzy Mascara
Date: 19 June 2014
Time: 14.26

Answer: nope

Re: Can a dead body be brought back to life?

JC
Date: 19 June 2014
Time: 14.32

Don't think of them as dead. Their soul has gone on to eternity – be glad they are on their glorious way to God the Father. It is a great opportunity.

Re: Can a dead body be brought back to life?

Fizzy Mascara Oh yeah, *really* great.
Date: 19 June 2014
Time: 14.36

Re: Can a dead body be brought back to life?

JC There is no death only change
Date: 19 June 2014
Time: 14.44

Re: Can a dead body be brought back to life?

Truestory Chocolate Moustache, thank you for telling me it
Date: 19 June 2014 is not obvious when death has happened. I did not
Time: 14.53 know that.

Re: Can a dead body be brought back to life?

ChocolateMoustache Glad to be of help. In 19th century Germany they had
Date: 19 June 2014 death houses so people could keep an eye on dead
Time: 14.56 bodies in case they 'woke up'!!

Re: Can a dead body be brought back to life?

Truestory Thank you, I will Google 'German death houses' for
Date: 19 June 2014 more information.
Time: 15.02

Chapter 43

Larry hung over my shoulder as I chopped the onion for the salad.

'Cut smaller bits not muckle big chunks.'

'Muckle big chunks,' I laughed. 'That's funny.'

'Here,' Larry put his hand over mine on the knife handle. 'Like this.' And he sliced the onion into slivers.

'Tomato salad is just tomato and onion then?' I said, 'I think even I can manage that.'

'There's more to it than *that*,' said Larry pretending to be offended. 'It's all in the mixing and the dressing. And it should have olives as well.' He raised his eyebrows. 'Got any olives?'

'What do *you* think? Olives!'

'No, okay then.'

Larry swept the chopped onion and tomato into the bowl.

'Do you think he'll come down for his tea?'

I glanced at the clock: 5.25pm. 'Well, I hope so. He must be starving; he's eaten nothing since breakfast.'

We stopped clattering about and strained to listen.

'Ssh. Here he comes,' I grabbed the quick-cook pasta, 'look normal!'

He was wearing my great big sunglasses and carrying a piece of paper, presumably to draw a map.

'You doing a map?'

No reply.

'What have you been doing this afternoon?'

No reply.

'Did you look at that Maths I sent you?'

Sam stayed silent. He stretched his arm across the table and leant his head on it while he worked on his map: Rectangle for House, squares for windows, farmyard, barn, Wildwood, Hell Fire Pass, big skull and crossbones and so on. He squinted at it as he kept his nose buried in his sleeve, presumably trying to avoid the smell of Larry's sauce simmering on the cooker.

I didn't bother asking him what he wanted – I put 19 pieces of pasta to boil and dug the butter out the fridge.

'Okay,' said Larry, dragging my attention back to the cooking, 'so the secret is the dressing which is olive oil . . .' He glugged a load of oil on the tomatoes. 'Plenty of salt . . . more than looks good for you . . . and a little drop of cold water . . . just a bit . . . a good mix round and that'll be perfect when Duncan comes in.'

We both looked at the clock.

'I'll go and give him a hand with the calves,' said Larry, then, lowering his voice, 'That might keep him quiet,' and he gave me a wink.

Sam was doing that trick of chewing each piece of pasta five times. He appeared to be fairly forcing it down, almost gagging on every mouthful. I wracked my brains for something to cheer him up. That goose thing had floored him.

Earlier on I'd got Duncan to take the Land Rover down the field to search for it and, if it really existed, to pick it up – I didn't want Sam seeing it again when he went to Jeannie's. Duncan found it down in the meadow like Sam had said and he'd brought it back and thrown it by the midden; the foxes would find it and make short work of it over the next night or two.

'Shall we go to Jeannie's in a bit?' I said, 'Maybe she'll – ' but as soon as the words were out Sam sat bolt upright and dropped his fork with a clatter into his bowl.

'No!' he shouted. 'I do not want you to go to Jeannie's.'

'Okay, okay.' His eyes were welling up and he buried his face in the crook of his arm. 'It's okay, Sam. The goose has gone.'

He raised his head and blinked at me. 'The goose has gone?' He sounded like he'd heard a miracle.

'Yes, it's gone,' I said, not mentioning the midden and the foxes. 'You'll not see the goose again, don't you worry. There's nothing to be frightened of.'

'Are you sure the goose has gone?'

'Yes, positive.'

I was pleased; it looked as if I'd done the right thing for once.

'So shall I come to Jeannie's with you then?'

'No!' knocking his fork on the floor and abandoning his pasta, he scrambled out of his chair and dashed upstairs.

Chapter 44

Welcome to U Chat

Home   Chat   Message Rules   Contact Us Log in   Sign up
                  Boards

Can a dead body be brought back to life?

Truestory
Date: 19 June 2014
Time: 17.45

Chocolate Moustache You were right when you said it is difficult to tell when something is really dead. I have had good news. Instead of seeing a death I think I saw a 'near death experience'.

Re: Can a dead body be brought back to life?

Sweet Cheeks
Date: 19 June 2014
Time: 17.49

Wow! Truestory! Did you see a long tunnel and white lights and things? My granny was met by a blue-eyed Burt Reynolds. She knew she was dead because in real life Burt's eyes were brown. She wasn't embarrassed even tho she was in her nightie because he was really nice. Can't ask her about it now tho cos she's dead for real.

Re: Can a dead body be brought back to life?

Sweet Cheeks   She died another time, not that time.
Date: 19 June 2014
Time: 17.50

Re: Can a dead body be brought back to life?

Truestory   I did not have the 'near death experience' I
Date: 19 June 2014   witnessed it.
Time: 17.51

Re: Can a dead body be brought back to life?

Sweet Cheeks   Oh, right.
Date: 19 June 2014
Time: 17.52

Re: Can a dead body be brought back to life?

Truestory   I have checked on the internet and it says near death
Date: 19 June 2014   experiences happen to 15 per cent of the population
Time: 17.53   of the United States of America. I have extrapolated
                       from that that they must also happen to 15 per cent
                       of the population of the UK. This is good news.

Re: Can a dead body be brought back to life?

Sweet Cheeks   If you say so Truestory. ☺
Date: 19 June 2014
Time: 17.54

Chapter 45

'This weather keeps up, we can mow Long Meadow tomorrow.' Duncan sniffed at his pasta sauce, a bit like Sam might have done if he'd dared go near it. He speared a single piece of pasta, examined it and in slow motion began to chew. His chewing quickened: 'Mmm,' he said, 'not bad.' Then remembering Long Meadow he said, 'Anyway, we'll be baling and carting the day after, so we'll need all hands on deck.'

The sauce was delicious but I didn't say anything. Duncan was going to need Larry's help with the haymaking over the next couple of days – it'd save paying anybody else. This was a chance to get Duncan and Larry back on good terms so I thought it best not to sing Larry's praises for his cooking.

'It's a team effort when we haymake,' he said.

'Aye,' said Larry. 'Well, whatever I can do.'

'I drive the tractor and trailer up and down the field,' I said. 'Duncan's on the trailer stacking the bales and usually we pay one of the Johnson lads to lift the bales onto the trailer, but we won't need them now you're here. Sam perches on top of the bales as lookout – though I dunno what he's looking out for. Oh, and Jeannie turns up with tea and cakes when she feels like it.'

I grinned at Larry. 'It's hard work, haymaking, but it's

quite good – it's a real team effort and Sam joins in too. You'll be a good help,' I said.

'Hope so.'

I passed the tomato salad to Duncan and he peered into the bowl.

'What the tomatoes in? Water?'

'It's dressing,' I said, resisting the urge to say 'Larry's dressing'. I leant over and helped myself to a big spoonful. 'It's delicious.'

Then Sam appeared at the bottom of the stairs. Again he was wearing the giant glasses and the bobble hat, but instead of coming to the table he headed towards the washroom door.

'What you up to?' I asked.

'I'm going to Jeannie's,' he said.

'Oh, right.' I watched him, head down as he dashed through the kitchen. 'Do you want me to come with you?' I shouted after him.

He shook his head. 'No, I do not want you to come with me,' he said, and he shot outside.

Three days later Duncan and Larry had done the mowing and the baling and we were ready to cart the hay back to the barn.

Sam came with us to ride on the trailer and climb on the bales as he always did, wearing his huge padded earphones over his bobble hat to block out the roar of the tractor. It was never easy to get Sam's attention and the earphones and hat didn't help but, as he clambered onto the trailer, he seemed even more distracted than ever.

He'd been down at Jeannie's a lot over the past two or three days and they seemed to be in the middle of some project or other. He wouldn't tell me what they were up to but it was keeping his mind busy. I thought they might be cooking up plans to get Sam away from the farm. I hoped so. Or maybe they were drawing up an outrageous wish list with crazy things like flying to Mars or travelling through time. Whatever it was, I wasn't invited. Sam insisted he go down there by himself. Perhaps they were planning a surprise – some crazy art project: a 3D map, a family portrait? Or maybe a tea party after the success of the barbecue? But I *really* hoped it was a project to get Sam away from Backwoods – even if only by a few hundred yards, for a few minutes. Anything would be a start.

Sam sat on the trailer beside Larry and Duncan. Before I pulled away I turned round to check everyone was ready and I was struck afresh by how distracted Sam looked. Instead of dangling his legs over the back of the trailer like usual, he was curled up in a ball with his chin resting on his knees, hugging himself.

Duncan banged on the trailer to tell me they were ready and I set off with a jolt. We bounced and lurched through the yard gate, across the lane and into Long Meadow, the field behind Jeannie's cottage. Larry jumped down and started to lift and heave the bales onto the lorry as Duncan stacked them.

I inched the tractor up and down the field, stopping every few minutes, to let Larry and Duncan catch up and snatch a breath. The bales piled up and Sam clambered on top of each new layer keeping out of Duncan's way. Eventually the bales were so high Duncan handed down the pitchfork to Larry who speared the bales and heaved them above his head on the fork for Duncan to grab and stack.

Eventually Duncan yelled: 'Load!' and I trundled out of the field, across the lane and to the barn and backed the trailer in. Duncan threw the bales off the trailer while Larry and I stacked them in the barn.

It was hot and dusty. Usually around now Jeannie turned up with a billy can of tea and a basket of cakes. We'd all shout 'here she is!' and 'what kept you?' and slump on a bale and gulp down the tea. But not today. Every minute or two, I glanced at the barn door but there was no majestic silhouette with a big cloak, a hat, a basket of cakes and a billy can.

'Not like Jeannie not to turn up,' I said to Sam.

He was heaving against a bale, trying to roll it off the trailer and he was still wearing his earphones even though the tractor was turned off. I stretched up and nudged the earphone off one ear.

'Why don't you go and see if Jeannie's about? It's not like her not to be here.' He frowned. 'She'll feel left out if she's not part of the haymaking,' I said.

'Well . . . ' He was thinking about it.

'Or I could run down.'

'No,' he said. 'I will go.'

He scrambled across the hay, jumped down and ran out of the barn. As he went I could hear him counting his steps.

By now Larry and Duncan were stripped to the waist. It was boiling and they were sweating. It was impossible not to compare them as they bent and lifted and stacked. Duncan was broad and muscular after a lifetime of physical graft and his skin was permanently tanned. There was no fat on him at all. Larry was much slimmer, muscly too, but more on the wiry side. There was no fat on him either.

'What's so funny?'

'What?' They'd finished and were both wiping their heads and necks with their shirts and looking at me.

'What's so funny?' repeated Duncan. 'You're standing there with a grin on your face.'

266

'Am I?' I could feel myself blushing. 'God, I don't know.'

Sam hurtled back into the barn out of breath and still counting.

'Jeannie can't make tea. She is busy.'

'Really? Busy?'

'Yes.'

'Busy doing what?'

Sam frowned then repeated: 'She is busy.'

'Oh,' I said. 'Right, okay.'

I was surprised; Jeannie liked to join in and it was always a fun moment when she unveiled the fancy chocolate cake or orange cake she'd whizzed up as soon as she saw us out with the trailer. We'd never asked her to bring the tea, but over the years it had become part of the ritual.

'Well, I suppose I'd better put the kettle on then.' I jogged across the yard and into the house. I leant against the kitchen wall and, as I bent over to knock my boots off, a pair of arms went round me. 'Hey,' I said, 'watch it,' and burst out laughing. I wrenched my boots off, still laughing as Larry squeezed my waist. 'I was just admiring you,' I said. 'You were born to work with half your clothes off.'

I straightened up and spun round and the smile froze on my face because it wasn't Larry, it was Duncan. He looked delighted at the compliment and it must have distracted him from the look of alarm on my face.

'Well, thank you, Madam, as a matter of fact I was,' and he gave a sarcastic little salute. Then he squeezed my waist again, ran his hands over my hips and pulled me to him and kissed me.

As he did so I saw Larry through the back door, wandering across the yard smoking a fag.

I gave a half-laugh and pulled away. 'Let me get the kettle on, Duncan. My throat's as dry as a bone.'

267

He didn't want to let go and he squeezed my hips again. 'You look good with some colour in your cheeks, Alice,' he said. 'You've caught a bit of sun.'

Larry watched halfway across the yard. He dragged on his fag and squinted through the kitchen door.

'Duncan, let me go, I'm gasping for a drink,' I said.

He laughed. 'Okay then, but that suntan suits you.'

He let me go and I strode across to the sink.

'Funny about Jeannie not coming,' I said, to change the subject. My heart was racing and I felt jittery. 'It's not like her.'

'Oh, she'll be busy with her cats and dogs or some spell or other.'

I grabbed the mugs from the cupboard. 'Don't be mean.'

'She'll turn up this afternoon, like a bad penny, don't you worry. We've got another few loads yet.'

Sam came in and ripped off his earphones and bobble hat. His hair was stuck to his head with sweat.

I handed him a glass of water and he gulped it down.

'Where's Larry?' asked Duncan. He looked at Sam who stared right past him so he repeated: 'Where's Larry got to?'

'Larry has got to his caravan,' said Sam, wiping his mouth with the back of his hand.

'He's probably sneaking a quick beer,' said Duncan and he laughed to himself. 'I gave him the hardest work this morning. I'm not sure he's used to it.' He plonked himself at the table. 'Perhaps he hasn't done as much hard graft as he reckons.'

'He did a good job,' I felt stung on Larry's behalf. He'd got the harder job and he'd done it well. Duncan shouldn't suggest he hadn't been up to it.

'Aye, well, we got it done.' Duncan watched Sam finish

his water. 'Maybe you'd like the job of throwing the bales up this afternoon?'

'Don't tease him, Duncan,' I said. 'You're fine on lookout, aren't you, Sam? You can tell me if I'm going to run over something – '

Sam interrupted me.

'I will not be on lookout this afternoon. I am going to Jeannie's.'

'Did she ask you to go and help her with something?' I said.

'No, she did not ask me to go and help her with something.'

'So what is it then? What are you both up to?'

Sam's eyes flew to my face, as if he was looking for clues.

'We are up to nothing,' he said, hardly moving his lips.

'I didn't mean you were up to something you shouldn't be. I just wondered if you were making plans or anything, but tell me it's none of my business if you want.'

'It is none of your business,' he said. He put his glass on the table and headed for the back door.

When he'd disappeared I said, 'I'm going to Jeannie's tonight to see what they're up to.'

'Leave them to it, Alice. Stop interfering. What harm can they do?'

'Well nothing, except anything can lead to trouble with Sam.'

'You're over-reacting, Alice. For God's sake, leave 'em alone.'

I took my cup to the sink and rinsed it. I didn't argue because I didn't want to have a row with the haymaking half done, but being accused of over-reacting infuriated me – only someone not in the front line could be smug enough to accuse me of 'over-reacting'.

'I'll go and get Larry,' I said.

'No.' said Duncan. He stood up leaving his tea half drunk. 'I'll go.'

I drove the tractor and trailer into the yard. I wished Sam was joining us. Haymaking was the only time he was anything like other farm kids. I was sad he was missing out.

Larry and Duncan came round the house.

Duncan shouted to Larry over the tractor. 'Do you want to stack on the trailer for this load? It's probably easier.'

'Nah,' said Larry. 'I'll do the lifting, no problem,' and he jumped on the trailer without acknowledging me.

Duncan knocked on the trailer. I turned round before I pulled away and I could swear he was smirking.

Larry ended up doing the hardest graft on every load. As the afternoon wore on there was less and less talking. Each time the tractor was turned off, as we unloaded in the barn, the only sound was Duncan doing a tuneless whistle.

We stopped for another cuppa, but there was neither sight nor sound of Sam or Jeannie, so I brewed up and we made do with digestives.

When the last bale was shoved into place in the barn, Larry and I were done-in but Duncan was fine and still whistling the same tune.

'We've earned a few beers tonight,' he said, grinning at Larry and me.

'Aye,' said Larry. His shoulders were burnt.

'You've caught too much sun,' I said, not wanting to stare.

'God, Alice,' said Duncan, 'stop fussing. He's used to working outside.' He started that annoying whistling again. 'I'm off for a cuppa before milking,' he said and he strode off to the house.

I stroked Larry's shoulder with one finger. 'I've got some cream,' I said. 'I'll put it on for you.'

Larry shrugged. 'I'm fine but you're welcome to fuss over me all you like.'

'I'll run you a bath. Don't use that old shower. Come in and have a bath but wait till you hear the milking parlour's on, okay?'

Larry nodded then pulled me to him and kissed me.

Duncan was swilling his tea and looking smug.

'You did that on purpose.' I said. 'Giving Larry all the hard work to do.'

'No. I offered many a time to swap, and it's not a piece of cake stacking anyway.'

'Yeah, but you only offered because you knew he wouldn't swap.'

'Well that's his lookout,' he said, and he grinned at me.

I slumped in an armchair by the fireplace. I'd planned to go to Jeannie's to see what they were up to but I was too knackered. Anyway I'd got other plans now. If Jeannie had had a phone I would have called, but she didn't.

'I'm going to text Sam to see what's happening,' I said.

I texted: Wot u both doing?

No reply.

'God Almighty, I wish he'd answer me.'

I texted again: Wots going on. All well?

No reply.

Wots going on? We've finished carting bales. You 2 busy?

Sam's reply came back.

YES.

Wot u up to?

NOTHING.

Ur busy doing nothing?

271

YES.

I sighed: Ok c u at tea time. Will u stay til then?

YES.

Ok c u at half 5

'Christ, that kid should get a job with MI5,' I said. 'Talk about playing his cards close to his chest.'

Duncan laughed. 'Well, he's never going to talk you to death, that's for sure.' He took the last gulp of tea. 'Well, them cows won't milk themselves.' He went outside, leaving his cup on the table and whistling that same tuneless tune.

I listened to his footsteps going down the yard and a couple of minutes later the hum of the milking machine being switched on. I dashed upstairs and started running Larry a bath.

I put some bath salts in and swirled them round. Leaving it running, I went halfway down the stairs and waited for the rattle of the back door latch. After a minute I heard it. I was about to call Larry's name but that seemed a bit reckless after the near-miss earlier on, so I ran down the last few steps and stuck my head into the kitchen. Larry was standing by the back door.

'Put that in front of the door.' I pointed to the small metal bucket full of clothes pegs. 'That'll make a right racket if someone comes in. I've already locked the other door. Come on,' I nodded towards the bathroom. 'We've got nearly an hour.'

I sat behind Larry with my back in the curve of the bath and used the old plastic jug from when Sam was little to pour warm water over his shoulders and head.

'Is that stinging?' I took a closer look at his red shoulders.

'The whole of my body is pretty much on fire,' he said, 'but I think this cure is working.'

He leant his head back and I kissed him upside down feeling the water trickling down his face.

'Duncan was being a prick today,' he said. 'He didn't think I could take it.' Then he laughed. 'Actually, he was nearly right.' He put his hand behind my head and pulled me down towards him and kissed me again. 'I'm making a pretty good recovery now though.'

'Good,' I said. I lathered up his hair and massaged his head before rinsing it off.

'Let's get dry,' he said, sitting up and sending a wave of bathwater slopping onto the carpet. He turned round and, leaning towards me, he took my nipple in his mouth and sucked it, causing a stab of desire behind my belly button. 'Come on,' he said.

When we were dry, Larry said: 'After all the work he got me doing today, I think I deserve a lie down,' and, taking me by the hand, he led me towards our bedroom.

He got on the bed and pulled me on top of him.

'After all the work I've done today, I think it's your turn,' he said.

I looked at the clock. We had twenty minutes.

Ten minutes later my heart leapt and I jumped off the bed as a crash came from the kitchen; the back door had knocked over the bucket of pegs.

'Get in the bathroom,' I said, lunging over to the door to listen. Someone's in the kitchen.' Larry stood behind me and traced a finger down my spine. I shivered. Then I felt him lift my hair and kiss the back of my neck. 'No!' I said, 'not now. Get in the bathroom, quick.' I turned, feeling the cold of the door against my bare back. He was half smiling and leant over to kiss me, pushing me harder against the door. He squeezed my breast and the latch dug into my spine. 'Go on,' I said, pushing my palms against his chest. 'And make a lot of noise sloshing the water about.'

I half opened the door and Larry strolled naked across the landing into the bathroom. I dragged on a T-shirt and some jeans – my hands shaking as I fumbled with the zip. Then I heard someone coming upstairs – it was the soft padding of Sam's footsteps. My breath froze in my chest as I leant my forehead against the bedroom door. I had to calm down; Larry was having a bath, that was all. After haymaking all day that was no big deal.

'I'll put tea on in a minute,' I shouted to Sam. I was taken aback by how normal I sounded – how clear and confident and everyday. No one would have known there was anything different, least of all Sam.

Chapter 46

Welcome to U Chat

Home   Chat   **Message Rules   Contact Us Log in   Sign up Boards**

Things are not working out right. What is the solution?

Truestory
Date: 22 June 2014
Time: 18.06

Things are different in a horrible way. I do not want this.

Re: Things are not working out right. What is the solution?

Razzamatazz68
Date: 22 June 2014
Time: 18.11

What was it Mike Jagger said – something about not getting what you want, but getting what you need, or needing what you get or wanting what you need. Anyway, you get the idea – make the most of what life hands you!

Re: Things are not working out right. What is the solution?

ChocolateMoustache
Date: 22 June 2014
Time: 18.16

Or as Robert Frost said: The best way out is always through.

Re: Things are not working out right. What is the solution?

Playmeright
Date: 22 June 2014
Time: 18.19

Or as I said: Stop moaning and suck it up. Nothing ever works out as we want.That's life. Deal with it.

Re: Things are not working out right. What is the solution?

ChocolateMoustache
Date: 22 June 2014
Time: 18.23

Well, rather brutally put Play Me Right, but yes, we are not necessarily happy if everything goes 'right' it's when things go wrong and we take decisive action to deal with it that we are at our most fulfilled.

Re: Things are not working out right. What is the solution?

Sweet Cheeks
Date: 22 June 2014
Time: 18.31

Your not watching titanic are you? When Jack died I could not believe it! Worst ending ever!! Mind you I still watched it five times. Why did they make Jack die though? Poor Rose. xx

Re: Things are not working out right. What is the solution?

JC
Date: 22 June 2014
Time: 18.34

Romans 8:28 *And we know that in all things God works for the good of those who love him, who have been called according to his purpose.*

Re: Things are not working out right. What is the solution?

Fizzy Mascara
Date: 22 June 2014
Time: 18.36

Yeah, like I've said many times, Truestory, do not rely on 'god' or 'magic' (same thing anyway) but take action and make it happen yourself. You don't have to announce it mind you. Sometimes you're as well making stuff happen by working behind the scenes. I'm all for being up front, but there are times you achieve more by being subtle about it.

276

Re: Things are not working out right. What is the solution?

SpiritLove
Date: 22 June 2014
Time: 18.46

Dealing with change is one of life's opportunities. Our leaflet 'Embracing Change with Spirit' is available on our site <u>here</u> at the introductory offer of $1.99. Come on over and chat about it. We are here to help.

Re: Things are not working out right. What is the solution?

Fizzy Mascara
Date: 22 June 2014
Time: 18.48

Honestly, action now (however small, however subtle) will make you feel better.

Re: Things are not working out right. What is the solution?

Truestory
Date: 22 June 2014
Time: 18.51

I have just looked up 'subtle' on my on-line dictionary. It says 'delicate and precise'. My maps are delicate and precise. It also says 'using indirect and clever ways of achieving something'. I will give this some thought. Thank you for your help.

Chapter 47

After tea Duncan turned the telly on.

'There's a good mid-week match on. United v Bayern. Want to watch? It's about to kick off.'

He headed to the beer fridge and brought back two bottles. He cracked one open and took a swig. The other one he noticeably left by the second armchair in front of the fire rather than bringing it over to Larry. He slumped in his chair, took another swig and made a loud 'Aah' sound. He actually smacked his lips as he plonked his feet up on the range.

'Aye, I'll keep my eye on the match,' said Larry, ignoring the bottle waiting for him across the room. 'But I thought I'd see if Sam here wanted to play cards first.'

Sam's head was low over the new map he was drawing.

'Do you fancy playing cards, Sam?' asked Larry, shuffling a pack he'd brought out of his pocket. 'Do you play?'

'We tried to play Snap once,' I said, 'but nothing else.' Sam carried on drawing – concentrating on getting the wiggles in the lane in all the right places. 'That wasn't so good, really.'

I shook my head at Larry. I hadn't thought about the Snap Episode for a while. Sam hadn't grasped the point of the game and when I yelled 'Snap!' and slapped my hand on the pile of cards he'd been stunned for a second before clapping his hands over his ears, slithering to the ground and producing a high-pitched shriek that I thought would never end. He was about five or six at the time. He hadn't shut up until I'd said we could throw the cards on the fire then he'd watched them curl and blacken and burn as he sat there whimpering.

Sam's head came up and he gazed at us as if he'd been dragged from under the sea.

'Larry says do you want to play cards,' I said, intonating carefully as though he was deaf.

'I can teach you to play Cheat. Have you played Cheat?' Larry was still shuffling.

'What is Cheat?' asked Sam.

'Well, it's a good laugh,' said Larry.

'I do not want to play Cheat,' said Sam.

'Hang on, I haven't told you what it is yet,' Larry shared the cards out between me, him and Sam. 'You need at least three people.'

'I do not want to play Cheat,' he said again.

'Wait a minute,' said Larry straightening his cards. 'Give it a chance.'

It was getting harder to hold Sam's attention because the noise from the football was getting louder and louder and we were having to raise our voices over the roar of the crowd. I could see Duncan pressing the remote.

'Okay, so the objective is to get rid of all your cards,' shouted Larry. He glanced over at Duncan, who was slapping the chair arm and shouting: 'For God's sake, pass it!' but he said nothing.

Sam studied Larry, then repeated: 'The objective is to get rid of all your cards?'

'Yes,' said Larry. 'First person to put down all their cards wins. But you lie and cheat as you put them down.'

'You lie and cheat, and then you win because you have nothing?' stated Sam.

279

'Yes,' said Larry. 'That's about it.'

'I do not want to play Cheat,' said Sam.

'You need a good poker face to play it,' said Larry. 'That means you mustn't let your face show what you're really up to. You've got to be a good liar.'

Sam felt his face as if he was checking whether he'd got his big glasses on or not. Then he slid his pens and ruler into his pencil case, placed his pencil case on top of the map, pushed the pile of cards back to Larry and said: 'I do not want to play Cheat.'

'Christ!' shouted Duncan over the telly. 'The kid doesn't want to play Cheat. Get the message.' He turned the telly up even more. 'This is a good match you're missing.'

Sam put his hands over his ears, wriggled off his chair and went scurrying upstairs.

I rolled my eyes to show Larry I knew Duncan was being annoying. 'Well, it looks like football's won,' I mouthed.

Larry gave me a wink so brief it was hardly there. 'So let's watch this match then,' he said, striding over to the armchair. 'You joining us, Alice?'

Duncan scowled.

'Nah, I'm a bit tired.' Then, without thinking, I added 'What with everything,' and I saw Larry smile.

'Yes, you've put your all into it today,' he said. 'You were good.'

He wasn't talking about the hay-making.

'Well I think it's an early night for me.' I grabbed my book off the table.

Duncan looked pleased. 'Night, Love,' he said, his eyes not leaving the screen.

'Night, Alice,' said Larry. 'Sweet dreams. And thanks . . .' he hesitated, 'for my tea.' And I saw another of his barely-there winks.

I went upstairs and straightened the quilt cover before sitting on it and messing it up again. Then I went in the bathroom and stared at the sodden carpet and the mass of wet footprints that looked as though half a dozen people had had a bath in there. Two wet towels were chucked on the floor. I put one in the wash and draped the other over the bath.

We mustn't get complacent.

The bed rocked as Duncan got up next morning to milk. I kept my eyes shut and lay still, concentrating on breathing slowly. I'd been awake for ages listening to the wind blowing round the house and imagining how much louder it must sound in Larry's caravan and how cosy it would be to be in there with him.

Duncan took his clothes from the chair and crept to the bathroom, not quite shutting the bedroom door so as not to wake me. I snuggled down a bit further.

When I could hear Duncan downstairs I stuck my hand out of the bedcovers and finger-tipped around the carpet to find my mobile. I wanted to hear Larry's voice. I pressed his number.

'*The number you are calling is not available. Please try again later.*'

I pressed redial.

'*The number you are calling is not available. Please try again later.*'

I let the phone drop onto the quilt.

Later when he came in for breakfast Duncan said:

'We were lucky to get that haymaking done. Forecast's bad today – wind's already up.'

Through the kitchen window I could see leaves skidding across the yard, making Bess bark and snap.

Where's Larry?' I said. 'What's he been doing this morning?'

'Nothing. Haven't seen him.' Duncan laughed. 'Recovering, probably, after yesterday. It's a good job I got him to check the anchoring on the polytunnel the other day. It's going to be bad.'

I looked back at the scudding leaves and hoped Larry was right when he said there had been no need to refasten the polytunnel.

Sam slid into the room and sat down beside his map and started organising his Weetabix.

I plopped three teabags in the pot.

Something was wrong.

'I'm going to get Larry,' I said, striding off before Duncan could stop me.

'Christ! He'll find his own way in for breakfast,' he shouted after me.

I strode through the washroom and had my hand on the back door handle when I stopped at the sight of the poly-tunnel. The plastic sheeting door had come unfastened and was flapping wildly and the wind was getting right inside the tunnel and blowing it up as though it was going to burst. I held my breath. Then a section of the covering broke loose from its anchoring and flapped straight in the air. The structure had the look of a ticking time bomb with a very short fuse.

'Duncan!' I yelled. 'The tunnel!'

'What?'

'Come here!'

I opened the door and a gust of wind crashed it back. I left it – the tunnel was about to take off. I charged outside. As I reached it the wind dislodged the next section of covering and it too shot in the air with a deafening racket.

'Christ's sake! I heard Duncan shout. 'Grab the fucking thing.'

282

I lunged at the tunnel, grappling with the plastic sheeting, but it was thick and heavy and hard to hold and it was as if the wind was doing what it wanted with it – playing with it for fun.

'Larry!' Duncan shouted. 'Where the fuck is Larry? Sam!'

I let go and ran towards the caravan. 'Larry!' I yelled. Larry could sort this out. 'Larry! Quick!'

Before I could reach the caravan there was a tremendous noise and I looked over my shoulder. Duncan had lost his grip on the sheeting and it was rising straight in the air and doing a slow twist. In trying to grab it Duncan was trampling on the small cannabis plants that were shuddering in the wind.

Duncan crashed over the plants as he chased the sheeting. Eventually as it snagged on the apple tree he lunged at it and, dragging it to the floor, he threw himself on it.

'Alice!'

I ran over and stood on it too and together we grappled it into a huge bundle.

'Keep a good grip,' yelled Duncan. 'Don't let go. Get it to the workshop.'

The wind whipped my hair across my face blinding me and sticking it to my lips and my teeth but my hands were full of sheeting.

Where was Larry?

We dragged the sheeting across the grass and yard and into the workshop. The relief of getting out of the buffeting wind was immense; the noise and force of it stopped you thinking, and I needed to think because I was panicking.

Where the hell was Larry?

'The useless bastard,' said Duncan. 'He doesn't anchor the thing down like I told him and then does nowt to help us rescue it. Fucking useless bastard.'

283

'I think there's something wrong,' I said.

'Well, he can fucking stew. The useless bastard. I told him to use them extra flagstones to weigh it down. And he fucking said he'd done it.'

We left the workshop and Duncan strode back to the house, still swearing and cursing.

I legged it to the caravan.

The cannabis plants looked as if they'd had it – pretty much what you'd expect after a thirteen stone man and a force eight gale had finished with them.

I hammered on the caravan door. 'Larry! It's me.' No answer. I turned the handle and it gave. 'Larry, for God's sake . . .'

I stuck my head round the door. It was empty. The only traces of Larry were umpteen cigarette butts squashed in the ash tray and two empty, crumpled cans of Carlsberg Special Brew. Everything else had gone: his rucksack, his books, his Golden Virginia tin, his clothes. Everything. I froze, half in and half out of the caravan.

'Larry,' I said 'What the fuck . . . ?'

I went into the caravan and pulled the blankets off the bed as though I expected to find him hiding under there. I strode round the caravan in a panic looking for clues. But there were no clues. Larry had gone. Larry had done what he always did – he'd moved on. I grabbed my phone from my pocket. My hands were shaking. I called his number.

'The number you are calling is not available. Please try again later.'

I chucked the phone across the caravan and it crashed against the metal sink and thudded on to the floor. He could be anywhere. I had no forwarding address, no way of getting in touch, nothing except that phone. I grabbed it and rubbed it against my jeans and checked it was still working. I called his number again.

'*The number you are calling is not available. Please try again later.*'

I took the blankets off the bed and held them in a great big armful and buried my face in them. They smelled of Larry's cigarettes.

My legs shook as I blundered down the caravan steps. I half ran, half walked back to the house.

In the kitchen Sam was drawing his map and Duncan was staring over Sam's shoulder. He straightened up as I came in and the look of rage on his face stopped me like a punch.

'The fucking bastard, I'll fucking kill him,' he said.

I was gasping for breath even though I'd only come across the garden. 'He's gone,' I said.

Duncan grabbed me by the shoulders and manhandled me out of the way and headed for the back door.

'He's gone,' I said again. 'Anyway, it's only a poly-tunnel.' But he shot out the back door.

I slumped onto a kitchen chair and glanced at Sam's map. He had his arm around it but I could see what he was drawing. Usually there were no people on Sam's maps and each map was the same – but today's was different. Today's map had two stick figures on it.

The stick woman had brown frizzy hair and boobs sticking out of a tight T-shirt, the stick man wore a bandana round his head and had a gold earring in. The stick couple were lying in the polytunnel and the stick woman had her stick legs wrapped around the stick man who was on top of her as they had sex. Both had big smiles on their faces.

My insides flipped and my scalp prickled. I grabbed the kitchen table.

Sam coloured the stick man's bandana in blue, concentrating on keeping his felt pen inside the lines.

I was shot-through with energy but I didn't know what to do with it. I jumped up and walked to the door then back again and collapsed onto the kitchen chair. Then I strode to the washroom door. Through the window I could see Duncan kicking hell out of what was left of the cannabis plants. Swiping and kicking and stamping on the plants which looked to be smashed to smithereens.

I searched around the armchair Larry was sitting in when I last saw him. Had he left a note? I couldn't believe he'd upped and left without a word.

There was nothing. I grabbed my car keys off the hook.

Duncan stormed back into the kitchen breathing heavily and with his fists clenched.

'Is this true?' he said nodding towards the map. Then when he saw the car keys: 'Where the fuck are you going?'

'I'm going,' I said. 'I'm not staying here without Larry.'

Duncan charged round the table and lunged for the keys, but I snatched them away and shoved them under my arm.

'Give me those keys.'

'I'm going,' I said again. I had no idea where, but I had to get out. The kitchen walls were pressing in on every side. I couldn't breathe.

'I brought him here. It's my fault.' Duncan covered his face with his hand. 'I'd like to break his fucking neck.'

I grabbed the back door latch.

'We'll be all right, Alice. We'll sort it.' Duncan was crying but my heart was full of Larry and I couldn't help him. I opened the door. 'Don't go, Alice,' Duncan said. 'We'll sort it out.'

I ran to the car and jumped in. The door flew out of my grip as a gust of wind snatched it away. The hedgerows blurred past as I headed down the lane, and my face was slippery with snot and tears however many times I wiped it.

When I reached the T junction at the main road I looked left to Lancaster and right to Preston. I had no idea where Larry was. And even if I knew, what difference would it make? He'd run away from me and Sam. He hadn't even left a note.

I didn't want to go either way. There was nothing for me to the right and nothing to the left. I had no friends in either direction, no family to speak of, none I wanted to see anyway. I had nowhere to go and no one to go to. I took my foot off the clutch, the car stalled and I rested my head on the steering wheel.

A car pulled up behind and tooted.

My heart was broken into pieces. It was a physical ache – an actual pain in my stomach and chest and throat that took my breath away.

The car tooted again, longer and louder. I felt for the ignition and turned the engine back on. I did a U-turn and, avoiding the other driver's eye, headed back down the lane.

I sat in the yard and saw Duncan briefly come to the window to watch me. I knew I had to find Sam. I'd blurted out that I wouldn't stay at the farm without Larry, right in front of Sam, and I felt sick about it.

Duncan jumped up when I went inside.

'Alice, sit down.'

'Where's Sam?'

He glanced around the room as though Sam might be perched on the units or the range or something.

'I don't know. Sit down, Alice.' Duncan sat down and pointed to the chair opposite.

'I need to see Sam.'

'Alice, do you love him? Do you love Larry?'

There was a crack in Duncan's voice but I couldn't talk to him now. I needed Sam. I walked past.

'Alice, don't walk away from me!'

'I'm looking for Sam.'

I ran up the stairs.

'Alice!' I heard Duncan's chair clatter backwards as he stood up. He stuck his head up the stairs as I knocked on Sam's door. 'Alice. You will fucking talk to me about this. I want to know what the fuck has been going on.'

I put my ear to the door then pushed it open. The bedroom was empty.

'He must be at Jeannie's.' I headed downstairs and tried to squeeze past Duncan part way down. He grabbed me and held me against the wall.

'How long's it been going on? Ever since he got here?'

'No.' I said.

'Tell me, Alice.' He shook me by the shoulders. 'I want to know. Do you love him?'

'Yes,' I said. Duncan's face fell and his hands dropped from my shoulders. I couldn't look at him. 'Well, I thought I did,' I said.

I slid sideways away from him and headed downstairs into the kitchen. Duncan followed slowly and stood at the bottom of the stairs. He looked stunned.

'I need to find Sam,' I said.

Duncan was staring back at that bloody map.

'I'm going for him,' I said.

'You were with him in the polytunnel and Sam saw you,' he said, as though he was talking to himself. 'He reckoned he was a friend.' He looked at me and said: 'But then you reckoned you were my wife.'

'I'm going to Jeannie's,' I said.

Duncan snatched Sam's map and took it to the bin and I thought he was going to ram it in, but he hesitated and seemed to think better of it. He took it back to the table and turned it face down.

That was the first time I'd seen Duncan do anything he didn't want to just to avoid upsetting Sam.

'I'm coming with you,' he said.

We struggled down the lane. I flattened my hair to my head to stop myself from being blinded by it. The wind fought us all the way – buffeting us and roaring in our ears. At Sam's Pile of Rubble Covered in Weeds, the wiry tufts of grass were flattened by the force of the gale. A group of heifers crowded under an oak for shelter from a world that seemed to have gone a little bit mad.

I tapped on Jeannie's door and stumbled straight in.

'Hi, Jeannie, it's me. It's us.'

Without waiting for a reply, I went through the porch and into the living room.

Sam was there but before I could get any words out I was struck by the stink and the unholy mess. The dogs had scattered their food all over the carpet and there was dog mess mixed in among it. There was a hum of flies.

'God, what's going on?' Then I focused on Sam and the breath froze in my body.

'For fuck's sake,' said Duncan.

Sam was standing beside Jeannie's wicker armchair. He was holding a comb and was gently brushing her hair.

Jeannie's face was dark purple. Her eyes were open as was her mouth; her lips had shrunk back in a grimace and her top set of false teeth were skew-whiff in her mouth. She was piled with blankets and had five or six cups of tea and plates of biscuits on the table in front of her and beside her on the floor.

'Oh, for fuck's sake,' said Duncan again.

She must have been dead for days. Sam was holding one of her clawed hands that rested on top of the blanket and with his other hand he continued to comb her grey hair.

'Sam, come away,' I said. I wanted to scream, I wanted to run, but most of all I wanted to get Sam away from the disgusting spectacle in that armchair.

'Put the comb down, Sam,' I said. 'You've helped Jeannie enough. Come here to me.'

Sam's comb hovered in mid-air and a bluebottle darted across Jeannie's eye.

'You can't help Jeannie now,' I said to Sam. I walked over to him, holding my hand out. 'You can't do anything more for Jeannie. Come on.'

'I cannot,' said Sam.

'Yes, you can.' My teeth were gritted and I had one hand covering my nose and mouth.

'Sam, do as you're told and come here,' Duncan's voice was raised.

'I cannot leave Jeannie. I did this and I must put it right.'

I looked at Duncan and saw my own horror reflected in his face.

'You didn't do anything, Sam,' I said. 'What do you mean? What did you do?'

Sam's eyes filled with tears. A bluebottle walked across Jeannie's hand and onto Sam's and I longed to dash it away but I stayed still. The fly's back shone iridescent blue as it washed its face, then it took off and buzzed towards me and I flapped my hands. 'No!' I said, knocking it away.

Sam took a cup of water and held it to Jeannie's cold drawn-back lips and let a snail's trail of water slide from the corner of her mouth down her chin and onto her blanket.

'She's dead, Sam. We can't do anything for her now.'

'She may not be dead,' Sam whispered. He looked closely at Jeannie's mottled fingers. 'This may be a near-death experience.'

'For fuck's sake', said Duncan. 'She's dead all right.'

Sam turned on Duncan. 'That goose looked like it

was dead,' he said and he looked at me, searching for agreement. 'That goose's head was twisted and its body dropped from the sky. But it got up and went.'

'What, that dead goose I threw on the midden?' said Duncan.

Sam's eyes were glistening. 'On the midden?' he said.

'Things don't come back from the dead,' I said.

'But,' Sam looked from me to Duncan and back again, 'but Chocolate Moustache said it is sometimes impossible to tell if something is alive or dead.'

'Who the fuck is Chocolate Moustache?' Duncan asked me.

I shook my head. 'That might be true, Sam, but not when you've been dead as long as Jeannie has.' I picked my way a step closer, avoiding a broken cup and saucer on the floor. I noticed that there wasn't the usual ticking of clocks. Jeannie obviously hadn't wound them up for a while. 'How long has Jeannie been like this?' I said.

Sam did not answer but stared down at her.

'When did Jeannie last speak to you?' I said.

'Wednesday,' said Sam. 'The day before I did the strongest magic available on the internet.' He put the cup down and picked up the comb and started brushing her hair again.

'Wednesday?' I said. 'Oh God. Five days.'

'For Christ's sake put that comb down,' said Duncan, 'and let's get out of here.'

'The magic got out of control and knocked the goose out of the sky,' said Sam. 'Then it did this to Jeannie.'

'And have you been making her cups of tea and getting her biscuits and things ever since then?' I looked at the table strewn with uneaten biscuits and cold cups of tea and lemonade and water. He nodded. 'Did you give her all these blankets?'

'She was cold,' he said. 'Even when it was warm outside.'

'Oh, Sam, Jeannie was an old lady. She was eighty-two and hadn't been well.' I had a memory of her telling me she'd lost her pills and my heart lurched. What had she said? Did she say she'd found them again? I hadn't really asked. I'd been too busy trying to escape real life with Larry.

'You haven't done this, Sam,' I said. 'Don't think for a minute that you've done it.' I held out my hand again. 'Come on.'

'But My Name is Magic said his magic was the strongest you can get on the internet. It might have done this.'

My Name is Magic? Duncan and I exchanged looks again.

'For God's sake,' muttered Duncan.

'No.' I shook my head. 'It definitely did not.'

One of Jeannie's cats leapt from the dresser and crashed onto the table sending other cups flying onto the floor. I screamed and Sam grabbed my hand.

'For Christsakes. We need to get these animals rounded up and sorted out,' said Duncan. 'I'll call the police.' He took his mobile out of his pocket and dialled 999. I saw the look of panic on Sam's face.

'Remember what I said, Sam. You have not done anything wrong.'

We listened to Duncan repeating Jeannie's address. 'An old lady has passed away,' he was saying. 'Yes, she's definitely dead. No, there is no pulse. Yes, she is definitely dead.'

'Come on, Sam,' I said. 'Dad'll stay here with Jeannie until the police come. We'll go home.'

I led Sam through the living room and gave Duncan a half-smile as we passed. 'See you at home,' I mouthed.

He nodded at us. 'No, I don't need to check,' he was saying. 'She is definitely dead.'

The wind grabbed the door as I opened it and I gulped a lungful of cool clean fresh air.

Sam and I clung to each other's hands as we struggled up the lane. If I let go of him for a second I was afraid he'd take off and fly away and I'd lose him forever.

A policeman came back to the farm with Duncan after Jeannie's body had been taken away.

'I'll see you in a bit, Alice,' Duncan said and he went outside to feed the calves. I knew he was desperate to talk to me.

The policeman introduced himself as PC Dale and hovered about, clinging to his hat, until I told him to sit down and I got him a cup of tea.

'I'm sorry for your loss, Mrs McCabe,' he said. 'I know you and the deceased were friends.'

'Yes,' I said. I avoided his eye; some friend I'd been. Her body had been rotting for five days before I'd even noticed.

'It's just routine, Mrs McCabe, I'll need to take a statement from your son.' He consulted his notebook. 'Sam, is it?'

He must have seen the look on my face.

'I can come back tomorrow to see Sam if you'd prefer?'

I shook my head.

'No, let's get it over with.'

'She came to my barbecue party for sausages and marshmallows on Sunday but had to go home before the lightning bolt because Elvis had an ear infection and may well have been stuck behind the sofa.'

PC Dale's pencil hovered over his notebook.

'So she was here and seemed fine on Sunday?'

'Yes. She ate some of my beautiful sausage and said I'd done a wonderful job.'

'Sausage,' repeated PC Dale jotting stuff down. 'So, when did you see her next?'

'On Wednesday but she did not want to talk about her wish list or her time travel and even though she was old she said she did not know anything about the creation of the 19th century toll roads.'

'Right,' said PC Dale.

I interrupted. 'She didn't look well. The cottage was upside down – even worse than usual. She said she'd been searching for her lost pills. For her angina.'

'Well, she found them,' said PC Dale. 'The paramedics said they were in her pinny pocket. She hadn't taken any though – the box hadn't been opened. Was it like her to lose her meds or forget to take them?'

'My mother said that Jeannie had a bit of a screw loose,' said Sam.

I shook my head.

'I doubt it,' I said. 'She was an eccentric but she was all there.'

'Okay. Was that the last time you saw her alive?'

'According to Chocolate Moustache it is not easy to tell if someone is dead or alive.'

'Well . . .' PC Dale grimaced a bit.

'Thursday the 19th of June was the lucky day that was unlucky and I did the strongest magic you can find on the internet and the goose fell from the sky and I found Jeannie cold and she did not speak. The goose got up and went again but Jeannie was not like the goose. She did not get up and go again.'

'So . . .' the policeman's gaze hovered between me and Sam. 'So, Sam, when you arrived at Jeannie's cottage on Thursday, was she sitting in her chair by the stove exactly as we found her today?'

'Yes. My magic went wrong.'

'Okay,' said PC Dale. 'And did you tell anyone, Sam?'

'No, I did not tell anyone.'

'And since then you've been . . .'

'Since then he's been looking after her, waiting for her to wake up,' I said. 'He's been giving her water and covering her in blankets and stoking the fire.'

'Oh, I see. Deary me,' said PC Dale and he shook his head.

We sat in silence as he carried on writing. 'Deary me,' he said again.

'Do you think she didn't take her tablets on purpose?' I said.

PC Dale pulled a face. 'Fraid I can't say, Mrs McCabe. Toxicology tests will show what meds she'd taken. All I can say is she told you on Wednesday that she wasn't well but that she'd found her tablets. She apparently died that night or the next day without opening them.'

'My Name is Magic said his magic was the strongest on the internet but my mother says that did not kill Jeannie.'

PC Dale gave a little laugh then, seeing Sam's deadpan face, he stopped.

'Magic? No, I don't think magic did it, Sam.' He smiled in what he must have thought was an encouraging way, but Sam did not smile back. 'Is My Name is Magic a friend of yours?'

'Yes, I have twenty-seven friends, but I have never met them. I also had two other friends, Jeannie and Larry, but Jeannie has died and Larry has left his caravan after having sexual intercourse in the polytunnel with my mother.'

PC Dale had a rictus grin on his face. 'Right,' he said. 'Right, well I think that'll be all.' He closed his notebook and tucked it in his pocket. 'I'll leave you folks in peace.'

'I did not like the polytunnel. It smelled funny and I never wanted to go in there. It was hot as a . . .'

'Okay – '

'Right – '

PC Dale and I stood up in a great clattering of chairs. Somehow I managed to show him out without either of us catching the other's eye.

'Alice, sit down and talk to me.'

I cleared the lunch pots into the sink and picked the kettle up.

'Forget coffee. Come here.'

I put the kettle down and slid onto the chair opposite him. Neither of us spoke.

'So, are you going to tell me what's been going on?'

I shrugged.

'Don't do that! Talk to me!'

I ran my fingers through my hair and blurted out:

'He was kind. He liked Sam. He was good with Sam – you could see that, it was obvious.'

He waited for more. When I didn't say anything else, he shouted, 'That didn't mean you had to sleep with him.'

'I know. I don't know. It was a mistake. It was stupid.'

'You can say that – '

I cut him off. 'You fight with Sam all the time. It's exhausting. With Larry I felt like he was on my side. I felt like he understood me. Like he wanted to help and support me.'

'Well I want to help and support you.'

'It doesn't feel like it. Ever since Sam was a baby – a really difficult baby – we've been fighting on opposite sides. Everything I do is wrong. Everything Sam does is wrong.'

'That's not fair. I'm working this farm to support you and Sam.'

'It doesn't feel like it. You're here because you want to

be here. Sam's here because he daren't be anywhere else. And I'm stuck here.'

'Well that's no reason to sleep with the first man who comes along.'

'That's not fair.'

'Fair! Have you been fair?'

'I'm sorry, Duncan. I didn't plan it. It was mad. I thought I knew him. I didn't.'

'Have you spoken to him today?'

'No, I . . . His phone's turned off.'

'So you've tried?'

'I did this morning.'

'And if he gets in touch – what then?'

I shook my head. 'I don't even know who he is.'

'Is that how you feel – that you are stuck here? Don't you want to be here?'

I put my face into my hands. That was the crux of it.

'I want to be able to choose. I'm in a straitjacket here. It's killing me. I just want to be able to choose.'

We sat in silence, and then Duncan said: 'What are we going to do about Sam?'

We both looked at each other. I shook my head.

'I don't know.'

The weather turned. Over the next few days the sun came out and burned my face when I went to hang the washing or put the rubbish out. The glare of the sun made everything unreal – like the three of us were going through the day-to-day motions but were suspended, waiting for something to happen. We hardly spoke, any of us.

Duncan worked outside all hours – finding jobs to do until it went dark – mending and fixing. One day I saw him attacking the weeds growing through the cobbles,

297

going at them with a trowel when all he needed to do was spray them.

We were scrupulously polite, especially in front of Sam, who seemed to be carrying on exactly as he always had done. My heart was in my mouth every time he produced a sheet of paper to draw another map. I'd watch him smoothing and straightening and preparing the paper and think: 'Oh God, what will he draw now?' But there were no more couples having sex in the polytunnel. There was no more polytunnel – not in the orchard nor on Sam's maps.

Outside, the wreckage of the plants had been abandoned and any that had survived Duncan's rage were withered and wilting as one hot day passed into another.

I kept being struck afresh by the shock of it all: discovering Sam giving Jeannie's corpse a cup of tea; finding the caravan empty and abandoned; seeing Duncan's expression as Sam drew the couple having sex in the polytunnel.

The couple having sex in the polytunnel.

If I could change anything it would be Sam knowing about me and Larry. And how could I have shouted in front of him about not staying another day without Larry? It made me sick to remember. I'd been on the point of apologising to Sam once or twice; I'd never got very far, though. I didn't have the nerve.

When Duncan *did* come inside, exhausted and filthy, we spoke to each other like guests in the household, skirting round each other, awkward and largely wordless. The only time I said anything was when I noticed him staring at my phone which was lying on the kitchen surface.

'I've not spoken to him,' I said. And it was true. I hadn't spoken to Larry since he'd strolled naked across the landing.

I'd checked my phone a lot, more than usual, although I was pretending that wasn't the case. But I wasn't sorry he hadn't phoned.

He'd as good as disappeared in a puff of smoke. It was as if he'd never been real – yet he'd changed my life and, even though he'd been a feckless waste of space who had done a runner, he'd changed me. He had made me look outside the family, look outside the farm and, for once, to think about me.

The following week we decided I'd go to Jeannie's funeral and Duncan would stay at Backwoods with Sam. It was to be a burial in a village churchyard about four miles away. She was to be put in with her parents. I thought there was something sad about an old person returning to their parents to be buried.

I'd kept a close eye on Sam – his two best friends, Jeannie and Larry, had disappeared in the same week and I'd been waiting for a reaction.

None had come. He'd carried on with his schoolwork and drawing his maps and going on his computer. The only time he'd mentioned Jeannie was to ask who was feeding her cats and dogs. I told her they'd all gone to good homes and then, in a panic, I phoned the police and tracked down one of her cats to a local cat sanctuary. I asked Duncan to get it.

When Duncan carried it inside, Sam held his arms out and buried his face in its tabby fur. The cat put up no objection and blinked out at the world from Sam's arms.

'It's Elvis,' said Sam.

Since then they'd been together all the time, the cat always purring and kneading Sam's quilt or his lap – a noise which didn't bother Sam at all. On the contrary, despite being given a bed by the range, the cat had taken to spending the night sleeping on Sam's pillow or sometimes on his head and appeared to have replaced the bobble hat.

The funeral fell on a Tuesday afternoon which was lucky; it meant I could leave home at my usual time and Sam didn't need to think about it.

We finished lunch and Duncan stood up and stretched.

'Well I'll get some weeding done while you're out.'

Sam, who was sitting at the table drawing a map with one hand and stroking Elvis with the other, announced: 'I am going to Jeannie's funeral.'

I stared at him. Duncan was pulling his boots on and hadn't heard.

'What?'

He must think Jeannie was being buried under one of the wooden crosses by her front door.

'I am going to Jeannie's funeral.'

'It's at Creighton. Down the lane.' I'd nearly said down Hell Fire Pass. 'It's four miles away.'

He drew the lane on his map.

'I am going to Jeannie's funeral,' he said again.

He coloured in the lane, and I waited for the inevitable, but for the first time he did not draw a skull and crossbones across the lane and no bright red sign in bold letters warning: DANGER.

Chapter 48

Welcome to U Chat

Home   Chat   Message   Rules   Contact Us   Log in   Sign up
                        Boards

The time is right.

Truestory
Date: 1 July 2014
Time: 10.04

My friend Jeannie Hope-Lamb (deceased) told me I would know when the time was right. She said when the time was right we would leave together. Jeannie is leaving today. So the time is now.

Re: The time is right.

Razzamatazz68
Date: 1 July 2014
Time: 10.08

Great Album. Love Lou Donaldson. Got the CD only issued in Japan.

Re: The time is right.

Blood Bro
Date: 1 July2014
Time: 10.25

Better a day too soon than a day too late I was told.

Re: The time is right.

AuntieMaud
Date: 1 July 2014
Time: 10.30

Very wise advice! My mother used to quote Socrates on this one: 'I would recommend you set off a day too soon rather than a day too late.' I am sorry to hear that you have a friend who is deceased, Truestory, and I hope you are still having fun with that map of yours. Much love.

Re: The time is right.

Blood Bro
Date: 1 July 2014
Time: 10.31

Nah, it wasn't that Socrates bloke who said it to me, it was Mr Shulberg the veterinary when he put down my ferret.

Re: The time is right.

Fizzy Mascara
Date: 1 July 2014
Time: 10.34

Go for it, Truestory, without going on about god or magic or spirits or anything else. Just go for it, whatever it is. We've got one life and one life only so it's up to us to make the most of it. Doing something beats doing nothing every time. Go for it big time, Truestory.

Chapter 49

As Duncan drove us to the funeral, I peered over my shoulder at Sam in the back. He was slumped in his seat. He had his bobble hat on with his earphones on top, not plugged into anything. The hat had made a reappearance after I'd explained that Elvis would definitely not enjoy coming to a funeral.

His eyes were open a chink and were on a level with the bottom of the window. He peeked at the world as it flew by.

With his messy blonde hair and his slight frame he didn't look so very different from the child I vividly remembered on our last journey down this lane – the child who had terrified me by stopping breathing. Now it was me who could hardly breathe.

'I can't understand what's happened to my suit,' Duncan said for the umpteenth time.

'Mmm?' I said, remembering brown paint splattering and dribbling all over the shiny lining as it disappeared under a pile of old floorboards.

'It's a good suit,' he said. 'I don't know what can have happened to it.'

There was only a handful of folk at the funeral, and I think most of them were from animal rescue places.

The coffin was waiting by the lychgate, covered in foxgloves and rosebay willow herb, flowers that grew in the hedgerow down the lane near Wayside Cottage. Among the flowers there was a photo of a young glamorous Jeannie in velvet and pearls.

The sight grabbed my throat and I felt my chin wobble.

'They've put weeds on the coffin,' Duncan said.

'They're wild flowers,' I said, 'resilient and untameable. They look lovely.'

I led us to seats at the back despite there being rows of empty pews. It was an old technique: when you were out with Sam you always made sure you knew your escape route, you could never afford to be one of those complacent parents without an exit strategy.

The organ wheezed into life and Sam clamped his hands over his earphones and pressed them hard and squeezed his eyes shut. He bent forward and leaned his forehead on the pew in front. I guessed if the pew hadn't been there he'd have toppled off the bench and curled into a ball on the stone floor. As it was he looked like he was praying.

My heart was in my mouth and I found myself praying, desperate words flooding my brain. 'I know I'm only in church for a funeral. I know I never set foot here one year to the next. I never pray. I don't even believe in God, but please, please make everything all right for Sam and get us through this next hour of our lives in one piece.'

My eyes were tight shut and my hands were gripped together and sweating. I didn't believe in God and I didn't know who I was praying to, but I meant every word.

The old Danger UXB memories; of being vulnerable to the entire world, of everyone watching and judging and finding us wanting – they were so close to the surface.

I took a deep breath and unclenched my fists. I had

to hide my fear and concentrate on looking calm and in control and not infecting Sam with my nerves.

The doors were fastened back and the bearers carried the coffin into church followed by the vicar.

'I am the resurrection and the life, saith the Lord; he that believeth in me, though he were dead, yet shall he live . . .'

'What language is that?'

Sam's voice was loud; partly because he was wearing earphones but also because I realised he'd never been in a church before and certainly never to a funeral.

I held my finger to my lips.

'What?' he said.

'Old-fashioned English,' I whispered.

'Jeannie was old fashioned but she never spoke like that.'

I held my finger to my lips again. I could feel the sweat starting to prickle under my armpits.

The vicar recited a psalm and I counted the moments as he intoned his way through the funeral service. Sam watched and even pushed his earphones off one ear so he could listen.

We shuffled to our feet for *The Old Rugged Cross* and I thanked my lucky stars there were hardly any mourners and no choir to make a racket. The singing was sparse, almost non-existent – and again I found myself saying thank you. Who to? I had no idea – possibly Jeannie – it didn't matter.

When the coffin was carried out of the church I thought we could do a runner back to the car but no such luck.

'They'll put her in the ground now,' said Sam. 'Come on.' He set off after the coffin into the graveyard. 'Jeannie had a wish list,' he said. 'She wanted to travel through space and time.' His eyes followed the coffin down the path. 'But she never mentioned going in one of them.'

I bit back a smile and caught Duncan's eye. He looked uncomfortable in his smart trousers and zip-up jacket.

When the committal was over I couldn't wait to get in the car and back down the lane. I could hardly believe we'd survived. There had been no meltdown, no screaming, no turning purple, no disaster that would knock me for six for a week, no turmoil that would make Sam hide or hurt himself.

'Come on,' I said, setting off.

Sam looked at his watch.

'It is 16.45 hours. The sun will set today at 21.21 hours which is four hours and 36 minutes from now. I want to climb a hill.'

'A hill?' I said.

'Yes.

'Big Hill?'

'No. Big Hill is not big.'

What's up?' Duncan said, catching up with us.

'He wants to climb a hill.'

'I want to climb a hill and see the pink road and the blue road that lead to Lancaster and to the Rest of the World.'

'Big Hill?' Duncan said.

'No,' I shook my head. 'We've been through that.'

'If we walk 200 yards in a northerly direction and cut across a field on the public right of way and climb the stile and follow the path through the copse, we will reach a hill,' Sam said. 'That is the hill I want to climb.' And he set off.

All those hours studying Larry's ordnance survey map meant he knew the landscape by heart: every lane, every field, every detail. Duncan and I jogged a bit to catch up with him.

'Climb a hill. Aye,' said Duncan.

'Yes,' I said, looking at my shoes. Thank God they were flat. 'Climb a hill.'

We fell in step with him – one on either side – and walked along in silence. As we rounded the corner the field gate came into view as Sam said it would and he climbed up and jumped over. Duncan did the same and held my hand as I jumped down too. Sam followed the hedge around the field and straight to the stile.

'Here's the stile!' I said, as though there had been any doubt about it.

'Yes,' said Sam. 'That is what the map said.'

I felt a rush of exhilaration and a laugh bubbled up in my throat.

'What are you laughing at?'

Duncan was watching me.

'I don't know. Everything.'

I gazed at the cows staring from the next field, looking suspicious and nosey and a bit put-out and the pair of ducks heading for the pond at the bottom of the field. I noticed the grey sheep's wool dangling from the barbed wire fence and the cow parsley growing in the hedgerows with the leggy buttercups.

The map was good but it couldn't show all this.

Sam marched along and I kept doing a little run to keep up. Walking through the wood the ground felt springy – there were so many pine needles and dead leaves underfoot.

'Hey look!' I jumped up and down. 'It's bouncy, see.' I stumbled and Duncan grabbed my arm.

He laughed. 'Steady on, Alice.'

I realised that Sam had never walked through a wood before as he stopped to stare up at the tree tops. Duncan and I did the same and we watched the sun glinting through the branches.

307

'It is just one tree after another,' said Sam. 'Like on my maps.'

'Yes,' I said, 'just one tree after another.'

Sam's pace slowed as we left the woods behind and the land began to rise. I was out of breath and panting and Sam hesitated and looked over his shoulder at me. I tried to smile but I was knackered. I held out my hand. He looked at it but didn't take it.

I put my head down and plodded on, each step burning my legs and my lungs. I felt a hand grasp mine.

'Come on,' Duncan said. 'Don't stop now, we're nearly there.'

At the top of the hill we sat down in a row and gazed at the patchwork of fields and the Pennines beyond.

'That's the A6, Sam,' said Duncan, pointing. 'And past that it's the M6.'

'The pink road and the blue road,' whispered Sam.

'Yep, the pink road and the blue road,' I said.

He pointed north. 'And that way are the graves hewn from rock where St Patrick landed from Ireland.'

'Yes,' I nodded my head. 'And we can go and see them any time. Tomorrow, if you like.'

He looked at me. 'Is that a true story?'

'Yes, Sam,' I said, 'it's a true story.'

He watched the tiny cars for a long time as they crawled to and fro.

'It is the rest of the world,' he said.

'Yes,' I said, 'it is.'